FIRESTARTER

RICHARD WILLARD

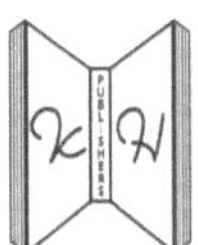

www.khpublishers.com

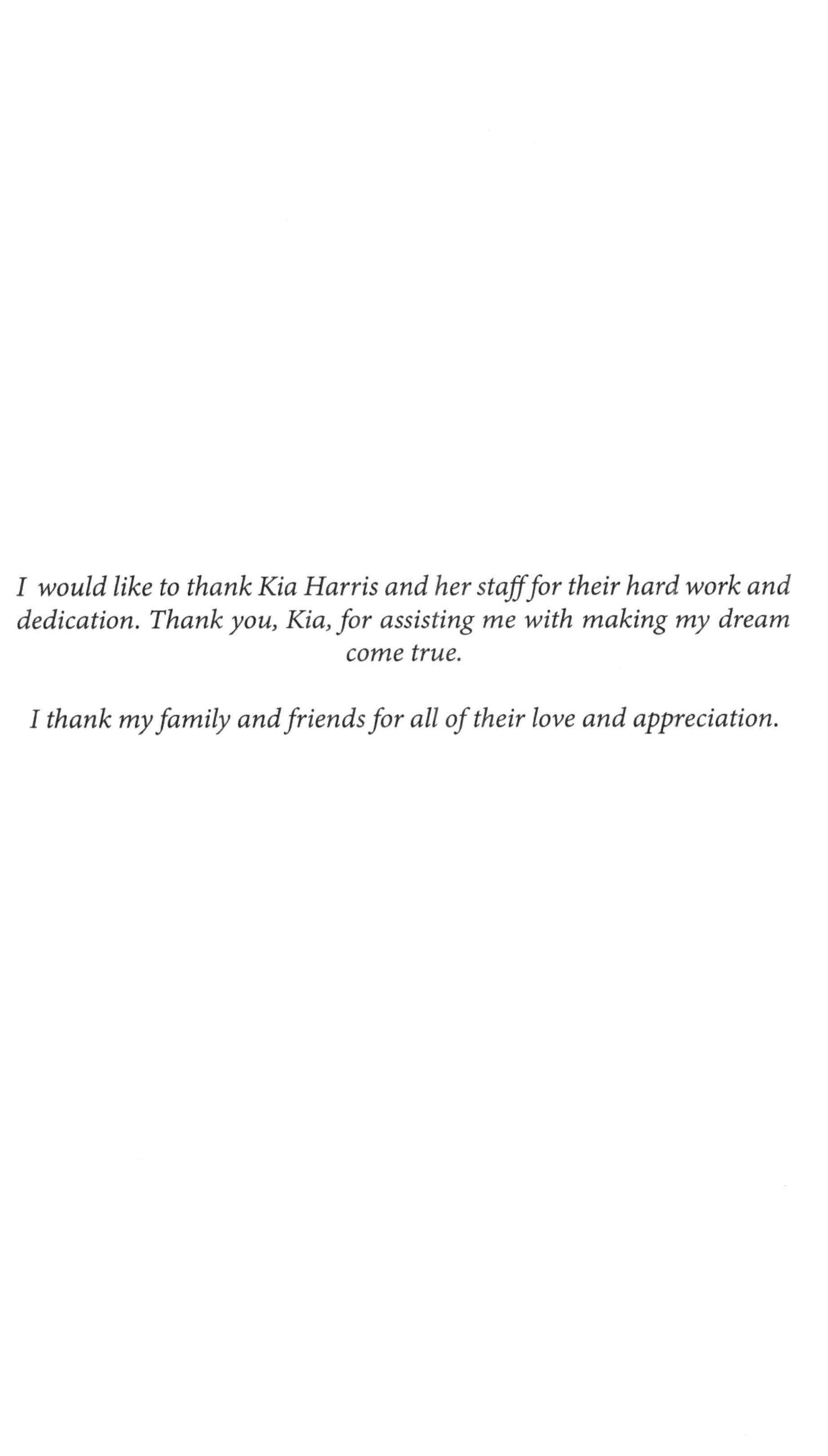

I would like to thank Kia Harris and her staff for their hard work and dedication. Thank you, Kia, for assisting me with making my dream come true.

I thank my family and friends for all of their love and appreciation.

Chapter One

Monica pulled the pillow slowly to her naked breast and cuddled it as if holding her man close to her. She had been awake since 10:00 p.m. that night, lying in her luxurious king-sized bed, trying her best to fall asleep. She looked over at the clock again.

"2:48! Shit!"

She was nude and horny, now going on seven weeks without making love to her husband. She could smell his Perry Ellis cologne on the silk pillow cover, Marcus' favorite. She lay on her side, her back to him, breathing in his redolent scent and caressing the pillow gently as her mind began its normal journey to her fantasy. Wet and hot now, she slowly rolled on her back, turning her head to a sleeping man who no longer desired her. Monica opened her long, chocolate legs and began the process of pleasuring herself.

She started to stroke her clitoris with her middle finger, at times pushing it inside of her hot, wet steamy pussy. She would occasionally take a quick peek at her snoring husband, making sure that he did not wake up from his deep, selfish sleep. When Monica was sure he would not wake up, she began stroking herself faster, still silent in her endeavor to please herself. Thinking of her husband on top of her, fucking her hard, she stroked herself harder and faster until her legs began to shake uncontrollably. She held her scream inside her sweaty body that yearned for her man's touch. When the orgasm was complete, she lay on her back, looking up at the ceiling. The tears began to roll down her cheeks as his snores roared louder and louder.

7 o'clock that morning, Marcus stood over the toilet relieving himself as Monica brushed her hair in front of the mirror. She gazed at him from the corner of her eye, his back to her, never acknowledging her. He hadn't said much to her lately and, at times, treated her as if she was invisible. She tried desperately to start a conversation with her husband each time he came home in the evening and early in the morning. But he was always short and hardly ever looked at her. *What have I done to this man?* She wondered.

They had been married for eleven years and had never gone this long without communicating, having sex, and going places together. Both thirty six, with a five-year-old daughter, lucrative careers, and in great physical shape, she couldn't understand why the marriage had lost its flavor. Monica excelled in the real estate business, owning her own franchise. Marcus earned his doctorate from the University of Alabama, majoring in computer science and owning his own computer business. Both had great businesses in Atlanta and were well known throughout the city.

Marcus and Monica had picked a home in a newly developed neighborhood in Powder Springs, twenty miles west of downtown Atlanta. Monica remembered the first day that they moved in. Marcus was very pleased with her choice. She remembered him hugging her as he lifted her into the air.

"This is our home, Baby!"

And for the first four years, she could remember them making love in every room. Getting their freak on, he would open her legs and taste all she could give him. The house held great memories of them. It wasn't only the sex that she treasured. He had a great sense of humor; he would act silly and always make her laugh. She loved him so much—more than he could ever imagine.

Monica watched as he slid out of his boxer shorts, never turning around, and stepped into the shower. She stared at him through the glass for a moment, watching him put his head under the running water. She turned slowly and walked out to the bedroom. She sat on the edge of the bed, listening to *The Tom Joyner Morning Show*. Sometimes it would take her mind off her situation. She always enjoyed the "Celebrity Snitch, Huggie Low Down," and would often wait to listen to his comedy at 8:30 a.m.

Marcus walked into the bedroom as she sat on the edge of the bed laughing from listening to the radio.

Monica looked up at him and said, "That Huggie is so funny!"

She could tell by the look on his face that he didn't care as he gave her a stare and walked to his closet. He had a towel wrapped around his waist, moisture running down his back. She thought about walking up to him and putting her arms around him. But it was just a thought, as usual. Each time she attempted, lately, he would shrug her off, saying, "Not now."

Monica walked to her daughter's bedroom to wake her for school. Taylor was sleeping soundly as Monica stood over her, reflecting on the night she was born. Marcus was nervous, she remembered, as they rolled her into the delivery room. The look in his eyes told her he loved her and would be there for her. She remembered looking up at her husband as the gurney rolled down the hallway. He stood six feet, two inches, and she thought, He's so handsome. Her mind slowly turned back to why she had gone into her daughter's room, to wake her sleeping beauty for school.

"Taylor Honey," she said softly. "Get up, Baby."

Taylor rolled over and looked up at her mother. She rubbed her eyes and said, "I'm up, Mommy."

Monica sat on the edge of the bed and began to stroke her daughter's head. Monica gazed at her daughter's dark skin and long wavy hair. She looked so much like Marcus. She didn't see any resemblance of herself in her daughter at all.

"I love you, Taylor," she said while stroking her daughters hair.

Taylor looked up at her mother and said, "I love you too, Mommy."

Monica's office was located on the outskirts of downtown Atlanta on Buckhead Street, giving her a view of the skyline. She sat in her office, her chair turned to the window, looking down at the people busying themselves through the streets of downtown Atlanta. It was a sunny September day, and the temperature was just right—in the high sixties. She had an important meeting scheduled for one o'clock that afternoon. Thomas McMichaels was a black millionaire in Atlanta looking to purchase property in a newly developed suburb ten miles outside of Atlanta. She would make a substantial amount of money if the deal went through. She liked Thomas' passion for making money and his willingness to give back to the black community. But she also couldn't deny that Thomas was a handsome man. She had been dealing with him for over four months and wondered why he had never flirted with her. He was 48 years old, divorced with two teenage children, and lived on a ranch 20 miles from Atlanta. He kept all their meetings strictly business, never giving Monica the inclination that he wanted her.

Thomas arrived at Monica's office 10 minutes early, carrying his expensive alligator skin briefcase and wearing a blue Armani suit with a red silk tie. He walked in and sat at the conference table, displaying his signature smile. Monica looked at him and smiled back. Her full lips enhanced her pretty smile.

"Hey, Thomas," Monica said as she walked over and shook his hand. "You look handsome as always." She sat across from him, taking in the smell of his Burberry cologne. "How is your day going?" She asked.

Thomas retrieved papers from his briefcase, looked up at Monica, and replied, "My day is going swell. And yours?" He asked with a full, bright smile.

Monica gazed into his eyes, trying not to give away her attraction to the man she was conducting business with. "My day is going okay, thanks."

Standing just under six feet tall, with a medium build, Thomas was what any woman would desire. And with his deep pockets and charming personality, Monica was sure that he had his pick of the litter.

"Okay. What do you think about the price of the shopping center?" She asked as she shifted to business mode but still adorned a warm smile.

"I think that we could come down another two hundred thousand. I am looking at another location for my project, and it's significantly cheaper. But I really do want the location we are negotiating. Can you make that happen?" He gave her a serious look, locking his eyes with hers.

"I know we can make this happen, Thomas. I believe that we could have this deal wrapped up by next Tuesday. Would that be ok with you?"

Thomas smiled at her and said, "You bet it's ok. What do I have to do?"

"You can meet me next Monday. We don't have to do any paperwork today. Let me contact my people and let them know that you are looking elsewhere, and I guarantee that we will have the deal you want."

Monica stood up feeling confident and very sure of herself. She shook Thomas' hand as he kept his seat and stared up at her. She could tell from the look on his face that he was confident he would get the deal he wanted.

When Thomas walked out of Monica's office, her mind drifted to a place she knew she had no business fantasizing about. She stared out of the window and fixated her thoughts on what Thomas was like in bed. Monica was married and never once stepped out on her husband; she never had any intentions of cheating on him. But she now found herself lusting for the affection Marcus no longer seemed willing to give her. She craved to make love and felt there was no sense in fighting the feeling that she missed so much.

Chapter Two

Marcus had just ended his meeting with THE DRAKE COMPUTER COMPANY when his cell phone rang.

"Hey, girl! What's up with you?"

The woman on the phone was Kyra Grant, who he had met at a business party his company hosted in the ATLANTA HILTON two months earlier. She was aware that he was married and had a five-year-old daughter. But after exchanging phone numbers and a few lunch meetings, their relationship had advanced to the bedroom. Marcus loved the color of her skin. Kyra had a light, silky complexion with short, black hair. She wasn't the typical light-skinned girl.

He teased her, "Your ass is too round. You definitely have white in you. But that ass is all Sistah!"

She loved Marcus' sense of humor and every moment they

spent together.

"Hey, Honey!" She bellowed into the phone. "Are you free to stop by at four o'clock?"

"You bet. Will you be butt naked when I arrive?"

She laughed and said, "Ain't I always?"

"Yeah! That's the way I like it!"

Marcus hung up and sat at his desk. He reflected on the night that he and Kyra met. When he looked at her, he knew that he wanted her. She was sitting at the bar, wearing a short black skirt that curved her body, and he was standing by the dance floor, holding a glass of cognac. He was mesmerized by her smile. Her full lips highlighted her beautiful white teeth. Kyra was a beautiful light-skinned Sistah. When their eyes met, they kept their gaze locked. Something told him to go over and introduce himself to her. The curiosity had gotten to him, forcing him to disregard his marriage.

Marcus arrived at Kyra's loft apartment at four twenty that afternoon. When she opened the door, she was completely nude. He looked down at her breasts as he walked in and closed the door behind him. His eyes slowly descended to the perfectly groomed black hair between her legs. She stepped to Marcus, pinning him up against the door. She looked up at him, grabbed his head, and pulled it to her. While looking him in his eyes, she forced her tongue into his mouth and began kissing him passionately. She then unzipped his pants and slowly slid down until she was on her knees. She pulled his penis out and began to suck it. Marcus looked down at her head, working back and forth. He began to grow longer and wider, watching her go to work on him. Before he reached his climax, he reached down and pulled her to her feet.

"Hey! You are going to make me cum with that great head!" Marcus groaned.

Kyra looked him in the eyes and said, "That was my purpose."

Marcus stroked her hair, gazing back into her eyes, and said, "I know. But I need that good ass pussy." He then walked her into the bedroom and undressed her.

Kyra lay on the bed and opened her legs. She loved the way he looked down at her when she was in that position. She knew he would dive inside her wet pussy with that long dick, fucking her just the way she needed.

"It's hot and wet," she said in a seductive voice. "Open for you to come in."

Marcus kept his gaze between her legs. "I see. I see. And it looks so good!"

Kyra put two fingers inside herself, soaking them with her hot juices, then slowly raising them to her lips and licking both fingers. She tasted the two fingers and said, "It tastes so good, too."

That excited Marcus, sending his head down between her legs, tasting it for himself. He looked up at her, watching her suck her two fingers, and asked, "Do you like that?"

"Hell yeah! Eat me, Baby!"

After Marcus made her cum by tasting her, he slowly climbed on top of Kyra and slid himself inside her. He loved the way she screamed as he fucked her. She was very vocal, talking shit and giving it back to him, and her shit-talking turned him on.

"That's it, Marcus! Fuck me! Give me that big dick, Daddy! You like this pussy! Huh? Do you like this hot ass pussy, Daddy! Make me your bitch! Fuck me, dammit!"

After their lovemaking, they both lay on their backs, breathing hard and fast. Marcus had met his match. Kyra had turned him out. She was twenty-five years old with energy. She knew how to please a man. She would go to any measure to ensure that her man was pleased and took pride in her work. She had told Marcus that and lived up to her word. He had never met a woman like Kyra before. A sex maniac. A FREAK! A woman who would go to any length to please herself while getting pleasure from turning a man out.

Marcus awoke at 8:00 p.m. that night. He began to not care about getting home late anymore, which had become irrelevant to him. His priority had become Kyra, ignoring the fact that he was married with a daughter. He had lost focus and was beginning to lose his love for his wife. He wanted every free moment spent with Kyra. Something about her made him deviate from his home and responsibilities, and she had taken him to a new world of sexual pleasure.

Marcus got dressed and sat at the edge of Kyra's bed. She had awakened and sat up in bed with the cover over her. They both stared at each other without saying a word. Marcus looked at her stroke her short hair. She looked away at the window, pensive and pleased.

"What are you thinking about?" He asked. "You look deep in thought."

She turned her head slowly towards him. "Just thinking that I wish you were not married and had to leave after every time you make love to me. I wish that I could sleep by your side all night."

Marcus began to feel sorry for her. He had told her that he wanted the same things that she wanted. But his situation would not allow him to stay nights with her.

"I know how you feel. I wish that I could too. But being married means that I have to go home. Believe me, my home is not what it is here." He looked into her eyes, hoping to convince her of the truth. He no longer desired his wife because of his relationship with Kyra. He tried to convince her of his desire to be with her.

Monica had become just a wife and nothing more. The mother of his daughter.

Marcus made it home at 9:30 p.m. that night. Monica was in her office reading over papers and contracts. She glanced over her glasses, watching him ignore her and walk up the stairs. He didn't communicate with her anymore about his business or whereabouts. Maybe he had been working on new deals just as I am. Perhaps he had been out with his friends for drinks and didn't bother to tell me. Could the business be weighing too heavily on him? Maybe he needed time to come back around to talk to me. She would wait and see. She loved him and wanted to stand by him. But she was in need of an orgasm from her husband's hard penis. Marcus' neglect of satisfying her hunger for sex started to drive her crazy. And the thought of being with Thomas was due to the fact that she wasn't getting any sex from her husband.

Monica went upstairs, hoping that her husband would be responsive to her. But he was under the covers when she opened the bedroom door, fast asleep. She undressed and got into bed, hoping he would awake and pleasure her. She turned her head and looked at him. His back was turned to her, and for a moment, she felt the need to touch and wake him. But something told her not to disturb his sleep. She looked up at the ceiling and began to fantasize again. She slid off her panties and opened her legs. Monica started to stroke herself, feeling the heat from her wet pussy. She stroked herself until she was satisfied. But it was not like the real thing; a man going in and out of her, looking up at him while he fucked her, the look on his face while he stroked her, the passion of a man telling her how hot and wet she was, and cumming inside of her after her orgasm.

Marcus was already gone the next morning when she awakened from a deep sleep. She glanced over at the clock. It was 8:00 a.m. She knew that Taylor was still asleep since it was Saturday. Monica lay in bed staring up at the ceiling. She knew that Marcus was probably at the gym. Or maybe he was at his office working on a proposal to sell more computers. He had stopped communicating with her about where he was going or what he was doing. *Could he want a divorce?* She thought. *If so, why? Have I neglected him in any way?* The questions started to mount, causing a sense of nervousness and anxiety.

The phone rang and startled her, taking her mind off her husband. "Hello?"

It was her sister, Tasha.

"Hey, Sis. How are you?"

Monica yawned into the phone and said, "I'm okay. How are you?"

"I'm doing fine. Are you going to let me keep my niece today? I promised her that I would take her to the movies."

"Sure. What time are you going to come pick her up?" Monica asked.

"I will be over at three o'clock. Is that ok?" Tasha confirmed.

Monica rose from the bed and brushed her hair with her hand. "I will make sure she's ready. Is she going to spend the night with you?"

"Yes. Brianna wants a sleepover with her cousin. She's been asking me when Taylor will come over and stay the night."

Tasha was two years older than Monica. She was divorced and had a seven-year-old daughter. Monica always looked up to Tasha, admiring her toughness and realness. Tasha was educated but gave the impression that she was only street smart. She was not the one to let a man call the shots on her. Tasha was fair but would not compromise her stand with any man. Maybe that was why she had trouble keeping a man, Monica thought. And the fact that Tasha could fight with the best of them and was quick-tempered often sent men packing. She was not the woman who a man could be physically abusive. And a few had attempted to control her with fear, only to discover that they couldn't hang around after hitting her.

Monica's cell phone rang, and she told her sister that she had to take the call. It was Marcus.

"Hey, Honey," she said, hoping for something positive.

"Hey. I'm going to be at the office all day. Is there something Taylor wanted to do today?" He asked.

"No. Tasha is coming to get her and take her and Brianna to the movies." She was disappointed that he wasn't calling her.

"Okay. Does she need any money to take with her?"

Monica thought, *silly ass question. You know she never needs any money.*

"No, she does not need any money. You know Tasha would not have that."

"Well, I thought I would just ask. Okay, goodbye." He was short.

Monica hung up the phone and sat down on the bed. She crossed her arms over her chest. Something was wrong with her marriage, if only she knew what and why. She began to cry, wondering what she had done wrong.

Chapter Three

Monica lay in bed thinking of her husband. It had been an hour since Tasha picked up Taylor. She wanted Marcus to come home because she was alone. They would have no one to disturb them. They could have fun, make love, get a bite to eat, and make love some more, just like it used to be. Monica began to drift off to sleep, thinking of how wonderful her husband's sex was. She would not pleasure herself this time. She would just have to sleep it off and hope that Marcus would come, wake her, and give her what she needed.

Monica jumped up, frightened by the loud sound of the fire alarm. She quickly put on her pajamas and ran to the bedroom door to see if there was a fire.

"Oh, God!" She screamed. She could see smoke coming from the attic. She ran down the stairs and out onto the front lawn.

She was terrified when she saw smoke coming from the top of her house. She could hear the sound of a fire engine approaching as she stood motionless in the front yard. She turned and saw the fire engine stop in front of the house.

"Ma'am, are you ok?" a white fireman asked as he hurried out of the fire engine. He was about six feet tall and had a southern accent.

"Yes," Monica responded, shaking with fear. She noticed a tall, dark, handsome fireman preparing to put on his safety gear. Monica watched as he put on his safety coat. He was wearing a tight blue shirt that showed his muscular build. After he was dressed, he motioned for another fireman to go inside the house with him. She watched as the two firemen approached her house while another two were preparing to get the hose ready in case of a fire.

"Ma'am. We have to ask you to step to the street, please," the white fireman directed her.

Monica waited by the fire engine until the two firemen came out of the front door. The black fireman she noticed came out and removed his air pack. She watched him as he walked up to the white fireman. Monica figured all was well because they hadn't used the water hose. She kept her eyes on the black fireman. He was dark but had hazel eyes. His hair was cut short, but it was wavy. She could not recall ever seeing a man that dark and handsome. The way he walked, Monica knew he was sure of himself. He displayed an air of confidence.

"Captain. It was an electrical problem. The wiring finally gave way, resulting in a shortage which caused a spark." As he told his captain what had caused the smoke, he occasionally glanced at Monica. He wiped the sweat from his face with a towel and placed the towel in his back pocket.

The captain looked over at Monica and nodded in her direction, "Go and check her out. See if she needs any medical attention from the smoke."

The tall, dark, handsome fireman stared at Monica and responded, "Ok, sir." He walked over to her and guided her back to the fire engine.

"Come with me," he said in a deep voice. "Are you okay? Did the smoke cause you to cough or have shortness of breath?"

She looked up at him while walking beside him. "No. I heard the fire alarm and ran downstairs immediately."

He looked into her eyes and smiled. "Thank God we got here in time. That wiring could have caused a fire." He asked her to sit down on the back end of the fire engine and pulled out his medical equipment. "Now we are going to check you out and make sure you are okay. Just standard procedure."

Monica could not stop staring into his eyes. She was mesmerized. "What's your name?" She asked, surprising herself at her question.

He smiled. "My name is Fireman Mann; Kenneth is the first name. Our station is in this neighborhood, about six blocks away."

"I know. I pass by it all the time. I never noticed you there," Monica said. She could not break her lock on his eyes.

He chuckled and looked away briefly. "I've been there. Maybe you noticed but just didn't register when you saw me again tonight."

"How old are you?" Monica got personal. His deep silky voice made her feel tranquil and intrigued to get to know him. She gazed into his eyes again and quickly said, "You don't have to answer that if you don't want to."

He laughed and answered, "I'm 35. I will not ask you your age."

Monica smiled and said, "I am 36. I am not one of those women who play the age guessing game."

"Well, ma'am. You are a beautiful 36-year-old black woman." Kenneth took notice of the way Monica's pajamas accentuated her curves. He noticed her round, tight ass, perfect breasts, beautiful smile, and full, luscious lips. Her dark caramel skin complimented her beauty. "Well, you are okay. Everything checked out fine. You need to call your electrician and get that wiring taken care of." He pulled out a writing pad and said, "I need to get your information for the report." He laughed and continued, "I would have known your age from your date of birth." Kenneth gathered Monica's information and said, "I am really glad that you are okay. You have a very nice day."

She reached out and shook his hand, "Thank you, Mr. Fireman." She flirted with him, hoping he would notice. But he shook her hand, not giving her a sense that he noticed her flirting.

"Take care, ma'am. I have to get to another call." Kenneth shared before climbing onto the fire engine.

Monica watched him intently. The fire engine sounded its sirens and headed down the street. Shen went back into her house, sat on the couch, turned on the television, and put her feet up. *Now, why did I put myself out like that?* She thought to herself. Was she missing the pleasure of a man that much? First, she fantasized about Thomas and now the fireman. Had her hormones gotten that far out of control? Was she thinking about cheating? No. It was just her imagination running wild. She would not cheat on her husband, she convinced herself. She would wait it out and find out the problem. Her husband was just under pressure trying to keep his business successful. When he wanted her, she would be available for him only.

Monica picked up the phone and called her husband. His cell phone rang until the voice mail picked up.

"Hey, Honey. The attic had smoke, and it set off the fire alarm.

The fire department came by and said faulty wiring caused it. They said it could have caused a fire. We need to contact an electrician about the wiring up there. Okay. Talk to you later."

Monica seldom called Marcus' office because he was always in meetings. She usually calls his cell phone and he would call her back when he had the time. She'd typically wait for him to call her back. Maybe he would come rushing home to see if she was ok. Perhaps he would be worried enough to run home, grab her, and pull her into his arms. And then, maybe, they could get back to where they once were, always laughing and enjoying each other's company. Her mind was now back to where it needed to be. On her husband. Who she knew loved her more than anything in the world. He just needed time. And she vowed to give him the time he needed. She would delete her thoughts and fantasies of being with Thomas and forget that she ever flirted with Kenneth. She would not be weakened from being deprived of sex. Marcus will come around soon, giving her the attention and pleasure that she so desperately needed.

Chapter Four

Marcus and Kyra lay in the bed talking, Kyra puffing on a cigarette and occasionally taking a sip of her wine. It was eight o'clock in the evening, and Marcus had not checked to see if Monica had called. Being with Kyra had become his only focus when he was with her. He had forgotten how Monica went to every measure to please him sexually. Whatever Marcus desired, she would submit to his sexual preferences. No questions asked. Marcus had neglected that he once told his wife that she had the hottest pussy he'd ever had. For some reason, Marcus dismissed his wife from his sexual desire. Kyra had somehow interrupted the truth now hidden inside of Marcus. There was something freaky about Kyra letting him have his way with whatever he desired. She had become a new toy for him.

Kyra looked over at Marcus, a serious look on her face. "Hey, Lover. You better get home. I'm sure she has called you."

Marcus looked into Kyra's eyes and smiled. "Maybe she has, and maybe she hasn't. I'm sure she is busy working on new real estate deals and probably hasn't thought of me."

"Now I find that hard to believe. You are not even mine, and I think of you constantly. I am horny for you, always," she said, smiling at him.

Marcus gave her his serious look and replied, "So you don't think that you are not on my mind constantly? That I am horny as hell for you all the time?" Before she could answer, he continued, "Haven't I been seeing you quite a bit?"

"You have been with me a lot. Yeah." She admitted.

Marcus got out of bed and began to dress. "I do have to get going. Will I see you Tuesday?" he asked.

"Sure. I will be looking forward to it." Kyra confirmed.

Kyra was the third woman that Marcus had been with within a year. His rise to success had brought much more attention from the *Sistahs* in Atlanta. Love-making with his wife had begun to dwindle, and he didn't notice that he was now neglecting the woman he had married. Kyra was the most exciting of his mistresses, and she had given him a sexual high that he had never experienced. Their relationship had taken him to ecstasy and made him lose focus of what was most important to him—his wife and daughter.

When Marcus got into his silver BMW X5, he checked his phone. He had a missed call from Monica. He had guessed that she called when he was with Kyra. But Monica wasn't the kind of woman to blow up his phone. He checked his voicemail and was alarmed by the messages she left. *Smoke from the attic? The fire department?* he thought to himself. Marcus quickly phoned home hoping that Monica wasn't downplaying the incident. He hoped that it was not an actual fire that had to be extinguished.

He yelled into the phone as soon as Monica answered, "Hey! What do you mean there was smoke coming from the attic? The fire department coming by?"

"It was faulty wiring up there. They said it could have caused a fire, but it didn't. We have to have something up there rewired." Monica responded.

"I'm on my way home. I will go up there to check and see if everything is okay."

"How long will it take for you to get here?" she asked

"I am about 25 minutes away. Why? Is there something else wrong?" Marcus was annoyed by her question.

Monica paused for a few seconds, thinking she should tell her husband that she wanted to make love to him. "No. Nothing is wrong. I just miss you, and we have the house to ourselves."

Marcus' voice became brusque. "Well, I am tired and don't feel up to anything. I just want to check the attic and relax before I go to bed."

Monica gave a long sigh. She hoped for a positive response from her husband. But she knew from the sound of his voice that something had gone wrong. What? She did not know, nor could she understand.

"Okay, fine. I will be in my office."

Monica sat at her desk and stared at the computer. Her focus now switched from her work to her marriage. She already vowed to give Marcus his space and was willing to give him time to come around. She yearned for a time when they danced in the bedroom, when he would act on impulse, take her upstairs to the bedroom, and pleasure her to the max—when silly pillow fights and tickling her feet were foreplay. She missed the moments when he looked into her eyes and told her she was the most beautiful woman he had ever known. And most important, the time when he would say, "Monica. I love you more than anything in this world."

Monica could hear the keys unlocking the front door. For some reason, she became nervous, and her palms began to sweat from anxiety.

When Marcus was inside, she called out to him. "Hey, Honey."

Marcus gave a dry response. "Hi."

She attempted to strike up a conversation. "How was your

day?"

Marcus walked by her office, gave her a quick look, and then looked away. "My day was busy, and I am going up to check the attic."

Monica knew there was no need to try and push herself on him. She had concluded that it would make things worse. So, she tried to redirect her focus back to her work. After a failed attempt, she turned on her CD player. The soothing beat of "By Your Side" began to play. And then the sexy crooning of Sade started. Monica began to sing along, rocking her head from side to side. "You think I'll leave your side, Baby? I wouldn't do that." She sang along, knowing that the words held a paradigm of her feelings for her husband. She held back her tears, not wanting Marcus to see her cry. Instead, she breathed deeply and concentrated on the song's calming lyrics.

Thirty minutes later, Marcus interrupted Monica's groove. "Hey," his voice was loud and cold.

Monica was startled as she reached for the volume button and turned the music down. "Hey, Honey." She answered

"I checked the wiring and will call the electrician in the morning. It's nothing to worry about tonight. The firemen must have cut some of the wires which cut off the power up there." Marcus looked at Monica without expression. "Sade again, huh?"

She smiled, almost letting out a laugh. She knew that Marcus liked Sade's music too. They had made love to every Sade CD. "Yes. Just felt like listening to her."

Marcus walked away and said, "Okay. I'm going upstairs to shower and relax."

"Okay, Honey. I will stay down here a while." She said as he walked up the stairs.

When Monica heard the bedroom door close, she went to the kitchen and poured herself a glass of red wine. She walked back to her office and closed the door. She was in the mood to listen to music. She flipped through her CD collection, lining up the CDs she preferred. She drank wine and listened to music deep into the night. With her wine and music, she would have her own private party. She popped in Tupac's *All Eyes on Me* and danced to its titled song. She held up her glass and shook her ass, rapping along with Tupac. Drinking wine made her horny, but she would somehow make it through the night without pleasuring herself. She would just rock to her music until she was too sleepy to think about sex.

Monica rocked her head back and forth and side to side. She felt freaky, so she dropped her hips and opened her legs, opening and closing them as if she was a stripper. The wine was taking its effect, making her loose and reckless. She had on a strapless sun dress that stopped just above her knees. She visualized Marcus being directly in front of her, looking at her goods and wanting to slide his piece inside her, taking what he wanted. Without hesitation, Monica slowly slid her panties off while still dancing. She threw them on her chair and raised her dress. She twirled her hips to the beat and smacked her ass with the palm of her hand. She was definitely in a zone, and it felt good to her.

She dropped her ass to Juvenile's "Back That Ass Up." She spread her legs and waved them open and close, repeatedly reaching down and touching her hot and wet pussy. *You know you want this hot ass pussy, Marcus! I don't know why you trippin' Niggah! Pull that long dick out and get to work! Now!* She was talking major shit in her head, making her want to run upstairs, pull the covers off her husband and ride him until he couldn't take it anymore. However, she opted to drink her wine and rocked until the wee hours of the morning.

The following day Monica was awakened by Marcus. She had slept on the couch in her office. She didn't remember lying on the sofa. The last thing she remembered was dancing to ZAPP's More "Bounce to the Once." She looked over at the table and noticed an empty bottle of wine. Her head was throbbing, and her feet ached. She looked at Marcus, who was standing at the door with a look of disgust on his face.

Marcus shook his head and snarled, "What the hell? You drank all that wine?"

Monica looked at him without responding. She felt ashamed. She had never partied by herself and gotten wasted with wine in her office. He'd seen her get tipsy before, but not in this way. She had done it because she was lonely and horny, and something came over her causing her to flow with impulse instead of reasoning.

Marcus shook his head again as he walked away. "I'm going to the gym." He slammed the door as he walked out of the house.

Monica looked over at her clock, which read 8:43 a.m. She continued sitting on the couch, trying to replay the previous night. The memories started to come to her slowly. She remembered telling herself, "Fuck Fred! And the goddam horse he rode in on! Shit, I'm horny and want my damn husband to want me!" She remembered dancing around the office, giving her stripper act. *Shit! I was tripping.* She thought.

Monica finally got to her feet and went upstairs. She undressed and sat on the side of the bed. She rubbed her face and then brushed her hair back with her fingers. She needed a shower in the worst way. She remembered the disgusting look on Marcus's face when he saw her in her condition. She was embarrassed and knew that she had lost points with him.

After she showered, she lay in bed, trying to gain her senses. Sudden sleepiness overcame her, and she did not try to fight it. She thought of the disappointed look on Marcus' face. How would she regain his confidence? She had gotten intoxicated with him many times, and he would take her upstairs and fuck her like he was a mad man. But having too much to drink and not being able to make it upstairs surely seemed to piss him off. Now she lay nude under the covers hoping that Marcus would have cooled off by the time he returned home. She wished he would pull the covers off her and give her a good fucking for being a bad girl. She fell into a hopeless, deep sleep.

Chapter Five

Monica drove through her neighborhood in her new navy-blue Infiniti G35. It was Tuesday, the day that she and Thomas were scheduled to close on the property they had negotiated. She passed by the fire station where Kenneth worked. She saw him pulling a hose on the fire truck. She slowed down and bit her lip, wondering if she should speak to him. After all, he was nice to her and made sure that she was in good health. She stopped and looked into her rearview mirror to see if any cars were coming from behind. The coast was clear, so she backed up and parked on the curb by the fire station. Monica looked into the mirror to make sure her appearance was on point. She got out of the car and walked near the edge of the driveway.

"Hey!" she yelled.

Kenneth quickly turned toward her and stood at attention. He remembered her and was surprised to see her stop by the station. He strolled towards her, keeping his eyes locked on hers. "Hey, you. How are you?"

Monica smiled with flirtatious eyes. "I am fine, Mr. Fireman. How are you?"

"I'm fine. Just washed the fire truck and checked the hose. What brings you by?" he asked.

"I was passing by, and I saw you." She looked at his muscles bulging through his tight, blue shirt. His eyes mesmerized her as he got close. "Hope I'm not intruding."

"No! No." He began to laugh as he extended his hand to her. "Glad to see you and glad to see that you are okay."

Monica laughed and said, "Thanks to you, I'm fine. Thanks for the quick response. If it were not for you arriving when you did, I would have burned alive."

Kenneth gazed into her eyes. He could not help but notice her natural beauty. Her skin was so dark and lovely. It was a silky chocolate, her lips full and luscious—the perfect combination of a gorgeous black woman. He had to tell her that she was a beautiful woman. "You are a very beautiful woman." He let out.

A feeling of excitement came over her, and she could not hide it. "Thanks for the compliment."

Monica wanted to know more about him; luckily, she had time

to ask. Her appointment was not until four o'clock that afternoon.

"Where are you from?" His southern accent told her he was from the south but not from Atlanta. He had a certain deep, southern twang to his accent.

"I'm from Arkansas. Did my accent give it away?" He chuckled.

Monica laughed and said, "It sure did. How long have you been in Atlanta?"

"I have been here for ten years. I played football for The University of Georgia, and after I graduated, I joined the Atlanta Fire Department." Kenneth surveyed Monica's long, slim, and fit body. "And are you from Atlanta?"

She followed his eyes as they moved from her breasts to her legs. She wore a tight red and white dress that stopped just above her knees.

"No, I am from Birmingham, Alabama. I have been living in Atlanta for quite some time now, and my family moved here when I was in middle school."

Kenneth's eyes quickly returned to Monica's beautiful, smiling face. "I see. And where are you going, all dressed up at two thirty in the afternoon?"

"I have an appointment at four o'clock at my office," she replied.

"Oh? And what is it that you do?" He asked.

Feeling proud of her accomplishments, she answered, "I have my own real estate franchise. Can I give you my business card?"

"Sure." Kenneth stared at Monica with a questionable look in his eyes. Then he asked, "Are you married?"

Monica looked down, and a feeling of shame came over her. At first, she didn't know how to answer his question. She took a deep breath and replied, "Yes. Yes, I am."

Before Kenneth could respond, Monica thought, *there's nothing wrong with being friends*, and rambled, "I don't see anything wrong with giving you my business card. Besides, I am conducting business, and there is nothing wrong with making friends in the process." She looked into his eyes and smiled. "Follow me, and I will give you my card."

Kenneth followed her to her car, his eyes glued to her ass. Damn! He loved her walk. She possessed the confidence and a style of pure class. He could tell that she wasn't an arrogant woman at all. Something told Kenneth that Monica was a friendly woman by nature. But most of all, he read something about her that intrigued him more. Something in her eyes gave away her secret. Something was missing in her life that made her look at him the way she did the first time he saw her. And when she stopped by the fire station, she gave him the same look, reassuring him that she needed special attention.

She didn't know it, but Kenneth was an excellent reader of people. Something he learned from his tumultuous childhood growing up in Arkansas. And there was definitely a nexus with her. Suddenly, her visit had given him a sense of fate. The look in her eyes and smile on her face told him that a special friendship was in the near future. He liked her from the first time he laid eyes on her and wanted to see her again .

Monica handed Kenneth her business card. "My cell phone number and office number are on there. Feel free to give me a ring."

"I will. Friends, huh?" Kenneth smiled at Monica. He looked at her car and said, "Nice car. It fits you perfectly."

Monica got into the car, rolled down the window, and called out, "Thank you, Mr. Mann."

A surprised look came over Kenneth's face. "So, you remembered my last name?"

She laughed and said, "No. It's on your tight shirt."

"Oh shit! I thought you had done some kind of research on me." He joked.

Still laughing, she said, "No. I have a feeling if I wanted to know something about you, you would provide the information."

Kenneth laughed along with Monica. "I sure will. And that depends on how much we get to know each other. Hopefully, we can become friends. A person is always in need of friends. Friends are very valuable."

"Friends we are, Mr. Mann. Call me." Monica waved goodbye and drove away.

Monica arrived at her office shortly before three thirty that afternoon. She sat at her desk looking over the contract that her attorney had drawn up. She had gotten the deal that Thomas wanted and felt good about making a huge profit from the sale. Thomas entered her thoughts as she looked out the window. She had vowed that her relationship with Thomas would only be about business. That's it. Nothing else. Her loneliness would be a thing of the past when Marcus decided to show her the love and affection she needed.

Thomas arrived at exactly 4:00 p.m. He wore a charcoal gray Armani suit with a red and white silk tie. He looked tempting. But she quickly focused her mind back on the business at hand. She could tell by his expression that he was pleased with the deal. The negotiations were done, and it was time to put pen to paper and move on.

"Hey, Monica," he said with a smile as he sat at the conference table. "I had faith in you all the time. Damn, you are good!"

Monica smiled back at him and said, "Thanks for having confidence in me. And thanks for giving me the opportunity to be your realtor. I owe you big time." Then she paused while still smiling, "Why don't I treat you to dinner and a drink? Is that asking too much?"

The smile on Thomas' face disappeared. He looked into Monica's eyes, his expression serious, and said, "Don't think that would be a good idea. I have a fiancé and would not want to give anyone any false idea that I was cheating. You are a very attractive woman, and I know that there would be natural jealousy from my fiancé. I do thank you for the offer."

Feeling a sense of relief, Monica said, "Well, I thank you for your honesty. I wish you and your fiancé the best. And I definitely don't want to start any rumors about you or me."

Then Thomas replied, "And besides. I have met your husband before, and you are correct. We don't want any rumors to come about."

Thomas had never mentioned that he knew Marcus until that moment. *Why didn't you mention that before?* She thought to herself. "Well, that's the end of that. But I want you to know that the dinner would have been only a business dinner. Just want you to know that." Monica sat down at the table and laid out the paperwork. "Okay, let's get started, shall we?"

After completing the deal with Thomas, Monica decided to treat herself to dinner and a drink. She chose an upscale Italian restaurant five minutes from her home. It was 6:30 p.m., and Giovanni's Restaurant began filling with many of Atlanta's bourgeois working class. Monica had frequented the establishment in the past but couldn't stand the shallow conversations of, "Oh, I just bought a Mercedes, and it cost seventy five thousand dollars." Or, "Girl, you wouldn't believe how much it cost me to remodel my home!" And, "Robert just bought me a ring, and it cost nine thousand dollars." Monica would think to herself, *these people are not used to having shit.* She was glad to have arrived before the crowd. She sat at a table near the back of the restaurant, where she had a clear view of the people walking in and out. She ordered the Italian Greek salad with shrimp and crab meat and a glass of red wine. She thought about Marcus while sipping her wine. She had called his cell phone before she left the office in hopes he would meet her there. But he told her that he had business to finish. Taylor was at Tasha's house and would not be home until about nine o'clock that night. The night was perfect for her and Marcus to kick it and share her enthusiasm for closing a lucrative deal. She wanted to share a glass of wine and a meal and then go home and have fun together. But being with her husband had become a lascivious fantasy with no hope of getting the real thing any time soon.

Chapter Six

That Friday evening, Monica labored in the kitchen, preparing one of Marcus' favorite meals. He loved her lamb chops prepared in garlic butter. Marcus had told her that he would be home for dinner and sounded pleased that she was preparing one of his favorites. Monica was elated to hear the satisfaction in his voice. She hadn't heard that from him in quite some time. Maybe after the family consumed her masterpiece and once she sent Taylor to bed, they could have some romantic time together.

Marcus arrived at 7:30 p.m., just as he promised he would. "Hey, Taylor," he said as he walked to his daughter. "How are you, my Little Princess?"

Taylor jumped into his arms and wrapped her arms around her dad's neck. "I'm fine, Daddy!"

"That's great! How was school today?" he said while gently

squeezing his beloved daughter.

Taylor yelled cheerfully, "We had field day today!"

Marcus eased Taylor down to her feet, and then he kneeled. "Give Daddy a kiss," he said and closed his eyes.

Monica watched the playfulness between Marcus and Taylor from the kitchen. It made her smile, and she knew that Taylor was his pride and joy. As she once was.

"Hey, Honey," she said to Marcus. "Hope you are hungry."

Marcus looked at Monica and walked to the kitchen. "Smells great."

Monica gave a euphoric smile and said, "Why, thank you! I aim to please my man!"

Marcus looked at her and gave her a tepid smile. Then he walked to the bathroom to wash his hands. He looked back at Monica and asked, "Will we be eating soon?"

Monica realized that Marcus wasn't all that enthusiastic about her cooking for him. The look on his face read, serve the damn food and let's eat. There she was, standing over the stove, asking herself the same questions for the last two months. *What is wrong with this man? What have I done? I just wish he would tell me what the fuck I have done to be avoided like this!* She wanted to grab him and scream, "What the hell is going on with you?" But she didn't want anything to ruin the dinner she had prepared. Maybe after dinner, once Taylor was in bed, they would talk. She could then tell her husband how she was feeling.

Dinner went rather quietly. Marcus seemed only interested in conversing with Taylor, occasionally asking her about school. Each time Monica chimed in, he would only look at her, and then it was back to Taylor. Maybe he didn't want to talk while in the presence of their daughter. Perhaps he wanted to save the talk between them for the bedroom. She hoped he would somehow open up and tell her what he was going through.

Monica left Marcus and Taylor downstairs playing checkers. Taylor was becoming a good checkers player after being taught by her father. She took a quick shower and put on a sexy silk nightgown; the red one was Marcus' favorite. She decided to surprise him when he showed up for bed. She put on his favorite jazz CD before spraying on a touch of perfume. She was setting the mood for a romantic ending. She vowed to give it to him just the way he liked it.

Marcus opened the bedroom door, and Monica was on the bed, her back against the headboard, her long legs open to show her husband that she wasn't wearing any panties. He shook his head as if disgusted and went to his walk-in closet without saying a word. Monica couldn't understand his disdain for her. He undoubtedly displayed a look of, I don't give a damn!

When Marcus walked out of the closet, Monica finally got the nerve to ask the questions she'd been screaming in her mind all along. She stood up and firmly asked him, "Marcus! What is your problem? What have I done to deserve the silent treatment and non-affection you have been displaying?"

He took off his tie, looked at her, and dryly replied, "I have been very busy, Monica. Trying to make sure you and my daughter are secure for the rest of your lives. I am sorry I haven't been giving you the attention you feel you need."

"That I feel I need? That I FEEL I NEED?" Monica kept her voice low but very serious and emphasized her question as she repeated it. "Marcus, you haven't touched me in…in I don't know when. You haven't told me that you love me in I don't know when." Her voice raised a few octaves and continued, "What do you expect of me? I have been trying to reach out to you, and you just blow me the fuck off!"

Marcus pointed his finger at Monica and barked, "You better calm your ass down! Don't get fucking loud with me. You know that I don't play that shit! Take your ass to bed!"

Monica started to move closer to her husband. She was not willing to give up the fight. "I will NOT take my ass to bed until you tell me what the fuck is going on with you!" She paused and then shouted. "So, fucking tell me, dammit!"

Marcus walked to Monica, grabbed her by the arm, and threw

her on the bed. "Don't you take that tone of voice with me! You know fucking better!"

Monica had to gain her composure. Taylor was down the hall, and she was sure her daughter had heard the commotion. Marcus had never once acted violently toward her. That was the first time he had laid a hand on her. Although he didn't strike her, his actions were something new to her. The Marcus she knew would never throw her to the bed like that. There was something different with her husband. Something had altered his behavior towards the woman he once held very high regard.

Monica leaped up from the bed, ran to Taylor's room, and opened the door to see if her daughter had heard the incident. Monica found what she had expected; her daughter was lying in bed crying. She had heard the fight between her parents and was now afraid. Monica quickly ran to her daughter and held her in her arms. She assured her that everything was okay.

"Me and your dad just had a little argument, Baby. Shhhhhh-hh. You can stop crying now, Honey. Everything is okay."

Monica lay next to Taylor and decided to sleep with her daughter. She was confident that sleeping by her daughter's side would ease the fright she felt. She rubbed her daughter's head until she fell into a deep sleep. She looked at her daughter and smiled. You are so beautiful, with your black self. I will always protect you, Baby. Monica began to cry as she turned her back to Taylor. Her life was spinning out of control. Her marriage was suffering, and she had no idea why.

At five o'clock the following morning, Monica went downstairs to her office. She knew Taylor would sleep in past eight o'clock, and she didn't want to bother her. Monica figured Marcus had not gotten up either, so she turned on her computer and began looking at properties for sale. She needed to take her mind off her problems, hoping that work would relieve her mind of last night's incident. Her husband's bizarre behavior was something new to her. She would not know what to say to him when she saw him. Something inside of her made her want to go upstairs and apologize for her behavior. Maybe she overreacted and caused the fight by pushing him to talk to her. Perhaps he was under pressure trying to ensure that she and Taylor were set for life. Maybe she didn't understand the pressures a black man had to compete in a world with many obstacles in their pursuit of wealth and happiness.

The more Monica thought about the night before, the more guilt she felt. She decided to make the first move and make things better. The last thing she wanted was that night to linger on. She headed upstairs to her bedroom to wake Marcus. She wanted to tell him that she was sorry and that she understood the pressure he faced. When she opened the door, he wasn't in bed. Oh, maybe he's in the shower, she thought. So, she sat on the bed, waiting for him to finish. But then she thought, I don't hear the shower. Maybe he's using the bathroom. She waited another twenty minutes, and still nothing. At that point, Monica got up and walked to the bathroom. The door was open, and there was no sign of her husband. Slightly confused, she went downstairs to the garage to check and see if his BMW was there. When she opened the garage door, her heart sank. He was gone.

Chapter Seven

Monday morning, Monica sat in her office staring into space. Marcus had not been home since their fight on Friday night, and he wasn't answering his phone. She picked up the phone and called him again; it went straight to his voicemail. She reluctantly left a message. "Hey, Honey. I have been calling you and decided to leave a message. I am sorry for causing the fight Friday night. I should have understood your being under pressure. I love you, Marcus."

After unsuccessfully trying to reach her husband, Monica called her sister. "Hey, Tasha. How are you, girl?"

"I'm doing fine. Has Marcus called you back?"

Monica had told her sister about the fight, something she wished she had kept to herself. Tasha was furious when Monica told her about Marcus throwing her to the bed. She should have known that her sister would be against a man using physical force on a woman. Monica knew that her sister was a no-nonsense type of woman and in no way would allow a man to push or strike her, no matter what kind of pressure a man was under.

Monica answered, "No, I haven't heard from him."

Tasha paused for a while and then gave her point of view. "Monica, I think Marcus is fucking around on you. Shit. You said he ain't fucked you in over a month, and he is acting like a jackass."

Monica interrupted her sister. "Wait a goddamn minute, Tasha! I don't need to hear that shit from you right now!"

"Well, you know I tell it like it is. And I don't want you to be surprised when you finally find out that Marcus is up to no good. I mean, why hasn't he called you? Even to check on Taylor?" Tasha retorted.

"Tasha, I think he is working too hard to keep his business afloat. Business can be a bitch when you are trying to stay on top." Monica defended her husband.

"Whatever, girl. Ain't that much pressure in the world. And besides, hasn't his computer company been at the top of Black Entrepreneurs? What fucking pressure can he be under? I read that he grossed over seven million dollars this year. That don't seem like pressure to me." Tasha snorted.

"There are other intricate details in running a business. Overlooking all the details to make sure your business stays successful is pressure within itself." Monica continued her weak defense.

"Whatever," Tasha ignored Monica's defense. "And also, with being a successful businessman, whether black, white, green, or yellow, here comes all kind of pussy."

Monica screamed into the phone. "Will you stop?! Just stop!"

"Bye, girl. Keep me posted and let me know how things are going." Tasha replied, not wanting to argue with her sister.

Monica stood up and stared out her office window. The conversation with Tasha had sent her into deep thought. *What if Tasha was right? What if Marcus was seeing someone else, and she was a better fuck than she?* Monica's head started to ache, so she canceled all her appointments and went home. She needed time to think.

When Monica arrived home, she pulled the car close to the garage and sat in the driveway listening to the soothing sound of jazz. The smooth sounds of Kenny G's saxophone relaxed her as she reclined her car seat and closed her eyes. She began to think about when she and Marcus first met. They were both freshmen at the University of Alabama. Marcus was eyeing her from across the room at a fraternity party. She was shy and remembered not wanting to go to the party. But her roommate talked her into going. She remembered Marcus walking over to her, her heart pounding and her palms sweating. She had to admit that she was watching him too. She remembered that he was nervous when he approached her, stumbling over his words, trying to strike up a conversation. She recalled laughing shyly as she looked into his eyes. After he gained his composure, the conversation became quite pleasant, and Marcus was the perfect gentleman. He had won her over and managed to pull her away from the party. Before she knew it, they were walking, talking, and laughing on campus. They had been together ever since.

Her cell phone rang and interrupted her pleasant thoughts of the past. It was Marcus. "Hey, Honey. Are you okay?"

"Yeah, I'm okay." He sounded angry. "I'll be by to pick up some things from the house. I need time to myself. I don't want Taylor to be there. So, I will be at the house in twenty minutes."

Monica's heart began to pound inside of her chest. She wasn't expecting this reaction. "Wait, Marcus! Let's talk about this. I'm sorry for overreacting! Don't do this to me! Please!" Monica begged.

"Look," he said in a calm voice. "I need time to myself. Whether you understand that or not, I am coming to get my things from the house."

"Well, I won't be here! You are acting like an asshole! Why won't you talk to me!" Monica screamed into the phone. "Why won't you tell me what the fuck is going on?!"

"I will be by in a few to get some things from the house, okay?" He reiterated and then hung up.

Monica started the car and pulled out of the driveway. She began to cry uncontrollably as she sped down the street. Perhaps Tasha was right. Maybe another woman was taking her time with her husband. *Maybe she's a bigger freak for him than I am. That definitely would explain him distancing himself from me. But how did he meet her? Where did he meet her? What does she look like? Is she prettier than me?* Monica's mind wandered.

Monica called her sister, who, despite how she got under her skin, was her best friend. "Tasha!" Monica cried into the phone. "I need to come by and talk to you."

Tasha could tell that her sister was crying. "Sure, Monica. I'm in my office grading papers."

When Monica arrived at her sister's office, Tasha got up from her desk, walked to her crying sister, and hugged her.

"Come in and sit down," she said as she held her sister in her arms.

Monica walked over to the small sofa. "Girl, he is at the house getting some of his things. I tried to tell him we could talk about what he's going through, but he didn't want to talk."

Tasha stood over her sister and shook her head. "Monica, let him go. He will be back if he loves you and cares about his family. Whatever he is doing or whoever he is doing it with, he will soon find out that she isn't you." Tasha tried to calm her sister.

Monica looked at Tasha, handed her a handkerchief, and said, "I don't believe it's another woman, Tasha."

"Well, let's hope not. But anyway, take your time and just let things play themselves out. Shit. You are a strong black woman. Mother taught us how to be strong in tough situations. Especially ones like this. All the shit Daddy took her through, and she still went on. She taught us about relationships and men." Tasha reassured Monica.

"I know all about that, Tasha. But each woman is her own woman. Momma was she, and I am me. Marcus and Daddy are two different men." Monica's defenses went up.

Tasha sat down at her desk. She stared at her sister, who was now gaining her composure. "Well, Monica. They are men, both the same. And I am not saying that Marcus is a bad man or nothing like that. But something has got him acting differently. That's all I am saying." Tasha explained her point of view.

Monica didn't give a response. She just sat on the couch and stared at the wall. *What if Marcus had another woman? How would I react to him having an affair?*

Indeed, she will be angry. And then she started to think of her father. He was physically and verbally abusive to their mother. He fathered two other kids while married to their mother. When her mother had enough of their father's corruption, she finally made up her mind to move to Atlanta. Their mother's decision to make a new start when the girls were young surprised everyone in Birmingham. They moved in with her older brother and never looked back.

Monica thought, *I would not separate my daughter from her father. We will work through our problems.* She vowed not to give up her love for her husband and stand by his side until he figured out what it was that he wanted to do. And she knew that he would come back around and see that she was the woman for him. She was the woman who stood by his side when he was struggling to get his business started, the woman who gave him all the financial support when his investments went down the drain, and the woman who gave him a beautiful daughter who looked just like him. She would continue to be his strong black woman regardless of the price she had to pay.

Chapter Eight

After making hot, sweaty love, Marcus and Kyra lay in the bed looking up at the ceiling, playing back the love scene in their heads. Breathing heavily, Marcus looked over at Kyra and said, "Damn! It gets better every time."

Kyra began to laugh as she turned her head to the man that had just rocked her world. "Shit. I thought you were drilling for oil in there. You were so deep! Damn, that shit felt good!"

Marcus looked at her sexy legs and then back into her eyes. "I love how you take it with those gorgeous legs up in the air."

Kyra turned on her side to face Marcus. "Any way you want it. You got it."

Marcus hadn't talked to Monica in four days now. He was too busy enjoying the company of his mistress, and he didn't even think of his neglect of his daughter. Marcus was in a new world of joy now, staying with Kyra. She had become Marcus' new toy, and he loved the ride she was taking him on. Her beauty and her personality intrigued him. And she was all he began to think about.

Kyra was a party girl who loved to hang out with crowds with money. She worked as a nurse at The Atlanta Methodist Hospital and had affairs with several doctors. Kyra was a groupie and wasn't ashamed of it. She kept up with all the conventions of those significant and had money. She was always invited to the professional athletes' parties, sometimes landing one and dating them until they were tired of her. Kyra was definitely proud of her ability to please a man sexually. And she was always careful not to get pregnant. She didn't want to raise a kid alone, so she ensured she had protection at her disposal.

Marcus got up and put on his boxer shorts. He looked back at Kyra and asked her to play her Best of the Isley Brothers CD. He watched her as she walked over to the stereo. She was naked, and he gazed at her ass. He watched as she leaned over to retrieve a CD with her legs unbent and opened. She looked back at him and smiled. She wanted to show him what she had just given him as she watched his eyes go to her hot, wet, soft place. Marcus began to rise again as he slid off his boxers and walked over to her. She looked up at him without changing her position. She knew exactly where he was going with that rock-hard dick. And she wanted it.

Marcus pushed his hard dick inside her as "Between the

Sheets" began to pump out of the speakers. Grabbing her ankles, Kyra closed her eyes and opened her mouth wide as Marcus filled her up with his long dick. She moaned seductively as he stroked her slowly. When she yelled, "Damn, Marcus!" she knew what was coming next. A hard fucking which she desired and begged for. "Fuck me harder, dammit!" she yelled. Feeling the hard thrust of his thighs against her ass made her cum and quiver. "That's it, Baby! That's what the fuck I'm talking about!"

Marcus' legs started to shake as he began to cum inside her. After he had cum, Kyra turned around and got on her knees. She began to suck him, licking their juices. She loved the way Marcus tasted, and she loved freaking him. She knew that she had turned him out. And she wanted to keep him coming back for more.

Marcus finally made it to his office that afternoon. He felt proud of himself as he thought about rocking Kyra's world. He sat at his desk and tapped a pen on it as he reflected on giving it to her doggy style. He refused to answer Monica's phone calls, only listening to the messages she had left and only concerned about his daughter's well-being. Marcus knew Monica was a submissive woman and subconsciously took advantage of her weakness for marriage. He didn't intend to neglect her. Kyra had just made it easy for him to desire her over his wife.

Marcus would have stayed the whole day with Kyra, but he had business to take care of. He had enough mental strength not to allow her great sex to come between his ambition to stay rich. But without realizing it, Kyra had already come between his purpose to show love for the woman he had married. She had come between his motivation to be the father he had promised Monica he would be for Taylor.

Marcus' cell phone rang and interrupted his thoughts. He quickly glanced at the phone and saw it was his friend Ed. "Hey, Ed. What's up?"

Edward Patterson was one of Marcus' best friends from his college days. Ed had taken over his father's warehouse business and was doing quite well financially. Patterson's Warehouse was one of Atlanta's largest and most lucrative warehouses. Ed had majored in business at Alabama under his father's wish. His father retired from the company and wanted to leave it to his son. Back in the day, Ed was a nerd and landed his ride to Alabama on an academic scholarship. Once Ed started hanging out with Marcus and his friends, he went from nerd to hip and cool. And most of all, he had become a player with arrogance.

"What's up, boy!" Ed yelled into the phone.

"Not much," Marcus answered. "Just looking over new ways to make money."

"I hear that. A man has to always stay on top of getting that loot." Ed laughed and asked, when are you going back home, boy?"

Marcus sighed and answered, "Who knows? Monica will be there when I get there."

"Have you talked to her?" Ed asked.

Marcus was frustrated by his friend's questions. He replied, "Look, Ed. I don't feel like talking about my situation. Okay?"

"Cool. Are you coming to Pop's birthday party next week? Man don't renege. I know Kyra has your nose wide open. But Pops is looking forward to my boys coming to hang out for the barbeque. And Bobby's dad is catering for us." Ed wanted to confirm.

"I will be there, and you know that," Marcus assured him.

Ed laughed as he confirmed, "Man! You better be there!" Ed knew that if a man left his family for another woman, there was a great chance that man would start to neglect other obligations. "It's next Friday. And it starts at six in the evening."

"I know, Ed. Count me in. I will be there." Marcus confirmed.

"One serious question, nigga. And don't get mad." Ed got serious.

Marcus took a deep breath and asked, "What is it, Ed."

"Are you bringing Monica and Taylor?" Ed knew that his father and mother wanted to see them; he wanted them over too.

"Ed." Marcus was about to disagree.

Ed interrupted and said, "Man, I'm just asking. You know Mom and Pops want to see them. They haven't seen Taylor in a while. Make up with your wife and bring them." Ed paused and asked, "Okay?"

Marcus hung up the phone and stared into space. He knew that Monica would be elated to go. Monica and Taylor loved Ed's parents. He knew that he could not bring Kyra along with him. However, the temptation to do so was there. But his better judgment told him to call Monica and make the date.

Monica answered the phone, her voice sleepy and weak. "Hello?"

"Hey, Monica. Ed's father is having his birthday party next Friday, and they want you and Taylor to come." Marcus rambled into the phone.

"That's fine, Marcus," she said in a low voice. "Just remind me by next Wednesday."

Marcus' voice rose. "I'm reminding you now!"

Monica cleared her throat and replied in an almost whisper, "Okay. We will be there." And then she hung up the phone.

Chapter Nine

Monday morning, Monica walked around her office as she talked on her cell phone. "Mr. Rogers. I know we can make this deal within the next couple of days." She had another lucrative offer on the table and was determined not to lose it. "I know the land is prime real estate, and they are asking for two million dollars. But I am sure that I can save you close to a million dollars."

After she hung up, Monica walked to the stereo and pressed play. Sade's *Kiss of Life* began to blow from the Bose speakers. The volume was just right for listening in her office. Monica sank into the oversized leather chair and leaned her head back. She closed her eyes and began thinking about Mr. Patterson's birthday party. She still hadn't seen Marcus since he left. She was tired of Tasha's accusations that he was seeing another woman. The office phone rang and snapped her out of her thoughts. She opened her eyes, picked up the receiver, and pressed the talk button. "Stewart's Real Estate." She was surprised to hear Kenneth's voice on the other end.

"Hey, you," he crooned with his seductive deep voice. "How are you doing?"

She lied and answered, "I am just fine. And yourself, Mr. Fireman?"

"Oh, I'm doing quite well. I'm off for three days." He answered.

"Must be nice." Monica's voice livened up. "We all can't have the hours of a fireman."

He laughed and replied, "Yeah, right! You own your franchise, which means you call your own shots."

"I guess you are correct." Monica turned her chair and faced the window. "So what made you finally call me? Were you bored?"

"No, I didn't call you out of boredom. I had been fighting the desire to call. I hope you understand." Kenneth confessed.

Monica's flirtatious spirit began its fervor. "Are you looking to buy some property?" she asked jokingly. She knew he wasn't calling her to inquire about buying property.

"No, Monica. I am just calling to see how you are doing, and I must be honest with you..." Kenneth paused before continuing. "I have thought about you since you came by the station."

"What kind of thoughts?" Monica asked.

"Just thoughts. You know. Wondering if you are doing well and hoping everything is going okay with you." He admitted.

"I am doing well, Kenneth. And thanks for asking." Monica got out of the chair and walked to the window. "It's a beautiful day outside, isn't it?" She made casual conversation.

"Oh, yes," he replied. "I am getting ready to flame broil some steaks on the grill." Kenneth shared.

"Sounds good!" Monica said with enthusiasm. "So, I guess you can cook?"

"I think so, yeah. People say they love my cooking. Hopefully, I can get you to judge it one day." Kenneth extended his indirect invitation.

"Oh, I don't know about that. Tasting your food may get me into trouble." Monica flirted.

"Well, it was you who said we could become friends. Was that just lip service, or were you sincere? I see nothing wrong with being friends." Kenneth reminded her.

Reflecting on the day she stopped by the fire station, she remembered telling Kenneth they could be friends. "Oh...yeah. Yeah! We can be friends." Monica agreed, paused, and then asked, "Friends only, right?"

Kenneth laughed and replied, "Yes! Monica, I will respect you. You don't have to worry."

Monica knew she needed a break from her work and to break the monotony of her everyday twisted life. "So, are you inviting me over for one of your steaks?" She asked.

"Monica, I would love for you to come and join me. I have been curious about you ever since responding to the fire alarm at your house. I am just being honest with you." Kenneth admitted.

"Well, curiosity could lead to things that we shouldn't do. So, let's just leave all that out of the equation. Is that alright with you? Friends, right?" Monica tried to convince herself more than she was trying to convince Kenneth.

"Don't get the wrong idea. By curiosity, I mean getting to know about your childhood, college days, and things like that. You know? Things friends talk about." Kenneth clarified.

"I see. Well, how far do you live from downtown Atlanta?" Monica asked.

"I live about 15 minutes away. Easy to get to." He confirmed.

"What time should I come by?" Monica asked as she took down his address.

Excited about Monica's arrival, Kenneth asked, "Can you be here at five o'clock?"

Monica sat back in her chair. She didn't think Kenneth would call her because she was married. She flirted with him because he was a gentleman and thought he was handsome. And now she had committed to going to his place for a steak dinner. She had mixed feelings and looked at the phone, wondering if she should call him back and cancel. *That would be so rude*, she thought.

Okay, Monica! Friends only! You are a strong woman, steak dinner and conversation only.

Monica picked up her cell phone and called her sister. "Tasha, can you pick up Taylor for me?"

Tasha never questioned Monica when she wanted her to pick up Taylor from school. She always figured it was business related.

"Sure. What time will you be by to get her?"

"It will be before nine," Monica assured.

"Ok. I will get her and call you when we are home." Tasha agreed.

Kenneth lived on the east side of Atlanta in a newly developed subdivision in Kirkwood. There were several vacant lots for sale. His spacious one-story brick home sat on a cul-de-sac with two-story houses on each side. Monica knew the area well. She had done business there several times. She pulled her car into the driveway and looked around. *I hope he doesn't have some crazy woman who will pop up uninvited.* Monica thought to herself.

She turned down the volume on her CD player and reached for her phone. When Kenneth answered, she said, "Hey, I'm out here."

Kenneth walked out of his house wearing all-white silk shorts and a matching silk shirt with black leather sandals. Monica's heart began to race. He had a fresh haircut and looked as if he had just shaved. He looked GQ-ish to her. She watched as he walked to the driver's side of her car. Monica looked from the window, smiling as he reached for the knob and opened the door for her.

"Come on. Get out. I promise I will be on my best behavior." Kenneth teased.

"I hope so," she blushed as she got out of her car. She looked into his eyes as she squinted at him. "I know karate. I can kick you where it hurts." Monica joked. She didn't know karate, but it was all she could come up with to break the ice. She hoped that a bit of humor would ease the tension.

"Trust me. No woman has ever had to use violence on me. And besides, you wouldn't kick a friend's ass, would you?" Kenneth kidded.

Monica laughed as he guided her into the house. She looked around, admiring his taste in furniture and black art. As she observed the living room, she noticed a large wooden shelf near the back wall. She walked over to look at the pictures on the shelves. Monica saw a picture of an older-looking dark-complexioned woman. She looked back at Kenneth and noticed the resemblance.

"This must be your mother," she said.

"Yes, it is. I guess you saw the resemblance?" Kenneth replied.

"Striking resemblance," she said as her eyes wandered to a picture of a younger woman. Curious, Monica asked, "Who is she? She looks like you too."

Kenneth sat at the bar, watching Monica glance over the pictures. He smiled and replied, "That's my older sister."

"Are they still in Arkansas?" Monica inquired.

Kenneth looked slightly uncomfortable. "No. Both have died.

"My mother died when I was eleven from breast cancer. And my sister died of the same when I was a junior in college. My sister was only 36 when she died."

He didn't like talking about the death of the two women he loved more than anything in the world.

He stood up and quickly changed the subject, "The baked potatoes are ready, so I had better start the steaks."

Monica looked over at the huge stereo and saw Kenneth's vast collection of CDs surrounding the tall speakers. "I see you are a man of music." She walked over and skimmed through the CDs. She located Brian McKnight's CD and asked, "Hey, I love Brian McKnight. Would you play it?"

Kenneth walked from the kitchen and put in the CD. "I like that brother, too," he said with a smile. "Look over the collection and play what you like."

He went back into the kitchen, grabbed the steaks, and continued, "I'll be outside grilling the steaks. It should take about eight to ten minutes, and we will be ready to eat."

While Kenneth was out back preparing the steaks, Monica sat and listened to the sounds of one of her favorite musicians. She rocked her head to "You Should Be Mine." She occasionally glanced over at the picture of his mother and sister. They were stunning with deep dark skin. She remembered the look on Kenneth's face when he talked about their deaths. She could tell it still hurt him by the look in his eyes when he spoke of them.

Ten minutes later, Kenneth came through the sliding doors carrying a plate with four nice-sized ribeye steaks. Monica could smell the flavor of seasoning and mesquite wood. She was hungry and couldn't wait to taste Kenneth's cooking.

Kenneth had set the table before her arrival. He prepared her plate with steak and a large potato, then called her over.

"That looks good!" Monica said with delight in her eyes. "Thanks for inviting me over."

"I'm glad you came over," Kenneth replied. "Hope you enjoy it. The toppings for the potato are right here," he said as he lowered the round large round plate to the middle of the table.

After dinner, Monica and Kenneth sat at the table on his back patio. Kenneth sipped a glass of beer while Monica had a glass of red wine. Talking to Kenneth during their dinner made her feel at ease. He was funny and easy to talk to. The conversation didn't get too personal, but it was enough to start a *friendship*. The getaway was just what Monica needed; she definitely needed a good laugh.

Monica looked over at Kenneth, who was staring out into space. "Hey. What are you thinking about?" she asked.

Kenneth turned his head slowly to her and said, "Nothing important. Just thinking about this evening and how glad I am that you came over."

Monica remembered the thought of another woman coming by unannounced when she was in the driveway. "There's no crazy woman lurking around here, is there?" she teased.

Kenneth laughed, "No, there better not be." He knew that was her way of asking if he was seeing someone.

Then she asked the question that she had held on to all evening. "Are you seeing someone, Kenneth?"

Without hesitation, he answered, "I was seeing someone. That relationship has been over for about four months now."

"And you haven't seen anyone since that time?" Monica probed.

Kenneth nodded and said, "I have seen someone else after. An old friend. A blast from the past." He paused for a moment and then continued, "I also have been on a few dates here and there. But nothing serious."

"I have no business asking you about who you've been with. That's none of my business anyway." Monica didn't want to seem like she was prying. However, she was curious about his love life but had to find some way to downplay her thoughts.

"It's okay to ask," Kenneth said. "I have nothing to hide. And besides, we are becoming friends, right?"

"You are correct. But your business is your business." Monica looked down at her watch. "Hey, it's seven forty five. I really must go. I have to get my daughter."

Kenneth stood up and said, "Okay, be careful driving home. And will you call or send me a message to let me know that you two made it home alright?"

Monica extended her hand to Kenneth and said, "I can do that. And thanks again for dinner."

"You are very welcome," he said while walking behind her through the door. "And hopefully, we can have a friendly meeting again soon."

"I don't see why not." Monica looked back at Kenneth as she walked out the front door. "The next time, I will treat you since you went through the trouble of cooking for me."

Kenneth opened the car door for her. When she was seated and had started the car, he said, "It was no problem cooking. I enjoy it at times."

"I understand. But I want to return the favor. And I will not be cooking," Monica laughed. She waved goodbye as she backed the car out of the driveway. "You take care."

Monica drove to her sister's house, relieved she had something else to occupy her thoughts. *Thank you, Kenneth.*

Chapter Ten

That Wednesday evening, Monica and Taylor were at Tasha's house having dinner. Tasha had called Monica that morning and insisted that she and Taylor come by because she was preparing her signature meatloaf, greens, and mashed potatoes. Tasha wanted to spend time with her sister because she knew her commitment to Marcus and his being away weighed heavily on her. Tasha also felt sorry for Monica because she always had a problem facing the truth regarding men. Tasha knew that her sister always wanted to accept the world the way she wanted it to be and not for what it really was.

Monica got off the couch, went to the kitchen, and stood by her sister, who was preparing a salad. "I told you that I would help. Is there anything you need me to do?" she asked.

Tasha looked at her sister and lay the knife and tomato on

the cutting board. "No, Monica. All I need you to do is relax and watch what you want on TV. I am done with everything; we will eat as soon as I cut this tomato."

Monica poured herself a glass of wine and sat at the dining table. She watched her sister slice the tomato and put it into the salad bowl. "Tasha. I just want you to know that Marcus' actions are not consistent with his personality. Something has happened to cause this reaction. You know Marcus yourself. And you must admit that something isn't right with him." Monica pleaded Marcus' case.

Tasha walked over to the table with the salad bowl. She sat down next to Monica and rubbed her sister's arm. "Monica, I know Marcus is a good man. And sometimes, the best of men stray from home. All I am saying is.be prepared to accept whatever has made him deviate from his family."

Tasha looked into her sister's sad eyes. "Monica, I love you, and you know that. And I am going to be here for you whenever you need me. You know that I face the truth no matter how much it hurts. I want you to do the same. Always have wanted you to look at things for what they are." Tasha comforted her sister.

"I know. I guess it's just easier for some people to accept the truth than others." Monica conceded.

Taylor and Briana were in Briana's room playing video games.

Tasha yelled for the girls to join them for dinner, and she and Monica laughed when the two girls came racing down the hall.

"I guess they must be hungry," Monica teased.

"I know Briana is. Girl, she can eat! I don't understand where all that food goes. She is so skinny and has an appetite like a cow." Tasha shook her head at the thought of her daughters' extra healthy appetite.

After dinner, Taylor and Briana hurried back to playing video games while Monica and Tasha sat on the couch with a glass of wine. Monica looked over at the TV and saw the 'Breaking News' flash across the bottom of the screen. The volume was muted, but she could see an apartment building burning behind the female reporter. To Monica's surprise, the scene switched to Kenneth carrying a woman from the burning apartment building. Her heart jumped, and she turned to face the TV screen.

"Tasha, turn the volume up!" Monica yelped.

Tasha reached for the remote and turned up the volume. The reporter continued to give her report on the scene that was taking place.

"As you can see behind me, the fireman is carrying a woman who was trapped inside one of the units. Reports are that the woman suffered smoke inhalation and minor burns but is expected to recover fine. The firefighters are believed to have safely gotten out everyone trapped inside. I'm Cynthia Starks reporting from WAGN 27."

Monica wanted to tell Tasha that she knew the fireman that saved the woman but decided that the time was not right. Now was not the time to divulge her having dinner with Kenneth, causing her sister to start asking questions and grilling her about something innocent. So, Monica played it off as if she was only interested in the news story.

"Wow," she said, looking over at Tasha, whose eyes were also glued to the TV.

Without looking at Monica, Tasha replied, "I know, girl! Look at that fire. I'm just glad that no one was hurt."

It was about 9:00 p.m., and Monica was ready to go home. She called for Taylor and thanked Tasha for having them over. She had to get Taylor prepared for school and herself for work. Monica knew her sister would be there for her whenever she needed her. She hoped Tasha's prediction about Marcus would be untrue or unfounded, and she was glad that Tasha didn't harp on Marcus having an affair.

Monica lay next to Taylor at home, reading her a bedtime story. Taylor loved "The Lion King" and asked her mother to read it to her. It was a little after 10:00 p.m., and Monica knew that Taylor would be sound asleep after a few pages; her prediction was correct. Once she heard heavy breathing from her daughter, Monica quietly eased out of bed and covered her sleeping princess.

After showering, Monica lay in bed looking over potential deals. She tried unsuccessfully to remove thoughts of Marcus. But the picture of them together taken at Ed's party was on the nightstand, and she couldn't take her eyes off it. They had fun that night, dancing, and drinking. She remembered Ed had rented the ballroom at The Atlanta Wyndham Hotel Downtown, and he reserved rooms for the party guests if they desired to stay the night. Monica and Marcus had gotten a suite on the 27th floor. She remembered the gorgeous view of Atlanta from the balcony. She also remembered her and Marcus making hot, passionate love on the balcony at four in the morning.

Monica reflected on the time when Marcus showed her affection and gave her attention. Not wanting to face reality, the thought of her husband's abandonment of loving her struck a hard blow to her already fragile psyche. Marcus hadn't really shown her love nor attention in nearly a year. Sure, they would make love, but when he was done, he would just roll over and go to sleep or get out of bed and go downstairs. He had stopped caressing and holding her. He stopped rubbing her back gently and stroking her hair. He stopped telling her that he loved her. The thoughts began to make her headache as Monica lay back. The tears started to roll down her cheeks slowly as she cried uncontrollably. Soaked by tears,

Monica drifted off to sleep.

Monica awoke from a light sleep and glanced over at the clock. It was three thirty in the morning. Her mind automatically went to her husband. *Where is he? Why is he acting like this?* She sat at the edge of her bed and rubbed her face with both hands. Her neck was tense, and she began to roll it to ease the tension. She stood up and gave a long stretch, her arms as high as she could get them. It relieved her tired body as she walked to the CD player. TLC's *Crazy Sexy Cool* came to her mind. She flipped through her CDs until she found the one she wanted. She put it in and programmed it to number four. "Diggin' on You" started to play as she sat back on the bed, soaking in the sounds.

The rain began to tap on the bedroom window, and thunder started to pound the skies. It was now 6:30 a.m. and Monica had not gotten much sleep. She had to wake Taylor for school. She knew that the way the rain was pouring, Taylor would not be up to getting out of bed. The rain always made her daughter drowsy and unwilling to get out of bed. Monica thought it was cute whenever her daughter heard the rain and rolled over, saying, "Mom. It's raining. I don't want to get up."

Monica looked at her beautiful 'Dark and Lovely' as her Infiniti eased down the street. She smiled as Taylor lay her head on the door, sound asleep. The rain tapped on the car's windows as Beyoncé's "If I Were a Boy" was at the perfect volume allowing Taylor to continue sleeping. Monica's focused on the lyrics as her mind multi-tasked, thinking about her situation. She began to associate the words of the song and her relationship with her husband.

After walking Taylor to the school's front door, Monica hurried out of the rain and sat inside her car. She knew that if Taylor was awake during the ride to school, she would have inquired about her father. Taylor was beginning to miss Marcus, and it started to show. Monica started to see a difference in Taylor, her spirit not as high and her smile not as often. Monica had to get her husband to come home for the sake of her daughter. Taylor was the most important thing in her life, and she didn't want anyone or anything to change that.

Monica thought about the birthday party that Ed's father was having on Friday. She knew she only had one day to get ready to see her husband and convince him to return home. She pulled her car away from the curb and drove back home. She decided not to work that day and focused only on how to get her husband to love her again. She would buy a new sexy outfit for the party just for Marcus' eyes. She would cater to him by being submissive and eager to show him how much she loved him. She would talk about only the things he wanted to talk about. Monica began to put her plan into place to win her husband's trust and show him she was all he needed.

Chapter Eleven

Friday evening, Monica sat on the edge of the bed listening to her Janet Jackson *Rhythm Nation* CD. It was 5:00, and she was dressed for Mr. Patterson's party. She had gone shopping at Macy's for her and Taylor the day before. She loved how the black silk dress sculpted her body and highlighted her round ass. The dress revealed enough cleavage and legs, ensuring her that Marcus would definitely take a second look. Monica stood in front of the long mirror, admiring her curves. *Perfect*, she thought to herself.

As Monica cruised the freeway, the mood was silent between her and Taylor. They hadn't spoken a word since Taylor told her mother she looked great. Monica would sneak a peek at her beautiful little girl every so often. Taylor kept a pensive gaze out of the window, looking down occasionally at the floor. Monica knew that her daughter had mixed feelings about seeing her father. She knew

Taylor didn't understand why her parents fought, causing her father to leave the house.

They arrived at the Patterson's house just before seven o'clock. Monica parked her car next to the curb and looked over at her daughter. "Hey, Sweetie. Daddy is going to be so glad to see you." She rubbed Taylor's hair and smiled. Then she looked her daughter in the eyes and said, "Give him a big hug when you see him, Okay?" Taylor nodded her head in agreement.

Monica held Taylor's hand as they walked toward the backyard. The Gap Band's "Humpin," vibrated the air as they got closer to the wooden fence. Monica could hear loud laughter and talking as she walked through the fence. She immediately spotted Ed and Bobby Dubose, another of Marcus' best friends. They both had a beer in their hands, talking loudly and laughing. When Ed noticed Monica, he quickly lowered his beer from his mouth and went to greet her.

"Hey, Monica!" he shouted as he approached her. He gave her a tight hug and a kiss on the cheek. "How are you?"

Monica smiled and said, "I am doing just fine, Ed. And yourself?"

"Couldn't be doing any better," he said, laughing. "Come on over and say hello to Pops."

Monica looked back at Bobby as she walked away. "Hey, Bobby," she called out. She didn't see Marcus as she attempted to locate him as she walked to a sitting Mr. Patterson, who was also laughing loudly as he told another one of his childhood stories.

When Lewis Patterson saw Monica approaching the table, he stood up excitedly. "Hey, Monica!" he shouted. "And look at my Little Princess," he said, laughing as he reached down and hugged Taylor.

Monica gave Mr. Patterson a tight hug and pulled away, looking at him with her wide beautiful smile. "Just look at you! Happy birthday! Still lookin' good!"

"Why thank you," he responded with his playboy pose. "And you look ravishing as ever."

She still hadn't seen Marcus. She gave Mr. Patterson his gift and begged him not to open it until after the birthday song was sung. After Mr. Patterson agreed, Monica's eyes scanned the backyard for her husband. The Patterson's estate sat on ten acres surrounded by pine and pecan trees near Gresham Park. The house was a huge one-story brick home with a game room separate from the rest of the home and located on a remodeled second floor. Monica always admired the estate every time she visited.

The Patterson's had exquisite and expensive taste in furniture and black artwork. They only shopped at expensive furnishers. And they order the most expensive artwork, mostly black art.

Monica always admired their art selections and even asked for Mr. Patterson's assistance with purchasing for her own collection. Mr. Patterson had given her famous pieces from Dr. Biggers and Charles Criner. She hung the artwork in her upstairs hallway so she could admire their beauty every time she climbed the stairs.

Monica sat at a table underneath a canopy near the edge of the backyard. Taylor joined her, sitting with her hand between her closed knees. Monica stared into the wooded acres. The sun descended, and the sixty-nine-degree evening temperature was perfect for the occasion. Then out of nowhere, Marcus appeared from behind the shadows of the trees. Monica could see he was on the phone, laughing as he approached the sitting and dancing guests. He was looking down as he walked, his laughter getting louder as he got closer to Monica's table. Her heart began to pound heavily inside of her chest. She was anxious to get back acquainted with her husband.

Marcus looked up, surprised to see Monica and Taylor sitting at the table. He quickly turned his back and whispered into the phone. "Hey, Baby. I have to go now. I have to pay my respects to the birthday man." He slipped his phone into its case and walked over to Monica and Taylor. "Hey, my little princess!" he called out to his daughter. "How are you?" He then gently grabbed Taylor and lifted her in the air. "I miss you so much," he told her as he looked into her eyes.

Monica gazed at them as Marcus kissed Taylor and rubbed noses with her. She was excited to see how happy her daughter looked. Taylor laughed loudly and held her father's face with her tiny hands. She noticed Marcus peeking at her as he held Taylor. She yearned for him to miss her so much that he wouldn't want to stay at the party but instead leave to take her home and make passionate love to her. Monica hoped that Marcus would freak her like he had never freaked her before, tasting all she had to offer and then some. She would treasure him sucking her toes as she moaned with ecstasy. She would accept his usurpation of her willing body, allowing him to do as he pleased.

Marcus interrupted Monica's fantasy of him making love to her. "Oh, hello, Honey."

Monica replied to his lukewarm greeting. "How have you been?" She didn't know how to respond as she tried to clear her mind of sweaty sex with her husband.

Marcus looked down at Monica as though she was transparent. In his deep voice, he replied, "I have been doing just fine." He looked her up and down and then returned his gaze to her eyes. "You look nice."

She smiled gleefully and folded her arms across her chest. "Thank you, Honey!" she said exuberantly. "You look quite handsome yourself."

Ignoring Monica's compliment , Marcus sat next to Taylor and began talking to his daughter. Monica held her gaze on her husband, understanding that spending time with Taylor was very important. She would wait her turn and hoped to make the most of it. She missed him and wanted him to know and understand that. Monica marveled at his fresh haircut and trimmed mustache; she couldn't get over how nice he looked in his designer jeans, blue and beige button-down Kenneth Cole shirt, and black Kenneth Cole shoes. She recognized a sense of confidence on his face. She sensed a cockiness about him that she hadn't known before; there was something definitely different about him.

Taylor decided to head over and keep Mr. and Mrs. Patterson company, sensing that her mother wanted to be alone with her father. Monica watched proudly as her daughter walked happily to where the Patterson's sat. She smiled at her little princess, wishing her family would restore the luster that had seemed to fade away so quickly. Monica turned around to face Marcus. He was leaning forward and checking his cell phone.

She took a deep breath and exhaled, "Hey, Honey. Would you like me to fix you a plate?"

Marcus looked up at her, a puzzled look on his face. He leaned back and rested his cell phone on his leg. "No," he answered and looked away, staring into the woods. "I've already eaten."

Monica took her gaze to the floor and then asked, "Well, can we take a walk? Maybe talk about us?"

Marcus was annoyed and replied with a terse answer, "No. I don't feel like walking nor talking."

A look of dejection came across Monica's face. Her husband's tone sent her into a deep sadness. She stared at Marcus for a moment, trying her best to hold her emotions inside. She wanted him to know what she was feeling; she pleaded, "Marcus, I am really hurting. I love you so much and will do anything to make this right." She took a deep breath and begged, "Please take a walk with me?"

Marcus stood up, got close to Monica, and through clenched teeth, said, "No. I don't feel like it, and this is not the time nor place for us to discuss this." And before he walked away, he told her, "I am going to the bar and get a drink."

Monica's emotions started to vacillate from sad to angry. *How could he treat me like I am just another somebody? I miss him so much and want to be all I can be for him. You bastard!* Her hormones were out of control, and she wanted him to fuck her. She wanted to leave the party early, take her husband upstairs and freak him out. What was up with his chicken shit attitude? His meanness for no reason. She needed to feel his dick inside of her. And she would not be denied; not tonight. She got up, walked to the bar, and stood behind him. She tapped his shoulder and said in a definitive voice, "Marcus. We are going for a walk, and we are going to talk about us!"

Marcus took a sip of his Hennessy on the rocks as he turned to face his wife. He looked down at her and growled, "Get the fuck away from me."

Monica became outraged. Before she could gather herself, she blurted out, "Fuck you, Marcus! You bastard!" Not caring if anyone heard her, she walked over to the table where Taylor and the Patterson's were sitting. "Come on, Taylor. We have to go." She grabbed her daughter's arm and pulled her as she walked to the gate. Monica was in a zone she had never been in, and she didn't give a damn if anyone at the party detected her anger. She just wanted to take her daughter and leave.

Marcus hurried, catching up with Monica after she walked through the gate. "Monica! What the fuck was that? In front of my goddamn friends?" he yelled.

Monica stopped and looked Marcus in the eyes. "I don't give a fuck about what you have to say right now! Get the fuck away from me and my daughter!" She turned around and began to storm away.

Marcus reached out, grabbed her arm, and swung her around to face him. "Don't you walk away from me! You ruined my fucking night! I told you this was not the time or place for this shit!"

Monica looked at Marcus' hand gripping her arm and then

slowly turned her gaze up at him. She had a pernicious look on her face. "Get your goddamn hand off of me! Now!"

He looked into Monica's eyes as he slowly released his grip. "Don't you ever do that shit again," he said in a low voice and then walked away.

Monica looked down at Taylor, who was crying. She watched helplessly as her daughter wiped the tears from her eyes. Monica bent down to console her. "I'm so sorry, Honey," Monica told her as she wiped the tears away from Taylor's eyes. "I am taking you home now, okay?" Monica was crying and couldn't stop the tears she wanted to hold back so bad. She tried to be strong for her daughter. Monica secured her daughter in the front seat and brushed her hair with her hand. "I love you, Taylor." She got in the car, tears still flowing down her face, and managed to start her car and drive away.

Marcus returned to the party and quickly noticed a waiting Bobby. Bobby was never serious about anything, and Marcus didn't feel like putting up with his jokes about what had just happened. Marcus pierced at Bobby and said, "Not now, Bobby. I don't feel like you playing now."

Bobby laughed and said, "Man, that was fucked up." He shook his head and walked away.

Bobby was always the jokester of the crew. No one knew how

he made it as an attorney. His family owned one of the most famous restaurants in Atlanta, and he and Marcus had known each
other since high school. Marcus introduced Bobby and Ed, and all
three became close like brothers. Bobby was divorced with two
young sons, one seven and the youngest four. He vowed never to
remarry again and be a player for the rest of his life; he was true to
his word He constantly emphasized that love was so overrated.

Marcus walked to the edge of the wooded area and pulled out
his phone. He knew that the guests were looking at him, and he
was now the focus of the party. He called Kyra in hopes that it
would subdue his anger.

"Hey, girl. What are you up to?"

He knew that if she wasn't busy, he could go over and take his
anger out by fucking her with everything he had, and she would
love every minute of hard fucking and getting her pussy eaten. And
Marcus wanted his dick sucked, knowing she would swallow all
he released into her mouth. He was pleased when Kyra said she'd
come over after the party. Kyra was what he needed.

Monica pulled into her garage at 9:30 p.m. She looked at her
daughter, who was asleep, her head leaning on the car door. She
let the garage down and leaned her head back. She had no idea

what she should do next. Her emotions were spiraling out of control. She didn't know why things had gone the way they had. She tried to figure out what she had done wrong. Why had her husband suddenly become disconnected and disinterested in her? She had no answers and didn't know where to begin to try and find the answers. She knew that she had to somehow pull herself together for the sake of her daughter. But her pain made her wonder how she could pull off being strong. Monica was devastated by her current love affair and knew that a miracle would be the only way she could gain her composure.

CHAPTER TWELVE

Monica sat at her desk the following Monday afternoon, sifting through papers. Business was going great, but it didn't make her feel any better. Her happiness had abandoned her to the point of depression. She hid her depression well when she was around her clients and friends. But her sister knew that she was depressed and wanted to be by her side. Tasha kept Taylor the Saturday after the party, allowing Monica to sleep all day. But now she sat in her office trying to regain her focus to perform her job.

She leaned back in her chair and stared at the wall. How could she focus on her job when all she thought about was her husband? He had left her and Taylor without giving any reason. Taylor missed her father dearly. And the questions that began to surface about his whereabouts began to weigh heavily on Monica.

The love for her husband sent her mind in and out of reality. Surely another woman wasn't the reason for dismissing his marriage and family. It had to be another reason for her husband to act the way he was. She knew that Marcus loved her. But could he have lost the love he once held so affectionately for her? *Had some other woman captured him, causing him to stray?* The thought of Marcus being with another woman caused her head to ache. She had to shake the thoughts of Marcus making love to the phantom woman that had begun to haunt her.

Monica turned her chair to face the window. In deep thought and deep depression, her office phone rang, taking her mind briefly away from her troubles. She picked up the phone. "Hello." It was Kenneth, his deep voice coming smoothly through the phone.

"Hey, Monica. How are you?" He sounded gentle and sincere.

Rubbing her hair and smiling, she answered, "Hey, you! I am okay, I guess. And how are you?"

Kenneth paused and took a deep breath. "I'm fine, Monica." He paused again and tried to get his words together. "I…" Then another pause.

Monica leaned forward in her chair. She was worried that something was wrong. His voice sounded low and nervous. "Kenneth. Are you okay?" she asked.

"Monica…I don't know how to say what I want to tell you. I

don't want to disrespect you in any way," he cautioned.

Her brow furrowed in concern. She stood up and began to pace around the office, phone glued to her ear. "Kenneth, what is it? Just talk to me." She urged.

Kenneth took another deep breath and then paused again. "Monica, I think about you all the time. I have not stopped thinking about you since you came by my house." He breathed deeply and continued, "You made a great impression on me. I have been wondering what you are like and what type of things you enjoy. And how beautiful you are," Kenneth confessed.

Monica was pleased with what she was hearing but had to slow Kenneth's expressions. "Kenneth, I appreciate that you like me and all. I really do. But you do understand that I am married?"

"Yes, I do, Monica. I was just letting you know my feelings. I can't help how I feel. But maybe you're right...I should have kept my feelings to myself." Kenneth sighed.

Monica sat in her chair and began tapping a pen on the desk. "Kenneth? What do you want from me?" Monica exclaimed.

"I just want your friendship. That's the first thing. Get to know more about you. You intrigued me the moment I first laid eyes on you." Kenneth replied.

Taken by his sultry voice and admiration, Monica asked again, "So, what do you expect from this friendship?"

She left the door open for him to give her the answer she wanted but tried so hard to fight. She was feeling neglected by her husband and yearned for some companionship. She had to admit that she was impressed by Kenneth the moment she saw him and when she visited his home.

"I don't want to rush into anything. I am just expressing my feelings to you. I will understand if you reject my offer." Kenneth began to concede.

A huge grin came across Monica's face. "And what is your offer?" she flirted.

Kenneth laughed and said, "Monica, I just want to see you again and have a nice conversation."

"Nice conversation, huh? And that's all?" she teased.

Laughing louder, Kenneth responded, "Look, Monica, I have to admit that you turn me on. But I am a strong man who can accept just being friends."

Monica's gut told her that Kenneth wasn't being totally honest with her. She had a feeling that he wanted more than friendship. She knew he wanted her and had seen it in his eyes. But she was in control of what would happen if he wanted more, and it would be her decision to give herself to him or keep it strictly platonic. Kenneth's friendship would be something of interest to her. She was lonely and depressed, and Marcus had abandoned her without reason, so she believed. And if he were seeing another woman, her decision to start a friendship with Kenneth would probably keep her from going insane.

"Kenneth, I would love to see you. As a friend." Monica gave an opening as she crossed her legs and tilted her chair back. She rested her pen on her bottom lip as she spoke into the phone. "When do you want to meet for a drink?" She was ready for someone to take her mind off her troubles other than her sister.

"Whenever it's convenient for you. I am off until Saturday," Kenneth shared.

Monica twirled her chair around and looked out the window. Giving in to her desire to see Kenneth as soon as possible, she asked, "So, what are you doing around six tonight?"

"Are you sure? I would like nothing better." Kenneth perked up.

"I'm sure. If it's okay with you and you don't have anything planned." Monica stood up and walked to the window. She figured that if there were going to meet for a drink, it would be near Kenneth's home. She didn't want anyone to see her out with Kenneth. And the possibility of being seen by anyone she and her husband knew would be slim.

"No! Nothing planned." Kenneth's voice exuded excitement. "I would love that." He paused and said, "Monica, I know you would prefer an inconspicuous spot, and I know just the place. It's close to me, and it has a great jazz band. Will that do?"

Monica was excited, "Sure! I love jazz. What's the name of the place?"

"A bar sat off Interstate 75, about five miles from my house. One of Atlanta's prominent DJs once owned the jazz bar and had sold it to a local businessman. *Jaay's'*. It used to be Frank Skies." Kenneth confirmed the location.

Monica had ventured there when Frank Skies owned it but had not been there since. She hadn't known it reopened under a different name. "Sure. Are you sure we won't run into one of your crazy women?" she teased.

Kenneth laughed and said, "No! Trust me. You don't have to worry about that."

Monica laughed along with Kenneth. "I will meet you there at six o'clock, Mr. Mann."

Monica arrived at Jaays' 30 minutes ahead of the agreed time. The weather was perfect, a still, dry evening with temperatures in the mid-60s. She flipped down the sun visor and opened the mirror. Feeling nervous and anxious, she put on a fresh coat of red lipstick. Keith Sweat's, "I Want Her," thumped lowly from her speakers as she looked into the mirror. She stared into her brown eyes, and a feeling of guilt invaded her conscience. She thought about calling Kenneth and reneging on the date. But the thought of going back on her word overruled canceling the date.

Monica sat back in her seat and tried to relax. *What am I doing?* she thought to herself. *What if someone sees me?* The more she thought of someone discovering her with Kenneth, the more uneasy she became. She looked down at her watch, and the time seemed to have crept up on her. *Shit! 5:50!* Before she realized it, Kenneth was standing outside of her window. She looked up at him, managing a feigned smile. She took an undetected deep breath, knowing there was no way of canceling the date at this point. She mustered up enough strength to open the door and get out of the car to greet her date.

Kenneth stood tall, wearing a navy-blue Armani suit and a beige button-down shirt with no tie. Monica stared into his hazel eyes, keeping her smile. Although nervous, she was curious to get to know the fireman that answered her alarm. *Damn, this man is fine!* "So, how are you, Mr. Mann?" She managed to get her first words out.

Gazing into her eyes and giving a half smile, Kenneth responded, "I am doing okay. A little nervous." He took a deep breath and then laughed. "Okay, I'm lying. I am a lot nervous!"

Monica laughed shyly as she looked down at her feet. "Join the club."

"I figured as much." Kenneth looked at Monica, knowing she

was attempting to gain her composure. He knew she was concerned about the risk of being seen and wanted nothing more than for her to feel at ease during the date. "Why don't you go inside first and see if the coast is clear, ya' know? Look around and if you don't see anyone you know, call me on my cell phone and tell me where you are sitting."

"No! We are walking in together." She reminded herself that she did have her own business and meeting male clients was a norm. But her knowing that meeting Kenneth wasn't business made her feel guilty. "If anyone I know sees us...well...it's a business deal," Monica hesitated with her excuse.

"Okay. Then let's go listen to jazz and have a few drinks." Kenneth let Monica walk ahead of him. Looking down at her round ass, he smiled with pleasure, and erotic thoughts began running through his head. *Damn! Her dress was form-fitting and stopped just above her knees.* She had a matching jacket that stopped at her lower back, leaving a full view of her plumpness.

An up-and-coming local jazz band was playing a rendition of Guy's, "Piece of My Love" as Kenneth followed Monica to a table near the back of the club. She hadn't spotted anyone she knew so far, and her nervousness dissipated. The club wasn't crowded yet, and Monica hoped it would remain a moderate crowd. But this was Atlanta, and every night was a club night. It could easily fill up with patrons eager to get their groove on. And the thought of running into Bobby Dubose would be a disaster.

Monica settled for a table with a full view of the jazz club. She could also see most, if not everyone, that entered the club. Kenneth sat across from her, relaxed and smiling. They listened to the jazz band, loving the soulful flow they were hearing. Monica hoped the waitress would hurry to their table; she needed a drink to help her relax and loosen up a bit. She looked across at Kenneth, who was eyeing the band. She could tell that he was enjoying the music. And she knew that he also needed a drink to ease his nervousness. His conspicuous nervousness turned on Monica. She liked the fact that he wasn't arrogant or egotistical.

The waitress finally came to the table. Kenneth watched Monica as she ordered a "Long Island."

The waitress turned to Kenneth, and he ordered a Crown on the rocks. When she walked away, he looked at Monica and joked, "Long Island? Acting grown!"

Monica lowered her head and squinted her eyes. "Grown? I am very grown, thank you," she said sarcastically.

Kenneth began to laugh. Her reaction amused him. He loved how she looked whenever she responded to his teasing or joking. Her neck jerked from side to side, and she batted her eyes. She was sassy but funny. It was cute, and he could tell she would be fun and exciting. Something about her started a fire inside him, and he wanted to find out all he could about the beautiful, dark, sexy woman sitting before him. He did not want to disrespect her position as a wife, but. . . he wanted what he wanted.

Kenneth stared at Monica's full lips as she enjoyed the band. She looked like she was in deep thought. But a few drinks would loosen them both up for engaging conversation. Kenneth wanted to become her 'friend' and hoped he would not say anything to ruin his chance. This fire burned inside of him the moment he saw her. And after she visited the fire station, he could not get her out of his thoughts. There was something special about this dark and lovely. Kenneth was determined to find out what unique qualities Monica possessed. Disregarding the risks and dangers, he had his mind made up.

The band took a recess, and a DJ took over. When Maxwell's, "Somethin' Somethin'" began to play, Kenneth stood up and extended his hand to Monica. She reached out, placing her small hand in his, and stood up. She led him to the dance floor swaying her hips back and forth while Kenneth was checking out her ass.

The dance floor wasn't overcrowded, but many couples were grooving to the beat. Monica began to swing to the beat as she glided across the dance floor. She turned to face Kenneth, whose eyes were glued to her swinging hips, as his body held the beat with hers. They were both dancing and having a great time. Monica was impressed with Kenneth's moves on the dance floor, surprised he could dance so effortlessly well. His moves mesmerized her, turning her on as the drinks began to take effect. Her moves and her beauty also turned-on Kenneth. *What a sexy ass woman!*

It was getting late, and Monica knew that she had to get home before doing something she would regret. The way she was feeling, Kenneth could have his way with her, and she wasn't ready for anything like that. "Kenneth, it's late, and I have to get going." She danced herself into happiness. And for four hours, she had left her troubled world behind. It felt good to get out, laugh, and dance with Kenneth. She learned more about his past and was intrigued that he had made it out of his troubled childhood, playing college football and becoming a fireman.

Monica definitely wanted his friendship and companionship. She was happy that he had called her, and they spent the evening together. The girlish feeling swirled inside her soul, a soul that needed to be touched and caressed, penetrated and satisfied. A soul that was on fire and needed to be extinguished. However, Monica vowed not to let that happen with Kenneth. *At least not tonight.*

Chapter Thirteen

The following morning, Kenneth sat outside on his patio listening to Marvin Gaye's What's Going On. The sky was clear, and the temperature was a pleasant 70 degrees. He knew that Atlanta's weather could sometimes be unpredictable, especially in the fall, so he wanted to enjoy the beautiful subtle breeze while he could. It was nearing October, and the temperature was pleasant. The thought of Monica's beauty and sexiness raged inside of him. After he arrived home the night before, he sat in his favorite chair, reminiscing about their night together. Now he was relaxing on his patio doing the same thing. She was his first thought when he awoke. And he couldn't help but wonder and hope that he was her first thought when she awakened.

Kenneth's cell phone rang just as he began to fantasize about Monica. He looked at the phone, and it read, Mark Boudreaux. "Hey, what's up, boy?" Kenneth answered.

"Not much. What do you have planned for the day, Mr. Mann?" Mark asked.

Kenneth stood up and took a long stretch. Sounding as if he had just woken up, he said, "Don't have anything planned yet."

"Well, you don't have to return to work until Saturday, so let's hook up and do something. I am off 'til Friday." Mark invited.

Kenneth knew his best friend wanted to call a few girls over and have him cook on the grill. He and Mark usually entertained women at either one's place, but Kenneth had stopped doing it as often as he used to. Mark would get upset whenever Kenneth declined his offer.

Mark was 42 years old, going on 19. Kenneth would joke. He was single, never married, and had two sons with two different women. He worked at the fire station with Kenneth, and although Mark was several years older than him, they had become close friends.

"What do you have in mind, Playboy?" Kenneth asked.

"Two nurses! You remember when I told you I met two nurses at Atlanta Memorial Hospital a couple of months ago?" His voice rose with excitement. "One dark and pretty and the other one a red bone!"

"Yeah, I remember." Kenneth sounded uninterested.

"Well, they agreed to hook up! Fine as a mothafucka! Both of 'em!" Mark exclaimed.

Kenneth rubbed his face and took a long sigh. "Mark, I don't think so," he paused as he thought about Monica the continued. "I met this woman, and we went out last night."

"Who is she, and when did you meet her?" Mark was curious, wondering why this was his first-time hearing of her.

"I met her about a month ago." Kenneth didn't want to tell his friend where and how he had met Monica. And he surely didn't want Mark to know that she was married. "I met her at the grocery store," he lied. "And she may come by tonight." He was hoping that she would.

"Ahhhh, man! I have two live, fine-ass women, and you don't wanna hook up?!" Mark yelled, giving his Rollo from Sanford and Son imitation. "You got to be shittin' me!"

"Maybe some other time. Okay?" Kenneth didn't feel like discussing the matter any further.

"Ken. You can hook up with that chick some other time. Man, I already hooked up with the dark-skinned babe. Man, I am telling you that she is a mothafuckin' freak! Love to be boned in the ass!" Mark paused before continuing. "Kenny, you know what they say. Birds of a feather flock together."

"I'm sure. But I am going to pass tonight," Kenneth told Mark. "I gotta go, man," Kenneth finally got his friend off the phone.

Mark was from Cleveland, Mississippi, and made Atlanta his home after he graduated from The University of Georgia. Kenneth visited Mark's hometown and loved his family. He would always get a kick out of how Mrs. Boudreaux teased about Mark's childhood. She always said, "My son wasn't the most handsome boy. But he grew up to be a good-looking man." Then she would let out a loud laugh. Mrs. Boudreaux always brought out the family photo album to prove her point. Mark was a light-complexioned, chubby kid. As he got older, he got taller, and the weight dropped. Staying involved with sports helped keep the weight off, and he vowed never to be chubby again, so he always worked out.

Kenneth retreated to his man cave and turned on the TV. He turned to his recorded shows and began watching Al Sharpton's *Politic Nation*. It was early, and he hadn't made any plans for the day. Monica stayed in his thoughts as he tried to concentrate on Al Sharpton. He wished that he could have kissed her full, luscious lips. Kenneth didn't want the night to end, hoping Monica would have mustered enough courage to come to his place. But he remembered his vow to be her friend. He sensed that she wanted more but also to remain faithful to her husband. And he also felt that Monica knew exactly what he wanted.

Kenneth had dozed off and was awakened by his cell phone. He looked down at the caller ID, and it read MONICA. He was excited and surprised. He gathered himself, took a deep breath, and then answered. "Hey, you! How are you?"

"I'm doing alright, thanks. I was calling to tell you that I had a wonderful time last night and to thank you again." Monica thanked Kenneth.

"You are quite welcome, Beautiful. And thank you for accepting my invitation. I had a great time," Kenneth acknowledged.

"And so did I. Well, I am at the office getting some work done." She laughed and then teased, "Unlike you, home relaxing. Not a care in the world."

Kenneth laughed at her joke. "Well, I deserve to take off some time, don't I?"

Monica responded sarcastically. "I guess, Mr. Mann."

"Monica, you know you can take off when you want. You are your own boss. Right, Sexy?" Kenneth couldn't help himself. He wanted her to know that he was being flirtatious.

Monica laughed. "Sexy, huh? Well, I better watch you, Mr. Mann," she responded seductively. "Well, I had better get back to work before I start giving out compliments," she laughed and continued, "I am getting off around 4 O'clock today. I will call you on my way home. Will that be okay, Mr. Mann?"

"That would be wonderful. I can't wait to hear that sexy voice later." Kenneth flirted.

Kenneth lay in bed and began to fantasize about Monica. He peeled off every piece of clothing and lay on his back. He couldn't help himself. Thinking about her doggy style on his bed, him standing behind her and pushing his dick inside her as she screamed out his name made him rise. He began to stroke his dick up and down slowly as the scene changed to Monica turning over on her back, her legs spread open and bent back to her head as he gave her his entire mule. He began to stroke his dick faster as he imagined her screaming his name. 'Kenneth! Ohhhh, Kenneth! Fuck this pussy!' Before Kenneth realized it, he had squirted all over his hand as he moaned loudly. He breathed heavily, and his body relaxed. He wanted Monica more than just a friend all along.

Chapter Fourteen

Marcus sat in his office, waiting for Kyra to call. She was supposed to stop by his office for a drink and a little sex play. He stopped using condoms when they had sex, becoming more careless in his relationship with Kyra. And Kyra had changed her point of view regarding unprotected sex. His feelings were growing for her, and he wanted her to feel the same about him. She had rocked his world the first time they had sex, and Marcus hadn't looked back since. Kyra knew how to make a man feel good, and she wasn't ashamed to let herself go all out. There were no limits to her freakiness. Anything a man wanted, just go for it. And Marcus went for it all.

Marcus' cell phone rang as he took a quick bird bath in his office's bathroom . He dried his erect penis off and then answered his phone. "Hey! Where are you?"

"I am on the elevator coming up now," Kyra replied. "Are you naked?"

"You damn right. Just as you ordered, now come and suck this hard ass dick." Marcus commanded.

"My mouth is watering for that big, fat dick. And I want to drink all of that nut." Kyra taunted.

"Hurry, Honey!" Marcus was so excited and couldn't wait to ease his dick in her tight ass. He loved the way Kyra got off on being fucked up her ass.

Kyra walked into Marcus's office wearing a tight blue dress with black high heel shoes. Marcus closed the door and locked it, watching as Kyra walked to his desk, looking back at him with a seductive smile. She went to the couch next to the window and eased down slowly. Smiling, she opened her legs and pulled her dress up to her waist; she wasn't wearing any panties. She then raised her legs, holding the back of her thighs.

"Come and taste this hot ass pussy, Baby," Kyra enticed Marcus in a low and sexy voice.

Marcus walked his naked body slowly to his awaiting freak. When he was in front of her, he kneeled slowly, looking into her anxious eyes. "Is this tongue what you want?" he asked, then extended his tongue and started to flicker it.

"Ohhhh, Daddy yes! Eat this pussy! Please stick that tongue inside and then suck the shit out of this pussy!" Kyra moaned.

Marcus reached out, grabbed her by the hips, and pulled her to the edge of the couch. He shoved his tongue inside her and whirled it round and round. He pushed his tongue in and out, making her jerk back and forth, grabbing the back of his head with one hand and pushing his face into her.

"Now suck this pussy, Marcus!" she screamed.

Marcus eased his tongue out of her and began to suck her clitoris softly. He then started to flicker his tongue up and down. She grabbed the back of his head with both hands. He knew then that she was about to cum as his head went back and forth, sucking and flickering his tongue, tasting all her hot juices. His dick was rock hard, knowing she was turned on by him eating her out. He loved to turn her on by eating her pussy. And he loved the way Kyra enjoyed him doing it.

Marcus stood up and ordered Kyra to turn over. "Stand your fine ass up and get doggy style!" Kyra stood up and faced the edge of the couch, placing her knees on the arm of the sofa to give her more height. Marcus palmed her round ass with both hands as she lifted it to him, stretching her upper body downward on the couch. He eased his dick inside her wet pussy, palming her ass cheeks.

Kyra looked back at Marcus and yelled, "Fuck me harder dammit! Hit this pussy Daddy!"

Marcus began to stroke her harder and faster. "Is this what you want!" he yelled. "You want it like this!"

Kyra began to push her ass back and forth, meeting his hard dick. "That's what the fuck I'm talking about! Yes!" She started to cum and pushed her ass back while gripping the couch. "I'm cumming!" She screamed as Marcus pounded her from behind. "Ohhhh, shit!" Kyra's body fell to the couch, her legs shaking vigorously. "Ohhhh, Marcus," she said in a low voice, her head laying sideways, and her eyes closed. "I'm sorry, Baby. I couldn't take no more." She slowly opened her eyes and stared into space. "Let me catch my composure." She continued to lay on the couch staring into space.

Marcus walked slowly to the front of the couch. "I understand, Beautiful. I ain't going nowhere. He sat on the couch, his naked body next to her head. He began to stroke her face and hair. He looked down at his hard dick, feeling proud of its size. He loved the way Kyra took all of him. And she loved every inch. He wanted to cum inside of her ass, and he couldn't wait. He knew she would cum again when he fucked her in her ass. Her loving it turned him on, especially when she would ask for him to go in there.

Kyra rose slowly to her knees, looking at Marcus' hard dick. "Are you ready to give me what I asked for?"

Marcus stood up, looking down at Kyra. "Are you ready to give me that ass?"

Kyra backed up to the arm of the couch and placed her knees back to their original position. She spread her legs and looked back at an anxious Marcus stroking his hard dick with KY lubricant. "Uhhhhhh! I want all of that dick in my ass!"

With a mischievous look, Marcus replied, "And that's what you are going to get. All of this dick in that hot ass."

Marcus slowly approached Kyra's round ass, glaring at her tight ass hole as he placed the head of his dick near the entrance of her ass hole. He pushed his thumb slowly into her ass, listening to her moan with ecstasy. He then played around her asshole with the head of his dick. After the foreplay, he popped the tip inside her tight entry and held it there. "Is that good, Baby?" Marcus asked.

"Yes," she responded seductively. "Ease it in slow for me, Daddy."

Marcus eased his dick deeper and deeper inside of her ass. He watched her as she gripped the couch, holding on for dear life. Easing his manhood back and forth, he said, "Damn! I'm in this ass! Damn!"

"Uh-huh, you sure are!" she screamed. "And that shit feels so good!"

Marcus began to fuck her harder while being careful not to treat her ass like her pussy. He knew how she liked being fucked up her ass, but he was sure to measure his force as he pushed back and forth. "Is that the way you like it!" he yelled, knowing she liked it the way he gave it to her.

"Ohhhh, yes! Just like that, Daddy! Just like that! Fuck this ass!" Kyra urged.

Marcus continued his journey deep inside her sensitive space ass , clutching both cheeks and spreading them open as he looked down at his work. Filled with excitement, he felt his dick throbbing inside of her ass. He knew that it was time for him to cum inside her. And the thought of her cumming with him excited him more. Kyra could always tell when it was his time to explode. And he had come to know when it was her time.

Kyra looked back at Marcus, who now had his eyes closed. "You getting ready to cum in this ass! Huh!"

"Ohhhh, yes! Shit yeah!" He opened his eyes and looked down at his dick going in and out. "Throw that ass back to me, Baby! Throw it!" Marcus instructed.

Kyra started to groove back and forth with Marcus, her ass hitting his thighs. "That's what the fuck I'm talking about! Ohhhhh! Fuck me! Hit that ass! Motherfucker!" She started to cum as her ass hole opened wider, taking all he had to offer. "I'm fucking cumming! Marcus! Ohhhhhhhh, Marcus! I'm cumming, Baby!" she called out.

Marcus yelled back at her. "Shit! I'm all in this mothafuckin' ass!" He started to ejaculate inside her. He looked down at his dick. "Shit! That looks so damn good!" He came inside of her and stood still as her body jerked. He then eased his dick out of her ass and waited for her to push his cum out. Seeing his cum dripping from her ass and knowing that she would reach back with her index finger, push it in her ass, and then taste it turned him on. And she did just that as he walked to her face, placing his dick near her lips.

Kyra tasted her finger and then started to lick Marcus' dick. "Mmmmmmm." She grabbed his dick and began sucking it. "Mmmmmm." Looking up at him with a smile, she asked, "You like that? Huh?"

Marcus looked down at her as her head moved back and forth. "You know damn well I love that shit!"

After freaking each other for almost two hours, Marcus and Kyra lay on the couch and dozed off. Both were still naked as they slept for over an hour. Kyra loved to freak Marcus at his office. It gave her a sense of ownership. A sense that she could call a shot if she desired, knowing that Marcus would not deny her request to have things her way. And Marcus knew he could call his shots with Kyra, having things his way whenever he wanted.

Chapter Fifteen

Monica and Tasha sat on the couch watching TV. Tasha had invited her sister over, wanting to ensure that Monica was not drowning in her depression. She had begged Monica to come to her house, if only to watch a movie with her. Tasha sipped her favorite wine while watching the film Boomerang and occasionally glanced over at her sister. Tasha could tell that Monica's mind wasn't on the movie, nor did she want to be there. But Tasha didn't care what Monica wanted. Her priority was to be there for her sister.

It was the middle of October, and the weather was getting cooler now. Monica and Marcus had talked on the phone a few times, but it was only concerning Taylor. He had come to pick Taylor up a few times to take her shopping. Whenever he came to get her, he sat in his BMW. His silent treatment was killing Monica inside. She would speak to him, only to get a mere "Hey" from her husband, with him only glancing at her. When Tasha asked her about Marcus, Monica would only give short answers regarding their separation.

Tasha got up and walked to her daughter's room. Briana and Taylor were watching cartoons and laughing. "Hey, girls. Are you two hungry?" she asked.

Taylor jumped up and said, "Yes. Are we having pizza?"

Brianna interrupted, "No! I want a burger!"

Tasha laughed as she folded her arms across her chest. "We can have both. How is that?"

Taylor yelled, "Yes! Pizza and burgers!"

Tasha returned to her silent sister, who had now folded her legs on the couch. Monica would not look at her sister, who was standing over her. She knew that Tasha wanted her to talk about Marcus, and she wasn't in the mood for any advice or ridicule. But she knew that Tasha wouldn't let the subject remain quiet. Tasha was as real as they come. And keeping problems bottled up inside was not her belief.

"I'm going out for food," she told Monica. "Do you want anything?"

Without looking at her sister, Monica replied, "No. I'm fine, thank you."

Tasha cruised in her Nissan Maxima and listened to Angie Stone's "Baby." She rocked to the beat as she pulled into Pizza Hut's parking lot. She could have had it delivered but instead wanted to pick it up. She needed the quiet drive to think. Monica was heavy on her mind, and Tasha wanted so much to be there for her. Tasha knew all too well how it felt to have a broken heart; she had gone through her battles with love and the loss of love.

After Tasha picked up the pizza, she drove to the Hudson Grill, one of Atlanta's most popular sports bars and burger joints, to pick up the burgers. The Hudson Grill sports bar made the biggest and best-seasoned burgers in town. It was located in Midtown and became a popular hangout, where some of Atlanta's elite would go for a good time and a great burger . Its popularity caused its expansion, increasing its square footage and adding large flat screen TVs. It had become the locals' favorite sports bar, many gathering for the Falcons and Hawks game.

It was Sunday afternoon, and the Falcons were playing the Saints. Tasha knew the manager and had phoned ahead to order her burgers and fries. When she arrived, she could hear the loud cheers of the zealous fans from the parking lot. The Falcons were doing well, and the city's hopes were at an all-time high. She was pleased that Johnny would have her order ready to go. Tasha walked inside and scanned the room for Johnny. To her surprise, she spotted Marcus at the bar with a light-skinned woman. They were hugging and kissing passionately, each oblivious to anyone watching them. Tasha was filled with anger as she made her way toward them. She squeezed through the crowd until she was standing behind Marcus. The look on Kyra's face gave away that she suspected that Tasha knew Marcus. Marcus looked at Kyra, who had pulled her lips apart from his. He followed her eyes, turned around, and astonished, his sister-in-law stood with a nefarious look on her face. Marcus stood up and backed away. He was speechless. He gazed at Tasha, looking her in her squinted eyes. He knew her well, and she was ready for battle. But Marcus didn't want to set anything off at the sports bar and instead wanted to ask Tasha to step outside. But his tongue was tied, and he couldn't move.

Tasha finally spoke, not mincing her words, "What the hell are you doing here with this bitch!"

Marcus tried to get a word out but couldn't. "I.... she...."

Tasha looked at Kyra, who had turned her head, facing down at the bar, and directed her question to her, "Do you know that Marcus is married to my sister?"

Kyra continued her stare at the bar, not wanting to face Tasha.

Tasha looked back at Marcus and then back at Kyra. She addressed him while staring Kyra down, "Marcus, you sorry ass motherfucker!" her words were intended to cut like a knife . She wanted to slap the taste out of Kyra's mouth, but something inside her told her to get the burgers and leave. The look on Kyra's face implied that she knew Marcus was married. Somehow, Tasha knew Kyra was just another gold digger, fucking rich men for their money. And she knew that she had to tell Monica what she had witnessed, even if it hurt her sister. She was relieved that Monica wasn't with her to see Marcus hugging and kissing another woman.

Tasha sat in her driveway, trying to gain her composure before she went inside. Her heart was racing, knowing she had to tell Monica what she had just saw. Tasha knew her sister would fall apart, but she had to know the truth. She knew that if she kept it away from Monica, she would never forgive her. The more Tasha thought about Marcus' mistress, the more she wished she had slapped her as hard as she could. The thought of Marcus kissing another woman in public also tempted her to kick him square between his legs.

Tasha walked into the house and went straight to the kitchen. She sat the pizza and burgers on the counter, never looking at her sister who was watching TV. She stood at the counter with one hand on her hip and the other tapping her fingernails on the counter. Feeling anger and sadness, she called for Monica to the kitchen. "Monica, come over here."

Monica turned her head to her sister. "Do you need help?" Monica noticed a disturbing look on Tasha's face. She knew her sister well, and Monica could read her. She easily recognized Tasha's happy faces, sad faces, angry faces, and all her emotional reactions.

"What's wrong, girl?" Monica asked, concerned.

Tasha took a deep breath before summoning Monica to the kitchen again. "Just come over here, will you? I have something to tell you, and I don't want the girls to hear me. Now, please just come over here," Tasha said with a sense of urgency.

Monica slowly rose from the couch and hesitantly walked to her sister. She stood in front of Tasha; curiosity heightened as she thought about what would be revealed. "What is it, Tasha?" she asked in a low voice.

Tasha leaned in toward Monica's ear. "I saw Marcus hugging and kissing another bitch at the Hudson Grill." She eased her head back and looked at her sister, nodding her head and biting down on her bottom lip. Anger still on her face, she continued. "I started to slap the shit outta her ass!" she said in a low but acrimonious tone. Tasha stepped back to gauge her sister's reaction.

Monica stood still in total silence. She had a blank look on her face as she stared at Tasha, whose anger and disgust had not left her face. Monica took a deep, jerking breath before tears welled up in her eyes. She tried her best not to let her emotions get the best of her, knowing that Taylor was in the house. Monica walked to the door that led to the garage and held the knob. She looked back at Tasha and said, "I will be in the garage, okay?" She walked into the garage and stood there, trying to gain her composure. She didn't want Taylor to see her all emotional and crying. She had to hold herself together; not knowing where her life was now going. Monica began to shake uncontrollably as the tears started to spill down her face. Her attempt to cry in silence had failed. The door to the garage was closed, and she hoped that Tasha could not hear her wailing.

The door opened and closed, and Monica knew it was her sister. Tasha walked to her crying sister and placed her hands on her shoulders. She slowly turned Monica around to face her. Monica kept her head hanging down as she cried uncontrollably. Tasha pulled Monica close and held her in her arms; she began to cry as she gently stroked the back of Monica's head. Tasha vowed not to let her sister go through her heartache alone. She committed that she would be there every step of the way, helping her sister through her pain and sorrow.

Chapter Sixteen

Monica sat at her desk, looking out of the window. It was a cool but pleasant Monday morning. After taking Taylor to school, Monica knew she couldn't stand to be in the house alone. She had to get away from the memories of her and Marcus. Being home would not allow her mind to focus on anything else. The horrible news of her husband abandoning her for another woman sent her into a deeper depression. She had tried her best to deny the inevitable truth about her husband and couldn't fathom him leaving home because of another woman. Monica was falling apart, and there seemed no end to her demise in sight.

She had called Marcus numerous times the night before and tried again that morning. She left low, sad messages for her husband, begging him to talk to her. "Marcus, please call me. Baby, I really need to talk to you." Monica didn't know if Marcus felt guilt or was too busy being with the other woman. *Is he staying with her? Does she have that much power and influence to make him move in with her?* Monica needed answers that she really didn't want to face. *Where did I go wrong?* The questions kept coming, sending her into a world of confusion. She loved her husband, and she vowed to forgive him only if he would allow her to re-enter his world.

Monica decided to go to Marcus's office that afternoon. Her emotions wouldn't allow her to remain passive. She had to make the undaunted effort of facing her husband in pursuit of regaining her family. She would not go out without a fight, and Marcus would just have to understand. And the other woman would have to leave her husband alone and find her own man. Marcus belonged to her, and that was never to end. Monica was still his as long as Marcus hadn't filed for a divorce. His sidepiece was in for a battle.

Monica sat in her car, nervous and afraid of what may lie ahead. Her fear of finding Marcus with another woman clouded her thoughts. She had seen his car parked in its usual parking space, so she knew he was in his office. *Could she be in his office? Could they be in his office laughing and joking? What if I walk in and Marcus is kissing this phantom woman?* A woman that Monica hoped never to meet. She finally gathered enough nerve to get out of her car and go to his office. Her legs were weak as she took a deep breath before she started to walk. *God, don't let her be here.*

Monica stood outside of Marcus' office, staring at the door. Then she heard loud laughter but not Marcus'. The laugh belonged to a woman. Monica listened to the woman say, "Marcus, you are so crazy! That's one of the reasons I love you so much!" Before Monica became too frightened and left, her anger took over. She opened the door and marched into Marcus' office, ready for war. What she saw infuriated her even more. Kyra was sitting on Marcus' lap while he was sitting in his office chair. Marcus and Kyra were caught off guard as they both turned simultaneously to face this mad black woman. Monica's hands were on her hips, and fury lit up her eyes. "Marcus! What the fuck?! You better get this bitch out of here! Now!"

Kyra jumped up and quickly moved behind Marcus's chair. Marcus jumped to his feet, nervous and angry. He looked into Monica's eyes and knew his anger would not change her position. He looked at Kyra and then back at Monica. Searching for words, he knew he was caught and had no way out. Tasha had told her sister about him and Kyra being at The Hudson Grill, and he could tell by her face that she knew of his public scene with Kyra. And now, with Monica standing before him, he didn't have any way out. The only thing that he could do was ask Kyra to leave, and she didn't hesitate after seeing the ferocity on Monica's face.

Monica's eyes pierced Kyra as she walked to the door; Kyra never looked up at her. After Kyra walked out the door and closed it behind her, Monica rapidly approached Marcus and stood in front of him. She squinted her eyes as she stared at him. She wanted to kick him in his nuts and punch him in the jaw. But she just stood there glaring at him. "You motherfucker! How could you?!" the words burst out.

Marcus stepped back, and his head dropped. He had been caught. And there was no way out. He now faced his furious wife. He didn't know what move to make or what to say. But his guilt quickly turned to anger. He decided that he would blame Monica. He justified his behavior by accusing Monica of not satisfying his needs.

Marcus lifted his head, looked Monica in the eyes, and said, "What the fuck do you mean coming to my office with this bullshit?! Get the fuck out of my office!"

Monica moved in on him and slapped him across his jaw. "You sorry ass motherfucker! How could you just leave your wife and daughter for some ho'?!" Monica screamed.

Marcus grabbed Monica by her neck and raised his hand. "Girl, you know better than to do that shit! I should slap the shit out of your ass!" But he lowered his hand and released her neck. He walked to the window and looked out while rubbing the back of his head. Without turning around, he said, "Why don't you just leave? Just leave."

Tears poured down her face; Monica turned and walked away. As she walked to the door, without looking at her husband, in a low, gloomy voice, she said, "Fuck you, Marcus." She felt defeated, alone, and proven wrong by her sister's suspicions of Marcus.

Monica parked outside of Taylor's school, waiting for school dismissal. Her tears hadn't stopped flowing since she left Marcus' office. She knew she had to gain her composure before Taylor came to the car. She tried her best to stop crying, but her tears won the battle. She needed something to take her focus off what she had witnessed. But nothing could erase the graphic memory of the encounter at Marcus' office. If only she could find a way to straighten up for her daughter. She didn't want Taylor to know that her father had abandoned them for another woman. Taylor loved Marcus, and the news of him being with another woman would be devastating.

Taylor walked to her mother's car, excited to tell her about her excellent grades. She knew her mother would be proud of her. But when she arrived at the car, her heart immediately filled with sadness. Monica's head hung low, and Taylor could see the tears streaming down her mother's face. She knew right then that her father wasn't coming back home, and she began to feel her mother's pain. Taylor missed her father and wished he would return home to them. But her mother's sorrow told her that her wish would not come true.

Monica opened the car door and watched her daughter as she got into the car. Taylor looked up at her teary-eyed mother. They stared at each other without saying a word. Sensing her mother's heartache, Taylor began to cry. Monica stretched out her arms and pulled Taylor into her chest. Her words could not come out as she held her daughter and began to cry uncontrollably. Taylor held on to her mother, hoping that she could comfort her.

It was six o'clock and Monica stood over the stove preparing dinner for her and Taylor. Her tears had subsided, but her heart was heavy with pain. She left Taylor upstairs to work on her homework while she moved about the kitchen. The thought of seeing an attractive woman with her husband caused her to pause from seasoning the fish that she was preparing. Kyra was very beautiful and had a gorgeous body. She was taller than Monica, and her ass was perfectly round. In the midst of all the drama, Monica took the time to observe her husband's mistress; an instinct naturally built inside every woman.

Taylor sat across the table from her mother, taking an occasional bite of her fish. She could tell her mother's mind was preoccupied. Taylor wanted to ask about her father but suspected that he was the reason for her mother's pain. She missed him too and wished it was some way to talk to her father to come home to them. Her mind returned to the terrible incident between her parents at the Patterson party. Taylor remembered how hurt her mother was that night. She remembered seeing a side of her father that she had never seen before. The whole situation was hard for Taylor to comprehend. *What went wrong?* Her mother and father seemed so happy together. Looking at her mother, Taylor knew things had changed for the worst. She lowered her head after peeking at her mother stare into space. The agony and pain on her mother's face made Taylor want to cry, but she held her tears inside. *Please come home, Daddy. She prayed silently. Please?*

Chapter Seventeen

Kenneth and Captain Franklin were relaxing in lawn chairs at the back of the fire station. November was approaching, and the sunny, 60-degree weather was perfect for grilling steaks for the team.

"Two more days 'til November," Kenneth said, taking a puff from his Cuban cigar. He and Captain Franklin loved to smoke cigars while manning the grill.

Captain Franklin looked up at the sky and said, "Yep. Gettin' close to the holidays. Time to start spendin' money."

Captain John Franklin was a redneck from Mississippi who had moved to Atlanta with his father when he was 11 years old. Now nearing sixty, he often reflected on his years as an Atlanta fireman. Captain Franklin was entering his 31st year with the department; times had changed, and he had to change with them.

Although difficult at first, 20 years of working with black firefighters had softened his position on the racial divide. He had grown to love Kenneth and treated him like his own son.

Kenneth stood up and went to the large grill to flip the steaks. He looked back at Captain Franklin. "A few more minutes, Captain. And it will be time for some good eating."

"Smells delicious," Captain Franklin said as he rose to his feet and walked over to Kenneth. He looked down at the ribeye. "Now that's what I'm talking 'bout. Nothin' like a good 'ole steak."

"Is Bryan still coming by to get himself one of these masterpieces?" Kenneth asked.

Bryan was Captain Franklin's son and had been in the Atlanta Police Department for eight years. Kenneth and Bryan had become good friends over the years, but competition in sports and chess often ended up in heated battles. And Captain Franklin was always on guard when Kenneth came by their home to play basketball with Bryan.

Captain Franklin took a puff from his cigar and looked at Kenneth. "He should be here any minute. He ain't about to miss out on a good steak if he can help it."

Bryan didn't date girls of his own race. He dated every race but white girls. He and Kenneth had double dated in the past. Kenneth hooked Bryan up with a few of Atlanta's finest black women. Bryan knew his father didn't like his choice of women but tolerated it. Kenneth remembered Bryan laughing as he told the story of him and Captain Franklin discussing Bryan dating outside his race. Bryan once told Kenneth that when he was in high school, his father asked him if he thought anything was wrong with white girls. Bryan told him no; he just preferred black and Hispanic girls.

Mark suddenly appeared out of the garage, dancing to the music in his head and jamming to his own singing. "Return of the Mack! Return of the Mack!" He did a spin and then started rocking his body to his own beat. "Captain, you wish you had moves like a brotha!" he yelled at Captain Franklin as he busted a few more moves. Mark loved giving Captain Franklin a hard time, all in fun and games.

Captain Franklin started to laugh, shaking his head as he watched Mark dance. Mark always made Captain Franklin's day with his jokes and clowning around. Captain Franklin looked at Kenneth and joked, "What are we going to do with him?"

Kenneth laughed as he watched his friend singing and dancing. "Captain, I don't know. It seems like he ain't paying attention to the music you're playing." Kenneth began to take the steaks off the grill and place them in a foil pan. Monica was on his mind, and he contemplated calling her. He hoped she would drop by and have a steak with him just by chance. They had spoken more often now, and she finally revealed that she and her husband had separated.

She told Kenneth that she was hurting too much to see him. She shared the story of her encounter with Marcus and his lover. Her desire for Kenneth's comfort grew stronger by the day.

Kenneth brought the pan of steaks to a group of hungry firemen sitting at the large table in anticipation. The crew of eight had their baked potatoes, loaded with sour cream, cheese, and onions, waiting for the arrival of ribeye steaks. Kenneth looked around at each of his fellow brothers as they laughed and joked. He and Mark were the only two black men at the fire station. Fire Station 69 had a strong tradition of white-only firemen for years, but the arrival of Kenneth and Mark slowly changed the dynamic. It took several years to accomplish the resistance to their arrival. Still, with the help of a few open-minded firemen, the others finally came around to accepting Kenneth and Mark.

Kenneth and Mark relaxed out back in lawn chairs after dinner. The sun was descending, and the late October air was comforting. Tony Toni Tone's, "It Never Rains" played as Kenneth and Mark puffed on their cigars. It was a slow day. All the men were satisfied without having to answer emergency calls and enjoy their steak dinners. Kenneth had hoped for a slow day, wanting to prepare dinner and relax with the crew. He enjoyed their wishes for his flame broiled steaks, especially from his captain.

Kenneth made it home around seven the following morning. He had received a phone call from Pam while he was at work the night before and had made plans to see her after he had gotten off work that morning. He had known Pam for five years now, and they hooked up whenever they could. Pam was a nurse at The Children's Healthcare Hospital and worked the midnight shift. Kenneth loved their relationship, an understanding of getting together only when both needed to get their freak on. Kenneth had gone a few weeks without sex and needed to relieve the air from his brakes in the worst way.

After a long shower, Kenneth put on his boxers and programmed his app to some of Monica's best slow jams. "Why I Love You So Much" began to play as Kenneth lay across his bed. He wasn't expecting Pam for another half hour or so, giving him time to think about what she had in store for him. Pam could definitely please him, having no limitations to her freakiness. He thought back to when he and Pam snuck inside closets at the hospital and had sex; it began to turn him on. He remembered her pulling down her scrubs and bending over, letting him slide his mule inside her. He remembered her trying her best not to scream as she got a quick orgasm. Kenneth began to rise inside of his boxers, anticipating her arrival.

Pam arrived at 9:15 p.m. Kenneth opened the door and watched her walk her sexy glide toward his bathroom to shower. She looked back at him and slowly ran her tongue across her top lip. Kenneth loved her dark skin and natural, wavy hair. Pam's round bottom was complemented by her soft full lips, which parted to make a gorgeous smile and perfectly pleased Kenneth every time she went down on him. By the look on her face, Kenneth knew that he was in for a long morning.

Pam was from Lexington, Kentucky. She was a sexy chocolate, 28-year-old woman. Kenneth often reminded her that she had a striking resemblance to Viola Davis. Kenneth knew that Pam's feelings for him were more than hot, passionate lovemaking and freaking. She wanted more. Despite Kenneth not wanting a commitment, Pam continued to allow herself to indulge in his pleasure; a pleasure that she had never felt from any other man before.

Kenneth lay across the bed on his back as Pam eased into the bedroom after her shower. She had a towel wrapped around her body, covering her breasts, and dropping just beneath her crotch. Kenneth watched as she dropped the towel to the floor. Damn, she's fine as hell! His eyes stayed focused on her shaved pussy and sexy thighs. He observed her as she turned around and began rolling her ass around and around before giving her ass a hard, loud smack. She looked over her shoulders and admired the look on Kenneth's face.

"Pull that big dick out, Baby," she said, narrowing her eyes and then putting her index finger in her mouth. When Kenneth slid his boxers off, Pam turned and walked to the bed. She laid between his legs and began to suck on an erect penis that stood without

Kenneth's help. Her head rose to look him in his eyes. "Shit, you have a big fat dick. And I love sucking it."

Kenneth moaned with ecstasy. He loved the way she sucked and licked him. "Ohhhh, damn!" he said as he cupped the back of her head. The more she got off into sucking him, the harder he became. "Yeah, Baby. Lick my balls," he demanded.

Pam's head descended lower, taking in his ball with a suckling sound. Her head started to go back and forth with vigor as she gingerly sucked and pulled on Kenneth. Without permission, she rose to her knees and looked him in his eyes.

"I'm not done yet, Daddy. But I am soooo fuckin' wet!" She crawled up and climbed on top of him. Pam straddled Kenneth and grabbed his stiff penis. "Ohhhh, damn!" she screamed as she began to guide him inside her wet, hot, steamy pussy. Pam began to roll her ass around slowly as she rode him, her palms resting on his chest. Then she maneuvered into a squat on top of him, never letting his manhood out of her hotbox. She began to jump up and down on him vigorously, screaming with every thrust. "Damn, Daddy! Damn! I'm riding the fuck outta this long dick! Ohhhh, shit! This shit feels so good!"

Kenneth let her have her way, enjoying the pounding she was giving herself. He kept his gaze on her bouncing breasts, another thing that turned him on while fucking Pam. Pam had major talent as a lover, the reason Kenneth kept in contact with her. For some reason, he trusted her enough to have unprotected sex. He felt that her occupation implied her health responsibility, which made him trust her. That and the fact that she told him he had nothing to worry about, not even her getting pregnant.

Pam slowly rose, enjoying the feeling of his formed dick sliding out of her. She backed up and began to lick her juices off him. When she was done cleaning her juices, she began to suck him vigorously. She grabbed his rock and began to massage it, sure to keep her rhythm. When Kenneth started to shake, she knew she had him where she wanted him. She loved swallowing every ounce of him, and she was not about to let go. Kenneth tried to fight her off when he began to cum, but Pam knew the pleasure overwhelmed him, so she held tight. She kept her grip, expecting the rush from his dick any moment now. Oh, cum for me, Daddy! she repeated in her mind. When she felt his dick begin to jerk, she lowered her head. Kenneth started to explode in her mouth. She gave a loud moan; her eyes closed and then opened to look up at him. She watched him as he yelled, his body shaking as he held her head. The pleasure of taking him in and him trying to lift her head always turned her on. She loved the fight between them, her continuing her bout to swallow all of him as he came in her mouth and his attempt at pulling her head up while he shot his load. She won every time.

Kenneth lay on his back, breathing hard, while Pam's head

rested on his chest. "Damn, girl. You sure know how to make me feel good." Kenneth gently rubbed the back of her head and looked up at the ceiling. "You know I got to hit that good pussy from the back."

Pam rose her head and looked into his eyes. "I sure do know that. Do you think that I'm leaving without it?" She kissed his chest, and then her head began to descend. She began her quest to make him rise again because she wanted him to fuck her doggy style. The position that made her cum the hardest.

Pam had come and served her purpose, leaving Kenneth satisfied to have relieved the buildup that needed to be released. After he showered, he sat in his living room. Toni Braxton's, "How Many Ways" played as he began to think about Monica. She had stayed on his mind since the time they'd gone out, and she hung at his house. There was something special about her. Deep down inside, Kenneth wanted her so much. She made an everlasting impression the first time he laid eyes on her. And she consumed his thoughts with her beauty, sexiness, and smile. But most of all, something mystical about Monica made Kenneth want to pursue the unknown.

He looked over at the clock on the wall. It was now after midnight, and he hadn't begun to feel sleepy. He reached for his cell phone and dialed Monica's number. Kenneth had mixed feelings. Not wanting her to answer so he could leave a message, and at the same time, wanting her to answer his call. The latter happened. Monica's sexy voice sounded low and weak. Kenneth's heart began to race as he rose from the couch. "Hey, Monica. How are you doing?" he said, walking to his bedroom.

"Hey, you," she answered. "What a pleasant surprise."

"Oh, a pleasant surprise, huh? Well, I have been thinking about you and wanted to talk to you."

"That's okay, Kenneth. I have taken some time off work. I'm dealing with some personal issues right now."

Kenneth sat in his chair and leaned back. "Personal issues? Is everything alright?"

"No...no, Kenneth, they are not. You know I caught my husband with another woman, and it's really bad right now."

Kenneth rose to his feet and began to pace the floor. He was speechless, but, for some reason, he felt jubilated. He finally asked, "Is there something I can do for you? You can depend on me to be a friend and be there whenever you need me."

"Thank you for that, Kenneth. I really appreciate that. I would love that."

Loving Monica's answer, Kenneth had to hold in his excitement. He took a deep breath and said, "Ohhhh.... kay. I'm here whenever you need someone to talk to." He sat back down in his chair. "Monica, just know that you made an impression on me the moment I met you. Something that I can't explain. I don't want to confuse you more than you are now. But I have wanted to tell you how I feel for quite some time."

Monica laughed softly. "I know that, Kenneth. I sensed that you were feeling something for me. And I have been flattered ever since."

Kenneth was happy to hear Monica laugh. He began to feel victorious with his efforts to comfort her. It seemed that his dream of getting close to Monica was suddenly attainable. His intuition told him something was special about her, and he was committed to being there for her. Monica started a fire inside him every time he saw her—a fire that continued to burn for her, a fire that he never wanted to burn out. Now that she had separated from her husband, Kenneth could move in on his dream girl. And when given the chance, he would not disappoint her.

Chapter Eighteen

The chilly November morning made it hard for Monica to get out of bed. She had taken Taylor to school, and when she made it back home, her bed was calling for her to come to lay down and drown in her sorrows. She had entered a depression that was foreign to her. She never felt like this and had no way of knowing how to deal with a pain that weakened her like a wounded animal, laying in the desert ready to die with no help in sight. She heard about heartache and broken hearts, but now she was evidence of its devastation. She felt all alone, even when her daughter tried her best to be there for comfort and support.

Monica heard the doorbell ring and then hard knocking. She looked over at her clock. It was 11:30 a.m. She had been asleep for about three hours. *Who the hell can that be?* Monica thought as she threw the covers off and put on her robe. The doorbell rang again, followed by the knocking. When Monica got to the top of the stairwell, she could hear her sister yelling her name. *Damn, I don't need this shit right now!* Monica flung the door open and placed her hand on her hip. She gave her sister a mean look and nipped, "What is it, Tasha?"

Tasha pushed past her sister and walked to the kitchen. "Come here and talk to me, Monica," she said as she stood by the kitchen table.

Monica ran her fingers through her hair and then closed the door. She reluctantly joined her sister in the kitchen, knowing what was about to come next; emotional support and husband bashing at the same time. Monica appreciated her sister's help more than she knew, but Tasha's expectations about how Monica should feel and what to do irritated her. Monica wasn't as mentally tough as her sister and surely didn't know what to do about her marriage. She knew that Tasha meant well and wanted only the best for her. But this was her fight and her fight alone. After all, the final decision would be hers.

Monica stared at her sister, who was pouring herself a glass of wine. "Pour me a glass while you are at it." Monica walked toward the kitchen counter while her sister retrieved another wine glass from the cabinet. She watched as Tasha poured the wine, looking her sister in the eyes. It was silent for a few minutes as Tasha never took her gaze from her sister. Monica would drop her head occasionally, looking up only to find her sister still staring at her. Monica couldn't hold it in any longer. "Tasha, what is it?" she asked.

Tasha sat on a bar stool next to her sister. She had a look of anger and sadness. She looked into her sister's eyes and paused before she began to speak. "Monica. I know that you are hurting. And I am here for you. You are my sister, and I love you very much." Tasha placed her hand gently on top of her sister's hand. She stared at Monica, glum, with her head lowered, gaping at the wine glass. Tasha placed a finger underneath her sister's chin and gently raised her head. She looked into Monica's eyes, and they both began to cry.

After Tasha left, Monica went back upstairs to her room to lie down. She turned on the TV and strolled through the guide while listening to Steve Harvey on The Family Feud. Monica didn't want to go back to sleep, knowing she had to get back up to pick Taylor up from school, so she settled on watching Family Feud to pass the time.

She positioned a pillow behind her back and watched the game show. Steve Harvey was his usual hilarious self. The thought of calling Marcus invaded her aching head. The shame and disappointment began to surface as she wondered where she had gone wrong. Had she not given him enough attention? Did she not please him sexually, the way that he wanted? She began to reflect on her marriage. Marcus was so into her, and then all of a sudden, he began to ignore her.

Monica sat in her car, waiting for school dismissal. Old School Jams were playing on her radio. She listened as The Temptations sing, "Just My Imagination." She began contemplating whether she should start seeing Kenneth. She could tell he wanted more than a friendship the day she went to his place for dinner. His sexy eyes gave it away. The way he looked at her and smiled at her told his inner secret. But she fought off the temptation, knowing that she would have succumbed to his desire if things were different. But now, her strength was weakening. Kenneth had begun to occupy her thoughts. She had fought off fantasizing about him. But lately, the fantasies began to creep into her mind, leaving her wondering what it would be like to have sex with him.

Chapter Nineteen

Monica and Kenneth had been talking on the phone more often, and Monica had let her guard down significantly. Kenneth always made her laugh, and she enjoyed his conversations. She could tell that he was a genuine and caring person. She had conflicting thoughts because of her marriage and her daughter. Marcus had left her vulnerable, confused, and wanting to be touched by a man. She desired to be pleased sexually and began to feel that she could no longer fight the sexual demons that haunted her.

She and Kenneth had made plans to meet for dinner. Although it was the second week of December, it was a calm 70 degrees, and the sky was clear, filled with sparkling stars. They agreed to meet at The Optimist Restaurant in West Midtown. Monica had a taste for seafood, and Kenneth didn't mind where they met, as long as he was in her company. Wherever her heart desired, he was more than willing to oblige her.

Monica arrived at the restaurant and sat in her car in silence. Her heart was racing, and her nerves were on edge. She thought about calling her sister, who agreed to keep Taylor for the weekend. But she decided against it. *What is wrong with me?* She took a deep breath and then turned down her visor mirror. She checked her lipstick, rubbing her lips together. She remembered Kenneth's deep voice telling her how he was looking forward to seeing her. She was flattered yet confused about getting so close to another man while she was still unsure where her marriage was going . She sat back and took another deep breath. *Ok. I'm ready. Let's have a great time.* She got out of her car and gave the valet her keys. As she turned around, she could see Kenneth standing at the front door. Her heart started racing again.

Kenneth walked towards her to meet her as she walked toward the restaurant. He could sense that she was nervous, her head looking down as she approached him. He knew that she had anxiety about seeing him. He understood that her reluctance to meet him was because of her marriage and her daughter. But there was something about her that he could not resist. Kenneth would do all he could to ease her mind and assure her that she would have no regrets. He was on a mission from the moment she told him about catching her husband with another woman.

Kenneth had called the restaurant ahead of time and reserved a table. They were led to a table near a window at the back of the restaurant. Kenneth watched Monica as she slowly lowered into her seat. He was nervous but anxious for their friendship to advance beyond conversation and casual meetings. He stared at her as she kept her gaze down. He perceived she was hurting inside, and he did not want to do anything to make her feel guilty. "You look so amazing," he said in his deep voice.

Monica slowly raised her head and smiled nervously. "Thank you, Kenneth." The words seemed to be a struggle as she spoke. "You look quite handsome yourself." She turned her gaze and looked out the window, staring at the clear starry sky. "It's a beautiful night," she said as she folded her arms as if she was cold. She could feel Kenneth's glare, and she would have to gather the strength to meet his gaze. She knew he would boast his handsome smile once she looked at him. She was conflicted as she wanted to resist him yet jump his bones at the same time.

"This is a nice restaurant," Kenneth said as he began to look out of the window.

Monica turned to Kenneth, and to her surprise, he was staring out the window, not at her. "Yes, this restaurant is very nice. I've been here quite a few times. They have an excellent menu."

Kenneth turned his attention to Monica. He looked into her eyes, hoping she wouldn't drop or turn her head. When she managed a smile, Kenneth's heart began to pound inside his chest, excitement rising at the thought that she was starting to relax. Kenneth focused on Monica's beautiful smile. Her full lips enhanced the beauty of her gorgeous smile. *Damn, this woman is so beautiful and sexy!* He couldn't help the thought from entering his mind. He had longed for her ever since he met her. Especially when she had stopped by the fire station for the first time, and tonight, Kenneth would make sure that Monica's marriage nor her problems would be a topic of discussion.

Kenneth watched as Monica ate her salmon. He loved that she had opened up and started to relax. They talked about sports, her business, and politics. She even managed to land a few jokes in the conversation, making Kenneth laugh. Kenneth was more relaxed as they listened to TLC's, "Diggin' on You" coming through the restaurant's speakers. He leaned back and took a sip from his beer. He was smiling and loved the way Monica smiled back at him. He knew that there was more to learn about her, and he would be patient in getting to know all there was to know about her.

Monica agreed to follow Kenneth to his place after dinner. He had not given her any indication that he was a forceful man. Kenneth had always shown Monica that he was considerate, passionate, and caring; she sensed that he wanted her badly. However, she began to worry that if he made an advance, would she have enough self-control?

Monica cruised as Kenney Lattimore's, "Never Too Busy"

banged from her Bose speakers. She enjoyed the dinner and conversation with Kenneth. She loved getting to know him and was more and more intrigued by his past. Something about his growing up poor, being around violence and drugs, and making it out thrilled her.

Monica pulled her car into the driveway and parked behind Kenneth's truck. She took a deep breath as she watched him walk to her car. She loved his smooth walk. He walked with confidence, and his posture was straight and perfect. He opened her door and extended his hand to her. Monica kept her gaze on his eyes as she rose from her car.

"Thank you, Mr. Mann." Her smile met his as he closed the car door. "Well, I'm back at your place. I hope that I'm safe," she shrugged and laughed.

"As safe as you will ever be," Kenneth said with his endearing smile.

Kenneth watched Monica walk as her sexy hips rocked back and forth. Her curves were round and perfect. *Damn!* As she walked to the front porch, his eyes were fixated on her ass. He wanted her in the worst way and felt in his heart that she wanted him too. He knew that the moment had to be perfect. He couldn't show her he was overzealous, being extra careful not to scare her off. It would be her willingness to give herself to him whenever it happened. Kenneth respected Monica in every way and was going to be careful not to lose her respect for him.

Monica sat at the bar as Kenneth made her a martini. "I guess you are a good bartender, huh?" she said with her legs crossed. She smiled at him and folded her arms.

Kenneth shook the drink as he turned to face her, "Well, let's just say I've learned to make a good drink.; it comes with practice."

"Good practice, huh? Well, what else have you been good at practicing?" Monica flirted as she gently bit down on her bottom lip.

Kenneth laughed, knowing what she meant. "I practice those things that I want to be great at. I'm sure the same goes for you, beautiful lady." He placed the drink in front of her and grabbed himself a beer from the refrigerator. Kenneth stood at the bar, watching Monica as he took a sip from the bottle. "Monica, you are so damn beautiful and sexy."

Monica took a sip of her drink and leaned back. "Well, thank you again, Mr. Mann. You are not bad looking yourself."

Kenneth laughed and said, "Thank you." He wanted to walk around the bar and kiss her full beautiful lips passionately. "You know? I've been with you all night and haven't gotten my friendly hug."

Monica put her glass on the counter and asked, "Well, Mr. Mann. What's stopping you?"

Kenneth walked around the bar, stood in front of Monica, and extended his hand to her. She placed her hand in his and rose from the bar. Kenneth looked down into her eyes. He then pulled her close to him. Her head rested against his chest as she hugged him firmly. He held her in his arms for what felt like an eternity. Kenneth didn't want to let her go as he took in the sweet smell of her hair. He began to rub her head gingerly. Kenneth felt her release her arms from around his back. He looked down at her as she looked up at him and closed her eyes. Kenneth's head began to descend. He placed a soft, careful kiss on her lips. Before he closed his eyes, he could see her mouth begin to open for acceptance of his advance. They began to kiss fervently. He gently placed his hands on her face, pulling in her wet, seductive kisses.

Kenneth pulled his lips away from Monica's and gazed down at her before taking her hand and placing it on his rock-hard dick. He began to kiss her again as she grabbed and massaged his manhood. Kenneth reached down, unzipped his pants, and pulled out hardness. Monica started to moan as she began stroking him. Her moans turned him on as he began to reach for the zipper on the back of her dress. Monica let out a loud, seductive moan as Kenneth unzipped her dress.

Kenneth led Monica to his bedroom as she walked backward, their lips never letting go. He stood in front of her, the back of her legs touching the bed, as he began to pull down her dress. Kenneth guided Monica's dress past her round ass and let it drop to the floor. He felt her step out of it as he kissed her and removed her bra. Kenneth gazed down at Monica's full breasts before he started to kiss and suck on them.

"Oh, Kenneth!" she screamed.

He laid her on the bed and opened her legs. Kenneth kneeled at the edge of the bed, grabbed both legs, and pulled her to him. He began to taste her, licking and sucking her.

"Oh, shit! Yes! Yes! Oh, yes!"

Monica loved the way Kenneth tasted her. She grabbed his head and began to move her hips round and round. "Shit!" she screamed. "Fuck!"

The more she screamed, the more intense Kenneth licked and sucked her. The sensation was so intense Monica wrapped her legs around his head and held her wet, hot pussy against his mouth.

"Eat me, Baby! Yeah! Taste this hot pussy! Yeah!"

When she felt herself about to explode, she released her hips from his mouth and lay on the bed with her legs still open. Kenneth was eating her like he was on a mission. It turned her on more as she watched his head moving up and down, back and forth.

"I'm cumming! Yes! That's it, Baby! I'm fuckin' cumming!"

Her body was dripping with sweat, and her juices overflowed. And Kenneth tasted it all.

"Oh, shit! Oh, shit!" She rocked and screamed as she tried to remain strong while Kenneth tasted her. She forcefully pushed his head away from her hot wet pussy when she could no longer stand the thrill. "No! Stop!" she moaned in overwhelming ecstasy.

Kenneth rose from his knees and stood over the bed. He watched as Monica lay there, breathing heavily and moaning. He slid off his pants and gently laid on top of her. Her eyes were closed as she spread her legs. It had felt like a lifetime since the last time she felt a man inside her.

Monica grabbed Kenneth and held on to him as he slid inside her. He wailed vociferously and then shrieked, "Oh, shit! This feels so damn good!"

He began stroking her smoothly, her legs wrapped around his back. She met his strokes as she began to moan.

"Fuck me, Kenneth! Fuck me! Harder! Harder!"

Kenneth rose, grabbed her ankles, and held them up. He looked down at Monica and began to give her the pounding he knew she had missed. He watched as her body began to quiver as he stroked her hard and fast. "You like that!" he asked.

Monica looked up at him, her eyes filled with excitement and surprise. "Yes, Kenneth! I fucking love this shit!" Fuck me hard!"

The following day, Monica was awakened by pots and pans banging in the kitchen. She looked over at the clock. It was 7:30 am. She sat up, rubbing her head. She was still naked and didn't remember when she had fallen asleep. Sex with Kenneth was more than she had anticipated. He was a terrific lover. *Damn! He knows how to eat pussy!* She began to smile as she thought of last night's hot passionate sex with Kenneth. *And now his ass is in there making breakfast*, she thought to herself and began to laugh.

Monica was now in unchartered territory and felt there was no point of return. Her husband had abandoned her and left her vulnerable. And now she couldn't get last night out of her mind. She wanted more of Kenneth. . . *after breakfast.*

Chapter Twenty

After leaving Kenneth's house, Monica arrived at her sister's house to pick up Taylor. She had reluctantly told Tasha about Kenneth and felt she shouldn't get involved with another man for some reason. But Tasha felt differently. After hearing about Kenneth, Tasha insisted that Monica venture out and discover what Kenneth was about. Tasha felt that what was good for the goose was good for the gander. Tasha was thrilled that her sister had another option, wanting Monica to experience the excitement of "the big payback."

Tasha opened the door with a big grin on her face. "Come on in here, girl! I can't wait to hear all about it!"

Monica gave her sister a sarcastic look as she walked through the door. She laughed and said, "Tasha, you are something else."

"I know that. I am something else and all that."

Tasha walked to the kitchen, knowing that Monica would follow. She was excited and very anxious to get the juicy info about her sister's date. She knew that Monica didn't go home and was prepared to set Monica straight if she tried to lie to her.

"Do you want some coffee?" she asked while looking back at Monica as she poured herself a cup.

Monica looked at her sister with squinted eyes. "Yes, I'll have a cup of coffee with you."

Tasha gave a big smile, letting her sister know that she wanted all the details. "You look like you had a freaky time. Yeah, you tried to fix yourself up before you got here. But I can see right through that, 'I got me some', morning-after look."

"Tasha!" Monica yelped. She lowered her voice to almost a whisper. "Stop it!" Monica looked around and asked, "What are the girls doing?"

Tasha stood at the bar and took a sip of her coffee. "They are in the back playing some game. I'm sure they are so into that game, they ain't even interested in nothing else."

Monica looked at her sister and shared, "We went out and had a nice dinner. After that, we went to his house for a few drinks." She didn't want to give Tasha the play-by-play of her experience with Kenneth. But she knew Tasha would be persistent, unrelenting in her quest to find out everything. "Okay, I stayed the night.

Now, are you satisfied?" Monica confessed.

Tasha put her hand on her hip and said, "Hell no!" She walked around the bar and stood in front of Monica. Tasha stared at her sister, her lips protruding. "I'll get all the juicy info when we are alone. I ain't gonna push you now because the girls are here."

Monica folded her arms and crossed her legs. "What if it's nothing to tell?"

Tasha walked back around the bar and said, "Bullshit. I damn well know you knocked boots with that fine-ass fireman. Remember, you are my sister, and I know your freaky ass."

Monica laughed and said, "And I know your freaky ass too."

Monica and Tasha were very close and could joke, push each other's buttons, argue, and then makeup. They couldn't stay angry at each other for a long period of time. And Monica was there for her sister during Tasha's time of need when she was heartbroken. She loved her sister and wanted nothing but the best for her. Monica knew that her sister felt the same way. Although annoying at times, she knew that Tasha had only the best intentions. But Monica knew that this was a time that Tasha would work her nerves like never before.

Monica and Taylor made it home just before five o'clock that evening, and the sun was going down. Taylor had asked her mother for pizza on the way home, so Monica called in the order for delivery on the way home. She sat in her home office going through papers while waiting on the pizza. Marcus called to talk to Taylor every day but didn't want to speak to Monica. She figured that since every time he called and she tried to have small talk with him, he'd brush her off. It saddened her every time Marcus would dodge her conversation.

The pizza arrived around 6:30 p.m. Taylor anxiously waited at the table. Monica sat the pizza down and watched as Taylor ripped into the box, devoured a slice of pizza, and then reached for another piece.

She laughed and said, "Girl, it's plenty of pizza. It's not going anywhere." She laughed again when Taylor looked up at her and started to laugh. She stared at her daughter, focusing on how much she resembled her father. She wore a smile on her sad face as she took in her daughter's beauty, adoring the child she gave birth to.

Chapter Twenty-One

It was Friday night, and a week had passed since Monica spent the night at Kenneth's. She took Taylor to her sister's house after getting her from school. Monica and Kenneth sat at a bar in West Midtown, having drinks and laughing. Whenever she was with Kenneth, she felt loose and free. Kenneth rejuvenated her soul with his compassion and charm. He began to lift the spirit in her, which had lain dormant for quite some time. She now felt brand new; letting her hair down and living it up with a man who began to sweep her off her feet.

Kenneth was into Monica and was mesmerized by her dark beauty and luscious lips. He loved her sense of humor, laughter, and how she talked—a Birmingham accent mixed with educated properness. And when she was tipsy, her authentic Alabama dialect was even more pronounced. He also loved her walk—a sexy glide, carrying confidence that spoke, I know I'm a fine ass black woman.

Monica ordered another drink and turned to Kenneth. "Now, about last week." Looking at him with a playful look and beautiful smile, she asked, "How many women have been getting that big thang?"

Kenneth looked away and chuckled. He shook his head and looked down. When he raised his head to look at Monica, she had her arms folded and her head tilted, looking straight at him. Kenneth didn't want to discuss his past sexual encounters. He only wanted to focus on Monica. He took a deep breath and answered, "Yeah, I'm a single man, and I have a past. But since we started seeing each other, you are the woman that has my complete attention." He leaned back in his chair and smiled at her. "Now, does that answer satisfy you?"

Monica took a sip from her drink and was silent as she stared at Kenneth. She was trying to read his demeanor as she investigated his love life. She nodded her head slowly as she bit gently down on her bottom lip. "Mm-hmm. Well, we were careless when we did it."

Kenneth agreed. "Yeah....yeah. To be honest, I wasn't even thinking about any protection. I just wanted you so bad; it wasn't even a thought. I apologize if that made you uncomfortable."

Monica took a deep breath and twisted her lips to the side.

"Well, you don't have to worry about me getting pregnant. I'm on the pill. But there are so many diseases out there…" She hesitated and continued, "…but for some reason, I was in a zone that night too."

"Well, concerning diseases, you don't have to worry about that. I'm clean, and I wouldn't jeopardize your health. I care too much about you to be that careless." He looked into her eyes with assurance and then gently grabbed her hand and said, in his deep, soft voice, "Monica, I really and truly enjoy your company. I love your spirit and your attitude."

Shyness and a feeling of elation began to run through her body. She looked into Kenneth's eyes, speechless; she could only muster up a long, deep breath. Her eyes began to vacillate from his eyes to the floor. She knew now that she had entered a whole new world of uncertainty and mystery. It scared her, but she wanted to take the risk at the same time. She was in her sexual prime, and here was a man sitting next to her, who had rocked her world the first time they had sex. He was a kind, gentle, strong, and handsome man.

Kenneth wanted to change the subject and get to know more about Monica. He released her hand and asked, "Hey, Beautiful? When are you going to visit Alabama?"

"I am thinking of going to Alabama this spring to visit my aunt and uncle." She took a sip from her drink and asked, "How often do you go home to visit?"

"I usually go home about two times a year." Kenneth's eyes fell to the floor. Without looking at Monica, he said, "I used to go to Arkansas for the holidays. But for some reason, the holidays don't have the same meaning to me anymore. Sure, I love the spirit of the holiday season, the music, and the decorations. But people have added so many other things that don't make it the same."

"I love the holiday season. Always have." Monica looked away and then back at Kenneth. "I enjoy the feeling of knowing that I can make others happy, even if it's just for that moment."

Kenneth agreed with her point of view. He loved the fire department's toy drive and giving to the less fortunate kids in the Atlanta area. "Yeah, I enjoy the looks on the kids' faces when we do our toy drive at the station. It reminds me of the joy I felt growing up in Arkansas as a little kid. My mother couldn't afford to buy my sister and me nice things. The police department would always have a toy drive and distribute toys in the poor neighborhoods."

"Fortunately, my sister and I didn't have to worry about going without."

She did know kids in Alabama that suffered from being poor and destitute. And seeing some of her friends growing up poor made her develop a warm heart for the unfortunate. "I love giving to kids, and I have always enjoyed the happiness it brings them. I don't just give at Christmas time. I always donate necessities to inner city school kids throughout the year ."

A curious look came over Kenneth's face. "Oh, yeah? What do you donate?"

Monica smiled and said, "I donate to the athletic program. I help with the basketball team's sneakers. I'm part of a program where we donate school clothes to the students. We help the girls get their hair done at local hair salons."

"Wow! That's impressive." Kenneth was intrigued by what Monica told him, making him want to be a part of her program. "Do you think that I can join your program? I would love to help with things like that."

"Sure, you can. I'll give you the info." Monica was pleased to hear that Kenneth was interested in joining her program for inner city kids.

Kenneth laughed and said, "Only one thing."

"What?" Monica asked.

"I'll help with the boys' haircuts, and I'll leave the girls' hair salon appointments to you," he said, laughing.

Monica looked at him and joined in the laughter. "Okay, okay. Let's change the subject. Do you hang out with the boys here in Atlanta? I mean, do you have any close friends?"

"Yeah, I do. Mark works at the station with me, and he's one of my closest friends. And there's Fred and Bryan. Fred and I played ball together in Georgia, and Bryan is a white dude; he's my Captain Franklin's son and a police officer here in Atlanta."

Monica nodded her head. "Oh, okay. So I'm getting to learn more about you. That's a good thing."

Monica and Kenneth laughed and joked well into the night. They opened up and shared much more about themselves, and both enjoyed what they discovered. They were getting deeper and deeper into one another's souls, cherishing each moment they were together. Monica was so intrigued by Kenneth that her marriage began to feel oblivious. He had pulled her out of her deep depression, and she appreciated him for that. If it wasn't for Kenneth, she didn't know where her state of mind would be. Now she was feeling alive and exuberant. She now looked forward to seeing the man who had swept her off her feet.

Chapter Twenty-Two

It was a chilly 40-degree December night. Kenneth and the fire department crew were passing the time playing dominoes. Waging bets: the games became more intensified the higher the stakes. Kenneth was a bit distracted, and his thoughts were on Monica, not the game he loved playing. He had lost two games, causing the crew to wonder if his mind was preoccupied. They knew how crafty Kenneth was at the game, often telling his taunting his opponent about what to play and what he had better not play.

The alarm bell sounded, and Captain Franklin yelled, "Looks like we got a biggun' fellows! Let's get suited and booted!"

The crew jumped up and ran for their fire gear and equipment. Kenneth was assigned to the emergency medical team that week and had helped save a heart attack victim the day before. And now, the call was a five-alarm fire at an apartment complex, and some of the residents reported injuries. Kenneth's mind jumped into full action mode, willing to save lives. He preferred riding on the fire engine more than riding the EMT because he loved the action it brought, hosing down the enemy fire and saving people from the fire's roaring blaze.

Kenneth's EMT team followed closely behind the fire engine. Flashes of Monica invaded his mind as he tried to concentrate on the task at hand. He took a deep breath and thought to himself, Okay. Let's stay focused. He stared out of the back of the window as the ambulance sped to the fire scene. He hoped and prayed that there were no fatal casualties. Although trained to be strong during horrific calls, Kenneth had a soft heart for those who perished in a fire, especially infants. He often struggled with nightmares and sleepless nights, thinking of the little infants' charred bodies taken away by the coroner.

He could hear Captain Franklin yelling as the fire engine team jumped out of the engine. "Get those hoses started! Quickly!" Kenneth and his partner ran to the injured people who had been helped out of the apartment building by their brave neighbors. It was total chaos and pandemonium. The fire was spreading out of control, its blaze lighting up the night.

Kenneth turned around to a voice screaming, "Over here! I don't think she's breathing!" Kenneth and his partner ran to an elderly woman lying on the sidewalk. He kneeled to check the woman's airway for a sign of breathing. She was barely breathing and had a slow pulse. Kenneth ran to the ambulance and got an oxygen mask. Let's save lives.

Kenneth and his partner resuscitated the older woman and placed her on the gurney. As they rolled the gurney to the ambulance, He could see Mark ascending the fire ladder, rising to the fourth level of the blazing fire. Kenneth wanted to be by his friend's side and help put out the burning fire. Although Mark came across as a comedian and living life on the edge, he was one of the bravest men Kenneth had known. When it came to facing the dangers of firefighting, Mark was one of the best. Kenneth took one last glance at his friend before the ambulance left for the hospital.

The ambulance arrived at the Piedmont Atlanta Medical Center. The older woman's breathing had improved during the ride to the hospital, giving much relief to Kenneth. He talked to her until the ambulance reached the hospital, encouraging her to, "Hang in there!" He constantly assured her, "Everything is going to be okay." They rushed her inside, and the hospital medical team ran to them. Kenneth told them she was pulled from a burning apartment building and barely breathing. After the hospital medical staff took control of the elderly woman, Kenneth and the EMT staff headed back to the fire scene.

When Kenneth and the EMT crew arrived back at the fire scene, he flung open the door to take a quick assessment of the scene. He could hear a fireman yelling, "Over here! We have a fireman who needs oxygen!" It was obvious that the fireman had been overcome with smoke inhalation. Kenneth had seen the signs many times and had been a victim of smoke inhalation a few times. Kenneth and his partner hurried to the injured fireman and gave aid. He was from another fire station, but Kenneth knew him from other fires they had assisted. And he also recognized him from the Atlanta Fire Department's parties.

The firemen fought the blaze well after midnight. Kenneth and his EMT crew were hard at work, giving aid to those who needed it. He looked at his friend, Mark, who was exhausted. Kenneth walked over to Mark and asked if he was okay. After Mark lowered his head from taking a long swallow from a bottle of water, he looked at Kenneth and shook his head. Mark had a sad look on his face. He touched Kenneth's shoulder and tried to speak, but no words could come out. Kenneth knew this reaction all too well. He looked at his friend and nodded his head. "It's okay, partner. We are all in this together."

No firemen were seriously injured, but the report was that three residents' lives were lost in the fire. The saddest was a nine-year-old girl trapped inside a hallway in an apartment. Losing lives always brought a fireman's confidence down, although many never wanted to admit it. There would always be second-guessing and self-blame. Guilt was something firefighters took home with them when fatalities occurred. And Kenneth knew that he had to be there for his friend. Just like his friend had been there for him.

Chapter Twenty-Three

Monica sat in her office looking over documents for a new residential sale. It was a week before Christmas, and Taylor was spending a few days with her father. Donny Hathaway's 'This Christmas played in the background. Monica made sure that Taylor knew nothing about Kenneth, being careful and not wanting to confuse her daughter any more than she already was. Monica had to admit that she was confused and lost in a wild love wilderness at times. Wandering around, seeking any direction that would tell her that she was free to do whatever she wanted with Kenneth.

Monica hadn't seen much of Kenneth lately, only talking to him on the phone. He told her he was taking extra shifts at the fire department because other firefighters were vacationing during the Christmas holiday season. She recalled Kenneth telling her how much he loved holiday songs and the city's holiday lights and decorations. He loved it when the fire department surprised the kids with gifts, enjoying the delight it brought to their eager faces. But he didn't like the commercialization of Christmas. He'd expressed his feelings regarding the greed of merchants during this time of year, especially those business owners who didn't believe in Christmas.

Monica leaned back in her chair and turned around to take in the view of Atlanta's Christmas-decorated skyline from her office window. Thoughts of Kenneth and the holidays invaded her mind. This would be the first Christmas that she wouldn't be with her husband and daughter since she and Marcus got married. The thought of Taylor's glowing face hugging and playing with Marcus on Christmas Day made her feel emotional. But she told herself that she had to be strong and accept the situation for what it was. Kenneth encouraged her to make the best of the holiday season for her daughter. She agreed with him, although she knew it would be easier said than done.

Monica sat looking out of the window, hoping that Kenneth would call her. Not only was he superb in bed, he was also a gentleman, and he seemed to care for her very deeply. She had texted him and asked him to call her when he got the chance. He texted her back and said that he would call her after he and his captain were done talking. Monica smiled as she thought of how Kenneth talked about his captain. Kenneth described Captain Franklin as a redneck who had a change of heart about black people. Monica enjoyed the stories Kenneth shared about Captain Franklin.

Monica looked at her watch as the sun began to set. She could use a drink after her busy day and hoped that Kenneth would be available to join her. He told her he was getting off work at 7:00 p.m. and would love to grab a drink. He told her that he had taken clothes to the fire department and would shower and change at the fire station. She wanted his company and his great sex. Monica was excited and wanted him to rock her world, taste her, and fill her up with all he was packing. Thinking about Kenneth began to make her moist and horny. *Please be available, Kenneth.*

Just as Monica had hoped, her phone rang.

"Hey, you!" Monica answered, her voice anxious and filled with excitement as she stood when she heard Kenneth's deep voice come through the phone,

"Hey, Sexy. What are you up to?" he asked.

Monica walked to the window, holding a glass of wine. "I just wrapped up some paperwork, and I'm still at my office." A naughty thought entered her mind, and she continued, "I really haven't seen much of you lately. Would you mind coming to my office? No one is in the building but me."

"Well, sure. I'll come by. I could use a drink, though. I'll stop by the store and grab me some Crown."

Monica laughed and said, "Kenneth, you don't have to do that. I have a private bar in my office. I'll save you the trip."

Kenneth started to laugh. "Oh, okay. Would you like me to grab you something to eat?"

Monica turned around and walked to her chair. "No, I'll order delivery. What would you like?"

"Whatever you get is fine with me. I'm open to anything."

"How about Chinese? I know a great restaurant nearby."

"That sounds great. I'll be there in about twenty minutes or so." Kenneth agreed.

Kenneth arrived at Monica's office at the time he predicted. She closed the door behind him as he walked inside her office. He turned around, taking in all of Monica's beauty. Damn, this woman is so beautiful! He had missed seeing her and could barely get her out of his mind. Walking to her, he touched her face gently, rubbing his large hand on her cheek. He then leaned down and began to kiss her passionately. Kenneth loved when Monica put her tongue in his mouth and how she sucked his bottom lip. She always smelled soft, sweet, and sensual. Kenneth had quietly begun falling in love with her. The woman that he was so intrigued with the moment he laid eyes on her.

Monica pulled away and looked into his eyes. She smiled and said, "Slow down, Mr. Mann. If you keep this up, we will miss the food that's being delivered."

Kenneth laughed and started to rub his head. "Yeah, you are correct, beautiful. I have to admit; I'm starving for you, not the Chinese food."

"I know," she teased. "But I can use something to eat. I don't know about you."

Kenneth looked at her and gently placed both hands on her face. "After dinner, you will be my dessert for sure."

Monica touched his arms and gazed into his eyes. "I know I will be. And you will be mine."

After dinner, Monica lay close to Kenneth on the couch in her office. She loved how he stroked her hair and gently rubbed her arms. She inhaled the tantalizing scent of his redolent cologne. Kenneth's sense of fashion impressed Monica. His muscular body was adorned with a white fitted, long sleeve sweater that boasted all the mountainous curves of his arms, shoulders, and chest. His blue slacks and brown shoes complimented his outfit. Monica could not contain herself as she pulled away and peered into Kenneth's eyes.

Kenneth looked back at her lovingly intense stare and recognized the fire and desire on her face. The woman he strongly desired sat right before his eyes, and he wanted her in the worst way. Kenneth thought back to when Monica confessed that sex with him was incredible. The thought made him grow even more excited. He pulled her face to his and began to kiss her fervently. He stood up and guided her gently up from the couch. "Will you join me in your private room?"

Because there were times when Monica pulled an all-nighter at work, she had a room at the back of her office with a bed and a 55-inch LG television mounted on the wall.

Monica began to walk toward the room, Kenneth following behind her. She knew he was admiring her curves. Without turning around, she teased, "I know you are staring at my ass."

Kenneth always told her how perfectly round her ass was. He constantly showered her with compliments; he loved the tone of her chocolate skin, her lips, hips, and more. She loved all the praises she had been missing for so long. And now Kenneth was here, in her office, ready to fulfill another of her fantasies. Monica was psyched about her sexual escapade with the man who had saved her from her loneliness and depression. And she would not disappoint.

Monica stood in front of Kenneth, kissing him as she unbuttoned his pants. She slid down his zipper and slid down to his rock-hard dick. She closed her eyes and put her luscious full lips around it. She began to lick and suck him, loving the way he moaned. The more Kenneth moaned; the more vigorous Monica sucked. It was her turn to display her talent to him after he'd blown her mind last time. She knew he would taste her, so she wanted to savor him before he weakened her with his tongue.

Monica pulled her head back, holding his manhood in her hand, and eased out, "Damn! You're big." She returned to pleasing him, confident that her head game was on point.

Kenneth pulled out of her mouth and shrieked, "Damn! Shit! I don't want to cum this way. You better stop."

Monica rose as she proceeded to disrobe Kenneth. She took off his shirt and began kissing his chest. She waited anxiously as he unbuttoned her skirt, letting it fall to the floor. Monica pulled down her panties as she stepped out of her shoes. Kenneth unbuttoned her blouse and glided it off. He stepped out of his shoes and eased out of his pants. Both completely naked, Kenneth kissed Monica as they made their way to the bed. He kissed her neck, arms, breasts, and stomach before making his way down to her hot, wet pussy.

Kenneth gently sucked her clitoris, and she began to moan loudly. Loving her seductive moans, Kenneth began to lick her with vigor. Monica screamed as he sucked and used his tongue at the same time. Kenneth wanted to pleasure her so badly and be the best she ever had. He loved when she came while he was tasting her. And he loved it even more when she came while he was inside her, filling her up with his sauce. Kenneth loved it when Monica screamed, "Ohhhhh! Kenneth! Fuck me with that big ass dick! Fuck me!"

Monica's body began to shake as she came while Kenneth flicked his tongue fast and briskly on her clitoris. "Ohhhhhhh, shit! Oh, shit! Fuck!" She couldn't take it anymore as she pulled her quivering body away from his mouth. She lay on the bed, breathing fast and rubbing her breasts. In a soft and faint voice, with her eyes closed, Monica whispered, "Oh fuck, Kenneth. That felt soooo good." She knew she needed to compose herself before he entered her; anticipating that she was in for a ride of hot steamy sex.

Monica loved how Kenneth filled her up with his big dick, stroking her hard and soft until she reached an orgasm.

After Monica had regained her composure, she got up from the bed and stood next to it. She looked at Kenneth seductively and demanded, "You are going to fuck me from behind."

Kenneth stood up and walked over to her. "Oh yeah? That's the way you want it?"

Without saying a word, Monica placed both knees on the bed and arched her back as her round ass rose. Then she looked back at Kenneth and said, "Put it in me, Daddy."

Kenneth gently slid his dick inside of Monica. Feeling the wetness and heat of her, he began to stroke. "Awwww shit! This feels good!"

Monica began to rock back and forth in rhythm with him. The good feeling mounting, she yelled, "Fuck me harder, Kenneth! Fuck me harder!" He caved to her demand and started to pound her harder. Monica screamed, "Ohhhhh, Daddy! Yes! That's what the fuck I'm talking about! Fuck this pussy, Daddy!" She was in a zone and loved every inch of him.

Kenneth was kind, considerate, and loving. He met her every sexual desire. Monica had come to adore him—he was so good to her, and it felt like he was heaven-sent. Monica would make sure to show her appreciation for him.

Chapter Twenty-four

It was two days before Christmas, and Marcus had come by the house to drop off gifts for Taylor. Taylor had gone to her room to watch TV before Marcus arrived. So, Marcus sat at the bar sipping Hennessy on the rocks which Monica had made for him. He noticed Monica's mood was upbeat like she was walking on clouds. She wasn't the same sad and miserable woman he had previously perceived her as. She glowed, and her appearance was radiant, not the unkept, stripped look she had just a few months ago. Marcus realized that there was definitely a change in her.

Marcus watched Monica as she poured herself a glass of wine. "So, how have you been doing?" he asked.

She put the glass to her lips, and before sipping, she smiled and responded, "I've been doing well, thanks." Her smile beamed as she caught eye contact with her husband. She walked over and grabbed a seat at the edge of the bar. She took another sip of her wine and asked, "How are things going with you?"

Her attitude and disposition began to make Marcus uncomfortable. He leaned back and took a sip of Hennessy. "Things are going great. Business is picking up, and I'm getting ready to expand."

"Oh, that's great, Marcus! I'm so glad to hear that," Monica exclaimed. She was genuinely happy for him and was always proud of his drive to be great and successful.

Marcus' facial expression changed from curious to concerned. Before he knew it, he blurted out, "So, what have you been doing with yourself? Are you seeing anyone?"

Not surprised by his question, Monica replied, "Well, Marcus. That's my business if I am or if I'm not." She smiled as she glared at him. She knew her response would make him uncomfortable, but she didn't give a damn.

Marcus raised his arms as to give a sign of surrender. "Okay, okay. I'm sorry for asking. You are right. I have no business asking." He looked into Monica's eyes and added, "But if you are. . . I would appreciate it if you kept it away from our daughter. I'm just saying."

Monica laughed and raised her eyebrow. "Oh really? Well, I hope you are doing the same with your girlfriend." She stood up, poured herself another glass of wine, then turned to him and said, "I don't want her to be more confused than she already is."

Marcus quickly responded, "Of course, she hasn't been introduced to another woman. I wouldn't do that. I know that would devastate her."

"Alright then. We've both established that she won't meet anyone we are involved with," Monica agreed.

Marcus began to feel uneasy after Monica's response. A sense of selfish, manly pride came over him. Suddenly, a deep feeling of jealousy began to burn inside his soul. And the way his wife was gliding around the kitchen only sparked his curiosity even more. The more he watched her, the more he wondered. His thoughts of the possibilities and the unknown bothered him. Why was he feeling this way? It was he that left her for another woman. But Marcus couldn't help what he was feeling.

It was nearing midnight, and Monica insisted it was time for Marcus to leave. She needed to get up early and finish her Christmas shopping. Besides, she wanted to get Marcus out of her business. The more he drank, the nosier he became. Since Taylor was asleep, she would have to miss saying goodbye to her father.

Marcus' visit didn't bother Monica all that much, although the thought of separation and divorce crept into her mind. Although she hated knowing how it would affect her daughter. And Taylor was the love of her life, her pride, and her joy, and she didn't want to see her daughter hurt.

Marcus walked to the front door, turned around, and said, "Tell Little Princess that I love her and that I will see her on Christmas."

Monica opened the door and said, "I'll be sure to do just that. You be safe driving home."

Marcus looked around, soaking in the view of the house. Safe driving home? Hearing Monica speak those words made it clear that this was no longer his home. He looked at her and said dryly, "I will, thanks. I'll call you tomorrow and confirm our plans for spending time with Taylor."

After Marcus left, Monica went to her room and called Kenneth. He didn't have to be at work until two o'clock the following afternoon, so she figured he'd be up. He was anticipating her call. Monica noticed the excitement of his voice. She had been honest with him about Marcus coming over to drop off gifts for Taylor. She didn't want any secrets between them. If Kenneth was to see someone else, just let her know. She understood that she was still a married woman and couldn't really make any demands on Kenneth. But deep down inside, she didn't want him to be involved with any other woman. The thought of another woman getting his great loving made her jealous.

"Hey, Handsome," she said as she positioned her back against the headboard.

"Hey, Beautiful," Kenneth replied. "How are you?"

Monica loved when Kenneth asked her how she was doing or feeling, and he was always concerned about her feelings. "I'm doing just fine. Tired from all this Christmas shopping," Monica admitted.

Kenneth laughed and replied, "You know that saying, 'shop til you drop.' I don't need you passing out at one of those malls."

In her seductive voice, Monica said, "Well, if I do, I know that you will rush to my rescue and give me mouth-to-mouth resuscitation."

"There you go. Being a naughty girl."

Displaying her wide and beautiful smile, she said, "And you like it when I'm a bad girl. Don't you?"

Kenneth laughed and then warned her, "You better stop while you are ahead. You keep talking like that, and you'll have to call your sister and let her know that you will be dropping off Taylor."

Monica and Kenneth talked on the phone until four that morning. She loved his sense of humor, his kindness, and the way he made her soul shine with his compliments. Kenneth brought back the confidence she had lost when she found her husband with his mistress. Kenneth bestowed the resilience she once had, giving her confidence that had been taken away from her by a husband who had abandoned her. And now she was a new woman. And every time she was with Kenneth, her light shined bright, and her fire burned hotter than ever before.

Chapter Twenty-Five

Monica and Tasha were up early Christmas morning, putting the finishing touches on their Christmas dinner. Monica had agreed that she and Taylor celebrate Christmas at Tasha's house. Monica enjoyed her sister's company, telling her all about Kenneth and what a wonderful man he was. Tasha was not the kind of person to hold back her thoughts or the way she felt, and Monica knew she would get unfiltered truth from her sister. Tasha was just like their mother; she didn't hold any punches, no matter how they may hurt someone's feelings.

Tasha looked at her sister as she prepared the icing for a cake. "This Kenneth, the fireman. You say he's a good man?"

"Yes, Tasha. Kenneth is a really good man. He's considerate and kind. He's neither arrogant nor a pompous ass just because he is a good-looking man, unlike most of the men in Atlanta who think that their shit don't stink, just because they look good and make a little money."

Tasha put the spoon down, walked to the refrigerator, and pulled out a bottle of wine. "Yeah, I hope that he stays that way. And if he does, then go for it. Shit, I saw bullshit in Marcus from the jump. All he had to do was achieve success, and he would show his true colors. Believe me, I can read people. I knew it was a matter of time before he started smelling himself."

Monica's voice began to rise, "Tasha! You knew of no such thing! Stop it!"

Tasha quickly corrected her sister. "No, you knew of no such thing. Believe me, I've been around longer than you, and I've seen these niggas show humility when they don't have shit. And the minute they have a little success, they think that the world is theirs and begin to treat women like shit. Marcus played the role of good husband for as long as he could before the real asshole came out."

Monica stared at her sister with squinted eyes. She wanted to respond vehemently, not wanting Tasha to start in on her husband. But she took a deep breath and said, "Tasha, this is Christmas. And I really don't want to get into that today." She walked over to the stove and began stirring the pinto beans. Without looking at her, Monica assured Tasha, "Besides, I'm doing okay, and I feel fine." Then she turned and smiled at her, "Just know I'll be okay, and let's enjoy this day."

Tasha nodded her head in agreement. "Okay, Sis." Then she teased Monica, "I'm so glad yo' ass finally learned how to cook. My god, you were a horrible cook!"

Monica rolled her eyes, and they both burst into laughter. Monica looked down at Tasha's wine glass and said, "Damn, girl! You starting too damn early. You'll be drunk before noon."

Tasha took a sip fand said, "I'm at my house, so if I do, I can go lie down. I'll recuperate and start again. You just mind your damn business."

Laughter rang out as they added the finishing touches to their holiday meal and sang Christmas songs.

They wanted to wake the girls up at 7:00 a.m. to open their gifts. They had allowed Taylor and Brianna to stay up well past midnight on Christmas Eve, knowing they were eager to find out what was under the Christmas tree. Monica and Tasha had watched Tyler Perry movies Christmas Eve as the girls played video games on the PS4.

Monica headed to Brianna's room to wake the girls up at seven sharp. She looked at her daughter as she arose slowly from the bed, rubbing her eyes. Brianna jumped up and quickly composed herself, knowing that gifts awaited her. Monica guided the two anxious girls to the living room, both smiling with glee as they followed behind. Monica anticipated the excitement and joyous screams as the girls ripped the packaging from their gifts.

While they were ripping into their gifts, Monica and Tasha snuck into the garage and wheeled in two brand-new bicycles. Brianna stood up and yelled, "Yay! We got new bikes!"

On bended knees, Taylor quickly turned around and faced her mother, who was standing next to her bright, new shiny bike. She jumped up, ran over, and wrapped her arms around Monica. "Oh, Mommy! Thank you!"

It was a sunny morning, and the neighborhood kids were out in the street playing with their new toys or riding their new bikes. Monica and Tasha watched as Taylor and Brianna enthusiastically rode their bikes, laughing and yelling. Monica smiled with joy, knowing how much Taylor wanted a new bike. She watched as Taylor rode, her short legs spinning fast as she sped past the house. Brianna was a more experienced rider, passing Taylor every time Taylor rode in front of her. Monica and Tasha laughed as Taylor tried her best to keep up.

Later that afternoon, after the girls were done riding their bicycles and playing with their toys, Monica and Tasha set the table for their Christmas meal. She called the girls over as she put the cornbread dressing on the table. Taylor and Brianna were hungry and anxious to eat. They stopped playing with their toys and ran to the kitchen table.

"Go wash your hands," Monica instructed.

They jumped up from the table and hurriedly ran to the bathroom.

After dinner, Monica and Tasha sat on the couch watching TV while the girls played with their new dolls in Brianna's bedroom. It was getting close to four o'clock when Monica told Tasha that she was going to meet Kenneth to exchange gifts around 7:00 p.m. She was excited about the gift she brought Kenneth and boasted to her sister about it. Tasha sat at the end of the couch, smiling at Monica. Monica could tell that Tasha was happy to see her out of her depressed state. They looked at each other without saying a word; their eyes said, I love you.

Monica's phone rang as she and Tasha talked and watched TV. It was Marcus calling to speak with Taylor. "Hey, Marcus," Monica answered. "She's in the bedroom playing with Brianna. I'll call her so she can talk to you."

Monica looked over at her sister, who was staring at her. She quickly turned her head away from Tasha's aggravated stare. Monica wasn't going to let anything negative ruin her Christmas with Kenneth. She was eager to see what he had gotten her, but most of all, she was excited to see the man that had come into her life and made a positive difference to her fragile psyche.

Chapter Twenty-Six

Monica agreed to meet Kenneth at The Historic Fourth Ward Park. It was 7:00 p.m., and the weather had dipped to a pleasant sixty five degrees. The sky was clear, and the stars shined brightly over the festive-lit park. Monica and Kenneth took in the beautiful holiday scenery as they walked through the park. She eased closer to Kenneth and placed her arm around his. He stopped, faced her, looked down at her, and said, "You are so damn beautiful."

After their romantic walk, Kenneth suggested they go to their cars and exchange gifts. The excitement brewed inside of Kenneth. He anticipated that Monica would love the gifts he had gotten her. He took notice of her taste in clothes and jewelry and knew exactly where to find what he was looking for. Kenneth had sneaked a peek at her clothing size one evening while she was soundly asleep. He had picked her out three outfits from Ann Fontaine and a collection of fine jewelry from Tiffany & Co. He had her gifts with a bow. Kenneth held a vibrant smile as he retrieved the boxes from the back seat of his truck. This was the first time he had felt this way since giving gifts to his mother and sister.

Kenneth let the tailgate of his truck down and placed the gifts on it. He looked into Monica's eyes and said enthusiastically, "Merry Christmas, Beautiful."

He watched as Monica unwrapped her first gift. She looked at the box and then at Kenneth, a cheeky smile on her face. She opened the first box and placed her hand over her mouth. Speechless, she began to unwrap the other boxes. After uncovering a necklace, watch, and a pair of diamond earrings from Tiffany's, tears welled in her eyes. Kenneth was happy that he had made her Christmas special.

Monica gave Kenneth a warm, tight hug. "Thank you so much, Kenneth." She cried joyfully, knowing that Kenneth didn't have to go all out for her as he did. She looked into his eyes, reached up, and gently touched his face. "Kiss me, please," she said in a near whisper. When Kenneth's lips touched hers, her soul melted into his. She held his head, not wanting the kiss to end.

Monica pulled her lips apart from his and joked, "We better stop this. Before you know it, we'll be getting arrested for public lewdness." She then hurried to her car and pulled out two small, gift-wrapped boxes. She handed the boxes to Kenneth. "I really didn't know what to get you, so I improvised. I hope you like what I got."

Feeling pleased that she had gotten him anything, Kenneth said, "Whatever you got me, I'm just grateful for the thought." He unwrapped the first box, opened it, and found a Versace Helenium watch. "Oh, Baby! Thank you! This is sweet!"

Monica knew that Kenneth loved watches, and she hit the jackpot on this one. Kenneth kissed her before unwrapping the other box. He unwrapped the box and found a bottle of Creed Aventis cologne. Kenneth nodded, loving her choice, "Oh, okay. You want me to turn you on, huh?"

Monica laughed and slapped him on the arm. "Stop! I hope you like the gifts." She hugged him again and said, "Looks like you went all out for me, and here I am just getting you a little something."

Kenneth pulled back, his hands on her shoulders, and said, "Baby, you went all out when you came into my life. You are worth more than any gift on earth."

Monica looked up at him, the look of love all over her face. She pulled in so his lips would meet hers and began to kiss him passionately. There was something indeed special about Kenneth. She could feel his warm and giving heart when he held her. She could feel his endearing care for her whenever they made love. She could feel a man with a soul that engulfed her own, coming together as one magnanimous heartbeat. Monica had fallen in love once again.

After exchanging gifts, Monica insisted that they go to his place. She wanted him in the worst way and knew the feeling was mutual when she hugged him and pressed against his pants. It would be a perfect ending to a night full of love and desire. And she was in the mood to give Kenneth all that burned inside her. Monica was a fire that he would have to bring all his fireman equipment to put out—a fire that would ignite over and over again. And she knew that he had the hose to put out her fire every time it would flame up.

Monica walked through the door and went straight to the bathroom to shower. They had talked naughty over the phone as they drove to Kenneth's place in their cars. They were like lovesick teens, so full of energy and not getting enough of each other.

After showering, Monica lay on Kenneth's king-size bed, waiting for him to finish grooming himself. She snuggled under the covers as she listened to the water run in the shower. Kenneth hummed to LSG's, Round and Round We Go, as he showered. She was naked and moist, anticipating Kenneth tasting her before he filled her up with his Mr. Mann. Oh, Baby! Hurry up, please, her mind marveled. Her desire was at a boiling point, about to spill over.

Kenneth walked into the room, aroused and hard. Monica

looked down at his manhood and rose to her knees. She arched her back as she rested on her hands and knees, not taking her eyes off his long and hard mule. Kenneth looked at her face, knowing what she wanted to do with him. He walked over to her and stood in front of her face. He watched as she grabbed hold of his hardness and began to suck. He watched as her head went back and forth, her mouth gripping him, pleasuring him as he had never felt quite before. Monica zoned in on pleasing him.

Kenneth couldn't take his building ecstasy anymore; he pulled away as Monica tried her best to hold on. "No! Stop now, Baby! I don't want to cum like this now!" he begged.

Monica reluctantly let go, still salivating over his mule. "Okay. But I wouldn't have minded drinking all of you."

Kenneth didn't say a word as he leaned in and lay her on her back. He slid down to her ankles and kissed her leg, moving up-ward to her calve and thigh until he reached her wet, hot jew-el. There, he went to work. Kenneth began licking all her soft-ness, tasting the juices overflowing from her fountain. Listening to her moans, he began to suck gently on her clitoris. When she screamed, he began to use his tongue, flickering it against her clitoris at a fast pace. When she grabbed the back of his head, he knew his mission was near accomplishment. He was now going in for the kill.

Monica's legs began to tremble, raising her hips, not letting go of Kenneth's head. She had never experienced such a feeling that Kenneth gave her. He definitely knew what he was doing. What are you doing to me? Monica screamed inside her head as she moaned with bliss. Feeling Kenneth's tongue on her tender spot while taking in the lyrics of TLC's Red Light Special blasting in the background made her hunger more. He spoiled her sexually and emotionally with his charisma and devotion to her. She was falling for him, the way that she knew he had already fallen for her.

Chapter Twenty-Seven

Marcus sat on the third-story balcony of his luxury apartment in East Point. Atlanta's skyline shined bright from a distance as he relaxed on his comfortable patio chair, sipping on Remy Martin, and puffing on his Arturo Fuente Opus cigar. It was an unseasonably warm night for December, and the weather was supposed to be perfect for New Year's Eve. He and Kyra were invited to attend a New Year's Eve party at the Hyatt Hotel on Peach Street. Ed had suggested that Marcus bring Monica instead of Kyra, but Marcus emphatically disagreed.

Ed was to arrive at Marcus' apartment any minute now. Marcus prepared himself for the argument about his decision to attend the party with Kyra. He knew his friend well, and Ed would not abandon his pursuit to persuade Marcus to bring his wife. Marcus didn't want to argue; he just wanted to sit on the balcony, have a sip of Remy and smoke a cigar with his best friend. He'd already decided and wasn't about to give in to Ed's demand.

Marcus was still admiring the Atlanta skyline when he heard the doorbell. He took a deep breath and one last sip of Remy before standing and going to the door. He opened the door, turned, and walked away. Without looking back at Ed, he asked, "What's up, my brother?"

Marvin Gaye's, Got to Give it Up was playing on Classic Soul 107.5. Marcus was in the mood for old-school jams, convinced it was a complement to the Remy and cigar.

Ed went straight to the bar and fixed himself a Crown on the rocks. "Give me one of those cigars," he told Marcus.

"You got it, my man," Marcus replied. "It's out on the balcony. Come on out and enjoy."

Ed's head started to bob to the beat of Marvin Gaye. "I see you got the old-school jams working."

Marcus walked to the balcony and slid open the glass door. He looked back at Ed and said, "Can't go wrong with old school jams, sipping on Remy and a nice cigar, my brother."

Marcus sat in his chair, waiting for Ed to come out. He started to think about Monica and Taylor. It wasn't that he had totally forgotten about his family and his marriage. He often thought about how things affected his daughter, surely sending her young mind into a state of confusion. But he had decided to move out of the house, letting the chips fall where they may. Kyra had turned his world around, and he had no regrets about getting involved with her. It was his life, and he was willing to face the consequences of his actions. He had vowed always to be a part of his daughter's life, continuing to love and spoil her to no end.

Ed walked out onto the balcony and sat across from his friend. "They are really jammin' tonight. Got that Al Green bumpin'."

Marcus smiled and looked at Ed. "Al is the man. He travels with time." He pulled a cigar from the box and handed it to Ed. "Now that's an Arturo Fuente Opus, my friend. Enjoy."

Ed rolled the cigar underneath his nose, taking in the scent before he clipped the end. "Certainly will, my brother." He lit the cigar and took a puff. "You always got to get the best, don't you?"

Marcus looked at his cigar and replied, "Why not? You only live once. Go for what makes you happy. Right?"

Ed's anxiety boiled as he prepared to bring up the subject of Kyra. He wanted to wait for the right moment. Ed knew that Marcus anticipated the conversation and would be ready to combat whatever heat he would bring. But Ed didn't care what Marcus thought nor how he would react. He would tell his friend what he needed to hear, not what he wanted to hear. No matter the outcome of the night.

Initially, Ed and Marcus reminisced about their college days.

Loud talking and laughter filled the balcony when Ed brought up a fight they had with two guys from Alabama. It was a campus party during their sophomore year at a hotel ballroom. Ed was sleeping with one of the guys' girlfriend; the guy found out from his best friend. Ed had no idea that the guy knew and wasn't prepared for the confrontation.

Marcus laughed loudly and yelled, "Man, that dude walked up to you and just landed one right on your fucking jaw! I don't know how the fuck you stayed on your feet!"

Ed laughed. "Man, you know I can take a punch. Shit. That shit did hurt, but I got on his ass! Turned the motherfuckin' party out!"

"Yeah! And then his friend stole on you! And I whooped that motherfucker's ass!" Marcus continued. "Next thing I know; the police had our asses in handcuffs and sitting in the back of the damn police car!" He stopped and paused. Looking down, he said, "Monica had to come and bail our asses out of jail. Good thing that shit was thrown out of court because we were college students and had never been in any trouble."

A serious look came across Ed's face. He went silent as he turned and looked at the Atlanta skyline. He stood up and went inside to pour himself another drink. Standing at the bar, he rested his hands on it with his head down. Ed had to say what was on his mind, and there was no reason to postpone the inevitable. He was going to say his piece, and that was final. That was his reason for coming over in the first place.

Ed walked out on the balcony and sat in his chair. He reached for his cigar and looked at Marcus, whose head was rocking to The Whispers' Rock Steady. "Marcus, we need to talk about your situation, man. You know it's been bothering me."

Marcus cut his eyes at his friend. He took a sip from his drink and then a puff from his cigar. "Ed, I really don't want to talk about this shit, man. Look. I know that you are my boy, and you have my best interest. But it's my life, and I'm a grown man."

Ed stood up and looked away. "Marcus, you know Kyra Grant's reputation! She's a fucking groupie who goes after any man with money! Shit, dude!"

Marcus stood up, offended by his friend's true remarks. He said in a low stern voice, "Look, Ed. Don't go there. That's all I have to say."

Ed turned and gave his friend the I don't give a shit how you feel, look. He managed to keep his cool and said, "Well, you are going to hear me. I am going to tell you what you need to hear. Not what the fuck you wanna hear. You know damn well if another lucrative offer comes Kyra's way, your ass is out."

Angry and frustrated, Marcus yelled, "Get the fuck out of my house! Fuck you!"

Angry himself, Ed put his glass and cigar down and shook his head as he looked at his friend. "Fine, my brother. But you know that I'm right. I'll holla." He left Marcus' apartment shaking his head, not looking back once.

Marcus was furious. He paced around the balcony, rubbing the back of his head. He knew of Kyra's past, and it didn't seem to bother him until now. *Why did my best friend have to come at him like that? Is he jealous of me?* After all, Kyra was the kind of girl that the ordinary man couldn't pull. She wasn't with the drama. She was submissive without questioning her man's desires and needs. She was game for whatever without any shame. And Marcus had been captured by Kyra's sexy yet classy wildness. He was caught in her trap, causing him to leave his family for a fantasy that he didn't want to end.

Chapter Twenty-Eight

Monica and Taylor sat on the patio at one of their favorite seafood restaurants. The Big Ketch Saltwater Grill in Buckhead had a moderate crowd, with people scattered inside and outside the restaurant. The weather was pleasant, with a slight overcast. Monica wanted to take her daughter out for a late afternoon lunch, and Taylor was excited. The next day was New Year's Eve, and Monica wanted to bring in the new year with her daughter. She and Tasha had agreed that the celebration would be held at Monica's house, inviting a few close friends and their families.

Monica watched as her daughter devoured the fried jumbo shrimp. This girl can eat! she thought to herself as she laughed.

Taylor looked up at her mother, ketchup on her face; she asked, "What are you laughing at, Mommy?"

Monica continued to laugh, leaning back in her chair with her arms crossed, she said, "You! Little girl, you know you can put away some food."

Taylor began to laugh at her mother. "But, Mommy, they're good!"

Shaking her head, Monica said, "I know, Sweetheart. Enjoy."

The waiter checked on Monica and Taylor. Monica sipped from her glass of water as she stared into space. Interrupted by the waiter, Monica was snapped out of her thoughts of Kenneth and her situation. She quickly shifted her focus back to her daughter. The waiter asked if she would like anything else to drink. Monica contemplated for a few seconds and said, "Yeah, I'll have a glass of your Romanee Conti fine wine, thank you." Her favorite wine would pair perfectly with her grilled salmon and salad.

Kenneth had told Monica that he would be working New Year's Eve night, easing her guilt for not being able to bring in the New Year with him. He'd put in for the shift months earlier. Deep inside, Monica wished that she and Kenneth could bring in the New Year together. But circumstances wouldn't allow it. She thought of taking him something to eat at the fire station that night if he wasn't out on a call. She was in deep thought about surprising at the station. She had considered surprising him at the firehouse with something to eat, but she knew it would be better to give him a heads-up before she went that late at night.

After lunch, Monica and Taylor went to Tasha's house. Tasha had invited them over for dinner. Mexican food was on the menu that night and Tasha wanted her sister over for tacos, nachos and burritos, refried beans, and rice. Tasha wanted so badly to meet Kenneth but knew that the timing wasn't right for him to come over. Monica had told her so much about Kenneth, causing great anticipation and excitement from Tasha.

Monica used her key and walked into her sister's house. "Hey, y'all!" she yelled as she closed the door behind her.

Tasha and Brianna met Monica and Taylor as they walked into the house. Tasha invited them to join them for movies. Tasha looked back at her sister and said, "You know I'm watching Tyler Perry movies."

Monica laughed. Taking off her jacket, she said, "Girl, I already know. What movie is it this time?"

Tasha looked at her sister and leaned her head down. "Madea's Family Reunion, one of my favorite movies."

The girls quickly ran to Brianna's room to play video games. Monica sat on the couch while Tasha went to the kitchen to get a bottle of wine from the refrigerator. It was always a perfect combo of good wine and movies when they spent time together. And Monica was prepared for Tasha to start bringing up old memories from their childhood after they had a few drinks. They would laugh uncontrollably, telling stories of when one had gotten caught with a boy, sneaking out of the house, and getting locked out.

Tasha came back to the living with two glasses of wine in tow. She gave her sister a glass and sat at the other end of the couch. Without hesitation, she said, "Christy told me that she saw Marcus and that heffa in Midtown the other day."

Monica kept her eyes on the TV as she took a sip from her glass. "I don't care, Tasha. I'm trying to move on. I don't need to hear about something I already know about."

Tasha folded her legs on the couch. "Well, are you going to file for divorce?"

Monica hadn't thought of a divorce. And her sister's question cut through her like a knife. A feeling of melancholy sent her mind into a spiral for a moment. "Tasha, stop. Please. Let's just enjoy movie night and dinner. I'll cross that bridge when it comes. If you care anything about me, please leave this subject alone."

Tasha realized that she had struck a nerve with her sister and agreed to stop with the subject of Marcus. "I'm sorry for bringing it up. I really apologize, Monica. It's just that I love you so much and only want what's best for you."

Monica looked at her sister and gave a genuine smile. "I know that, girl. We good. Now let's get to what I came here for."

Tasha got up and walked over to her sister. "Stand up and hug me because God knows I could use one."

Monica shook her head and began to laugh. She stood up and embraced her sister with a tight hug. "Girl, you know you get on my last nerve!"

Tasha laughed and said, "I know, I know. But you love me."

Monica unwrapped her arms and stepped back. "Now, get your wine, and let's get tipsy. How about that?"

Tasha got her glass of wine and held it up. "A toast. To us."

Monica held her glass up and tapped her sister's. "To us. There will always be us. Sisters."

Chapter Twenty-Nine

Marcus and Kyra walked into the Hyatt Ball Room at 9:30 p.m. on New Year's Eve. Marcus sported a charcoal gray Armani suit with a navy-blue Armani shirt. He was feeling good after having a few drinks with Kyra before the limousine arrived. He was going all out that night. He wanted Kyra to feel like a queen. He had given her two-thousand dollars to shop for whatever outfit she desired. He wanted her to surprise him, and she did not disappoint on that mission. Her tight-fitting black dress showed all her curves and luscious cleavage. Marcus' ego was at an all-time high, knowing that the girl he was with would turn everyone's head when she walked by.

A host led Marcus and Kyra to their reserved table. Marcus looked around the ballroom, searching for Ed and Bobby. He and Kyra were to sit at the same table as Ed, Bobby, and their dates.

The dance floor was packed with people dancing to Notorious B.I.G.'s, Hypnotize. Marcus started to rock his head and body to the beat as he smiled and looked at Kyra, who was jamming to the beat herself. Marcus knew that she wanted to hit the dance floor and stood up. He held out his hand to her and told her to join him on the dance floor. Kyra quickly jumped up and led Marcus to the dance floor.

Marcus danced as he watched Kyra shake her round ass with her back turned to him. She was feeling the beat, dropping, and rolling her ass, as she looked back at Marcus. Marcus knew then that the new year would be brought in proper that night. All she was dropping and shaking would be his to do whatever he desired later. And the look in her eyes told him that he wouldn't be disappointed. Marcus looked at his prized trophy with total admiration, confident that he was the only man who could tame this wild beast—making her his and his only.

Marcus and Kyra danced to a few more songs before heading back to their table. When they arrived, Bobby was sitting at the table with his date. Marcus looked at Bobby's date, who was sipping on a margarita. She had on a black blouse with a red skirt. Marcus had never met her before but approved of his friend's taste. Bobby had an affection for light-skinned women with long hair. And she was just Bobby's type.

Marcus introduced Kyra to Bobby and his date. "Kyra, meet my boy. This is Bobby. One of my best friends."

Kyra smiled sheepishly and said, "Nice to meet you, Bobby. I've heard so much about you."

Bobby stood up and took Kyra's hand. "Nice to meet you, Kyra." He turned to his date, who stood up. "This is Melissa." Melissa introduced herself to Marcus and Kyra, smiling as she shook their hands.Marcus and Bobby talked as the girls became more acquainted. Bobby knew about the argument that Marcus and Ed had. He wanted to be the mediator for his friends and insisted that they both squash the beef. Marcus told Bobby he was done with it and hoped Ed would leave the subject alone. Bobby disagreed with Marcus' decision to leave his family but knew that Marcus was a grown man who understood whatever consequences he would face.

Ed arrived at the table with his date just before 10:30 p.m. Marcus and Bobby knew Desiree from previous gatherings and parties that Ed hosted. Ed introduced her to Kyra and Melissa before they sat down. Ed watched as Desiree hugged and kissed Marcus and Bobby on the cheek. Ed smiled with closed lips, a look of despair on his face. Marcus and Bobby knew that Kyra being there made him uncomfortable. And they knew that their friend's emotions showed on his face when something was bothering him. Marcus tried his best to downplay the incident he had with his friend. "Look at Desiree! Looking all pretty and shit!"

Desiree smiled and then laughed. "Stop it, Marcus! With your crazy ass!"

Ed looked away and watched the people on the dance floor. He hadn't gotten over their argument on the balcony the other day. And sitting at the table with Marcus' side piece gave him a feeling of guilt that he couldn't shake. He knew that it was supposed to be Monica sitting at their table. He was the best man at their wedding, and Monica was like a sister to him.

The DJ kept the floor packed with his selection of music. Marcus' party danced and drank as the time neared midnight. The ballroom was crowded with people at their tables and on the dance floor. Ed and Desiree were on the floor, getting their groove on, while Marcus and Bobby sat at the table, laughing, and joking with their dates. Kyra glanced back and forth at a tall, slim gentleman standing near the bar. The man wore a black suit, a white shirt, and a red tie with a gray design. He was talking to another man, but he also glanced back and forth at Kyra.

The waitress was busy placing several other orders and hadn't been to their table for a while. Impatient, Marcus suggested to Bobby that they go stand by the bar and order drinks. He asked Kyra if she would like another drink as he stood up.

"Yes. I'd love another Martini with an olive." Kyra answered.

Marcus smiled as he rose from the table. "Sure thing, Beautiful. I'll be right back."

Ed and Desiree returned to the table while Marcus and Bobby stood at the bar waiting for their drinks. Ed looked at his watch, anticipating the countdown to midnight. In fifteen minutes, the crowd would be holding their drinks in the air and yelling, "Happy New Year!" Ed couldn't wait for the party to be over. He wanted no part of Marcus and Kyra and didn't want to be in their company. No matter what he did, he just could not shake the feeling of guilt he had, watching his friend entertain a woman that was not his wife. Deep down inside, Ed knew Monica was hurting because she loved Marcus so much.

Ed had called Monica on occasion to check on her. He remembered at first that Monica would cry, telling him that she didn't understand what had happened or what had gone wrong. Ed would tell her to be patient and stay strong. He hated being caught between his best friend's infidelity and Monica's hurt and pain. Ed's mixed emotions were getting the best of him that night, and he didn't want to cause another argument with Marcus. So he would let the night play out, take his date home and enjoy the rest of the evening.

Marcus and Bobby arrived back at the table with five minutes to spare before the countdown. Marcus sat down and quickly looked at Ed, then looked away. The crowd was getting antsy as more people began to flock to the dance floor. Marcus looked around the ballroom, watching people leap to their feet from their tables, cheering and yelling. Marcus and his crew stood up as the countdown began.

They all held their drinks in the air and yelled, "Happy New Year!"

Each put their drink down, hugged one another, and wished each other a Happy New Year.

Marcus and Ed embraced for a moment and stepped away, looking each other in the eyes. Marcus smiled at his best friend and said, "I love you, bro. Thanks for a strong bond."

Without smiling and with a somber look on his face, Ed responded, "Always, my brother."

After the countdown celebration, the ladies agreed to go to the bathroom and freshen up. Each grabbed their small purses and told the men they would be back. Marcus and his friends sat at the table, talking, and laughing. Marcus noticed that Ed was trying his best to enjoy the night. He knew that Kyra being there haunted his friend. He wanted Ed to understand but knowing Ed; there would be no such thing. So Marcus would just let the night take its course and hope for the best.

While glancing around the ballroom, Marcus noticed Kyra talking to a tall man in a black suit. The man had a serious look on his face, and so did Kyra. Marcus rose to his feet after he saw Kyra try to walk away, and the man grabbed her arm. Marcus recognized the tall man. He played basketball for the Atlanta Hawks. Marcus quickly maneuvered through the crowd, reaching Kyra. The man in question noticed Marcus moving swiftly through the crowd and released Kyra's arm. He kept his gaze on Marcus while Kyra stood there yelling at him.

Marcus had a fierce look on his face as he approached him. "What the fuck are you doing!" he yelled.

Kyra turned to Marcus and said, "Let's go, Honey. It's nothing."

Marcus yelled at the basketball player again, his ego damaged and angry, "I asked you what the fuck were you doing, grabbing my girl's arm!"

The tall man looked at Marcus, also wearing the same fierce face and standing his ground. "Man, I was just talking to her. I didn't know that she was your girl."

A crowd had gathered around the three of them, some men ready to spring into action to stop a fight. Ed and Bobby slid through the crowd after seeing the confrontation between their friend and the tall gentleman. Neither man was backing down as they stood face to face. Kyra grabbed Marcus' arm and insisted they return to their table. But Marcus' pride just wouldn't allow it. It was a mixture of drinks and a big ego that wouldn't allow Marcus to walk away without an explanation from whoever this man thought he was. Marcus felt disrespected, and this dude had to be put in his place.

He looked at Marcus and said, "Me and Kyra go back a ways and are still friends. That's all."

Marcus shot a look at Kyra, feeling like he had been punched in the stomach, and asked, "What is he talking about? Still friends?"

Kyra looked at Marcus and insisted that they ignore him and go back to their table. "Marcus, it's nothing. Let's just go and have a good time."

The man's face became more agitated. "Nothing?! What are you talking about? You were with me last week, and I've been trying to call you!"

Marcus' blood began to boil. "What the fuck are you talking about!" he yelled at the tall man.

The Atlanta Hawk took his gaze off Kyra and turned to Marcus. "Man, I'm not trying to talk to you. You can get the fuck on. I'm talking to her."

To his surprise, he felt a hard blow to his jaw, sending him crashing to the floor.

Chapter Thirty

Ed and Bobby grabbed Marcus while others held the tall man back after he leaped to his feet. Five police officers working the party had arrived and separated the two in order to interview them. They were both detained while the police interviewed witnesses for statements. Ed knew the basketball player. He had attended a few of the player's parties and had become acquainted with him. Ed knew that Marcus would be sent straight to jail for his actions once the police determined that he was the aggressor.

Two police officers walked Marcus to the patrol car, waiting to transport him to jail. The tall gentleman yelled at Marcus as he was being escorted out by the policemen. "Hey, bitch ass nigga! How do my dick taste?!" He insisted on pressing charges against Marcus. He was furious with hurt pride after not being able to defend himself.

Ed and Bobby knew exactly what the basketball player meant when he yelled at Marcus. There was only one explanation. Kyra had recently been with the basketball player and had sucked him off. Ed knew his friend was angry and disappointed, knowing he had been played. Ed quickly gathered his senses and told Desiree that he had to meet his friend at the jail to post bail. She insisted on going with him, and he agreed.

After being booked into the Fulton County Jail, Marcus was placed in a holding cell. He sat on a bench in a corner, away from the other inmates, and began to reflect on the night. Should he have just walked away? Was the basketball player telling the truth about him and Kyra? The thought of what the man had yelled as Marcus was escorted away kept ringing in his head. How could she?! The more Marcus thought about Kyra being with the basketball player, the angrier and more agitated he became.

Two hours later, a deputy called his name to be released. Marcus ambled to the deputy as he pointed to the jail cell door. He told Marcus to walk in front of him as he escorted Marcus to the property desk. Marcus was handed his personal belongings and then was escorted down a hallway to a sliding gate that rose as he neared it. He walked out, looking around for Ed's car. He knew the first thing Ed would do was to go to a bondsman. A feeling of embarrassment and shame overcame Marcus as he spotted Ed's car.

Marcus got into the back seat without saying a word. He first tried to thank his friend, but the words were stuck in his throat . Ed and Desiree didn't say a word as Ed drove away from the jail. Marcus stared out the window as the car cruised down Rice Street. Ed entered Marietta Blvd and picked up speed. He looked into the rearview mirror at his friend. Marcus' head lay on the back of the seat, his eyes closed as if he were sleeping. Since Desiree rode in the car, Ed thought it was best to wait and talk to his friend.

Marcus got out of the car and began to walk toward his condo. Ed hopped out behind him and followed. Marcus heard the car door slam and looked back at Ed. He turned around and said, "Thank you, Ed. I really appreciate it. I'll pay you back tomorrow."

Ed stood in front of his friend, hands in his pockets and looking down. "Man, don't worry about that. Money is not on my mind." He looked up at Marcus. "How are you doing? Do you need me to come up and talk for a while?"

Marcus looked at Ed, then up toward the sky. He rubbed the back of his head and took a deep breath. "Naw. I'm okay, my brother. We'll talk tomorrow. I just need to go and get some rest." Marcus gave his friend a handshake and a hug. "Once again, I really appreciate you. Thanks again." Marcus then walked away, still feeling ashamed of his actions and Kyra not being upfront with him. He knew he was in for a long night of unrest and worry.

Ed watched his friend walk toward his condo and decided to call out to him.

Marcus turned around to face his friend. "Yeah, Ed?"

Ed walked up to Marcus, not wanting to tell him what Bobby had called and told him. But Ed felt that Marcus had to know. "I know that you are mad and hurt as hell. But you have to know this." Ed paused for a few seconds as Marcus stared at him. Ed looked down and then back up at his friend. He took a deep breath in, then exhaled. "Bobby called and told me that Kyra left with the ball player. I just had to let you know. We boys, and it wouldn't be right to keep that shit from you."

Fury began to rage in every inch of Marcus' soul. Looking away from Ed, he laughed angrily, punching a fist in the other opened palm. Not able to say a word, Marcus turned around and walked away.

Chapter Thirty-One

The following day, Monica was sitting at her kitchen table talking to Tasha when her cell phone rang. It was a friend of hers who worked in the real estate business. "Hey, Diane! How are you, girl?"

Monica and Diane would go out for dinner and drinks on occasion. Diane was very brilliant at her business, and Monica admired her for that and had learned a great deal about the business from Diane. Diane was not the type who thought she was more important than anyone else in the real estate industry and was always willing to share her knowledge with up-and-coming realtors.

There was a pause on the phone after Monica answered. "Diane?" Monica called.

"Yeah, girl. I'm here. There is something that I have to tell you. It's about Marcus."

Monica's heart began to beat heavily inside her chest. Is he hurt or dead? were her first thoughts. "What's wrong, Diane?" Monica said as she walked to her home office. "Is Marcus okay?"

"Yes, he's okay. Last night, he was in a fight at the New Year's Eve party at the Hyatt."

Surprised, Monica asked, "A fight with who?"

"There was an Atlanta Hawks basketball player at the party, and Marcus was with another woman. I'm sorry for having to tell you this. I'm really sorry, Monica. But Marcus was with another woman."

Monica took a deep breath before responding. "Girl, I know. Marcus and I are separated, and I know all about the other woman." Monica walked around her office, curious as to what had caused the fight. "Diane, just tell me what you know."

"Well, this basketball player apparently knew the woman that Marcus was with. They exchanged words, Marcus hit him, and the guy fell to the floor. The police working the party arrested Marcus for assault and took him to jail."

Monica's heart began to race. The only words she could muster up were, "Thanks, Diane. I'll have to talk to you later." She hung up the phone and stared into space. She was angry and wished that Marcus was in front of her so she could slap the taste out of his mouth. That stupid bastard! She knew that her reputation was at stake. Monica and Marcus were well-known throughout the Atlanta community, and she knew that Diane was not the only one who knew about Marcus' going to jail for assault.

Monica walked back to the kitchen, where her sister sat and ate breakfast. Monica had an agitated look on her face as she sat down. She looked at Tasha and asked, "Guess what Marcus did?"

Tasha could tell that something was concerning her sister. "Girl, what?"

"That son of a bitch got arrested for assault last night at the New Year's Eve party at the Hyatt."

Tasha immediately stood up; her mouth opened with a surprised look on her face. "Assault! Who did he assault?"

Monica rubbed her forehead. "He assaulted one of those Atlanta Hawks basketball players." She looked up at Tasha. "And from what Diane told me, it was over the girl Marcus was with." She slammed her hand on the kitchen table and yelled, "Shit! I don't need this kind of shit in my life!"

Tasha walked over to her sister and began to rub Monica's shoulder. "Girl, don't worry yourself about this. Marcus is a grown-ass man. He should have known the consequences of his actions."

Monica replied without looking at her sister, "Taylor don't need this confusion. She's already having a hard time without her father living in the house. Shit! And now this bullshit!"

Monica jumped up and quickly walked to her office to call Marcus. She hoped he wouldn't ignore her call. She was furious and wanted to let him know. When Marcus answered the phone, Monica started in on him, her voice high with intensity. "Marcus! What the fuck were you thinking? Assaulting a basketball player over that bitch!"

Marcus struck back quickly. "Don't you call me with this shit! You call me when it is dealing with my damn daughter!" He hung up on her.

Without giving it another thought, Monica texted Marcus.

Fuck you! You sorry motherfucker!

She wasn't looking forward to discussing her husband's wrong decisions with anyone who knew them. She wanted to keep her life as private as she could. But now Marcus had interrupted her privacy by moving out and now being seen with another woman. The woman who caused him to assault a professional basketball player.

Monica distracted her thoughts from Marcus onto Kenneth. After her New Year's Eve party, she had gone by the fire station. Kenneth anticipated her coming by with the food she had prepared. Kenneth had come out to her car as she stood leaning against it. She thought about his wide smile as he approached her. She recalled their sloppy, wet, and long kiss. She began to laugh as she remembered the other firemen yelling and cheering as she kissed Kenneth. They were nosy, and their sense of humor made her laugh.

Monica met Mark that night and immediately liked him; he made her laugh. "Where's my damn plate?!" she remembered him joking. She wanted to meet Captain Franklin, but he had taken the night off. Monica hung around the fire station and met the other firefighters, laughing and joking.

A tall white and husky fireman told Kenneth, "K Mann. Looks like you hit the jackpot with this one!"

Monica smiled as she reminisced about the night at the fire station. Kenneth made sure she was at ease and welcomed by the guys. And she left the fire station feeling important and like one of the guys.

Taylor and Brianna were still asleep after staying up until for in the morning on New Year's Eve. Monica decided that she would let them sleep until they decided to wake up. Monica and Tasha sat in the kitchen talking while the food was cooking. Both girls liked chitterlings and hog maws, growing up on them in Alabama. And they kept the tradition going each New Year's Day. Monica recalled when she told Kenneth she would bring him a plate of chitterlings with the hog maws, greens, and black-eyed peas later that day. And she remembered Kenneth being enthusiastic about her bringing him chitterlings and hog maws. She smiled as she remembered joking with Kenneth, "Okay, country Arkansas boy. I'll be sure to come by with your chitlins."

Monica joined Tasha in the kitchen to help finish up the cooking. Tasha cut up the onions as she kept her eyes on her sister. There was a long period of silence before Monica got up and started to cut the celery. She shook her head, looking back and forth at Tasha. The thought of Marcus going to jail for assault angered her the more she thought about it. Although her sister could sometimes be pushy, forcing a conversation, she knew that Tasha wouldn't bother her until she was ready to talk about it.

Monica's cell phone rang while she was cutting the celery. She wiped her hands on a towel and walked to the table to answer. She looked down and saw MR. MANN on the caller ID.

"Hey, you!" she answered, smiling.

"What's up with you, Beautiful?" he replied.

Monica sat down at the table and crossed her legs. "Well, we are preparing New Year's dinner. We should be done soon."

"Oh, okay. I'm sorry for disturbing the chef. I have Mark and the guys over watching football. So when you come over, they will be here. Just giving you a heads up."

"That's no problem. Enjoy your football games," Monica responded.

"Well, that's not the reason I called you. I am having a get-together at my house this Friday, and I would love for you to come."

"What's the occasion?" she asked.

"Well, since I worked on New Year's Eve, it's a late New Year celebration. So I'm having a get-together with Mark and a few friends and their dates, and I'm having food catered."

Monica stood up and walked to her office. "That sounds great. I would love to come over. What time on Friday?"

"We are going to get started around eight in the evening. But you know that you can come over before that if you like."

Excited, Monica replied, "Sure thing, Mr. Mann! I'll be there around six thirty or seven o'clock. Is that okay?"

"It sure is. Well, I'll let you get back to fixing my food." Kenneth started to laugh.

Jokingly, Monica said in a submissive tone, "Okay, Daddy. Mama is going to the kitchen now to prepare her man's food." Not able to hold it in, she burst out laughing.

Kenneth laughed and said, "Girl, you know you are crazy! I'll see you later. What time do you plan on coming over?"

"How about six?" she asked.

"That sounds good. I can't wait to taste those chitlins. I know you and your sister did a good job. Two Alabama country girls in the kitchen doing their thing."

Feeling prideful and confident, Monica replied, "You better know it. And don't you forget it."

Kenneth laughed, loving her playful sassiness. "I'm sure you won't let me forget it. Enjoy your day, and I'll see you around six."

Monica headed back to the kitchen with a changed look on her face. She smiled at Tasha. Tasha knew Monica had talked to Kenneth from the glow and excitement on her face. Monica looked at Tasha they burst into loud laughter. Nothing was going to ruin Monica's mood that day. Whatever Marcus had going on, he had to deal with it himself. Monica was not going to feel sorry for him. He made his bed, and it was now time for him to lay in it.

Chapter Thirty-Two

Monica arrived at Kenneth's house at 6 O'clock, as agreed. She and Tasha had cooked enough food to feed an army, and she was sure to bring Kenneth plenty of food. She sat in her car in his driveway, and a feeling of joy consumed her. Also feeling nervous, Monica hoped he would enjoy the meal. The last thing she wanted was for Kenneth to be disappointed in her cooking. She'd brought enough for Kenneth to share with his friends if they wanted to eat some of her chitterlings and hog maws.

Kenneth met Monica in the driveway to help her bring in the food. "Hey, Sexy Lady," he greeted her.

Monica gave her wide, beautiful smile and said, "Hey, Handsome." She grabbed him, and while looking up at him, he planted a soft kiss on her lips. As Kenneth's lips met hers, they closed their eyes and kissed passionately.

"Now that's what I'm talking about!" Monica said.

Kenneth warned her, "We better stop. My boys are in the house. You gonna have me kick their asses out."

Monica responded playfully, "I'll kick their asses out for you."

"Girl, let's get the food and go inside. You've met Mark, and now you can meet Jeff and Bryan," said Kenneth.

Monica walked into a loud, cheering house. Mark and Bryan were high fiving each other while Fred sat on the couch with a sad look on his face. When Bryan and Jeff saw Monica, their eyes stayed glued to her as she walked to the kitchen with Kenneth. Mark walked over to Monica and hugged her after placing the food on the kitchen counter. Kenneth introduced Monica to Jeff and Bryan. Monica shook their hands as she smiled, feeling a sense of the significance of meeting Kenneth's friends.

Kenneth and Monica walked over to the bar. He got himself a beer from the refrigerator and turned to Monica. "Would you like me to fix you a drink?"

"I only have time for one drink," she said. "I told Tasha that I wouldn't be long."

"Okay, what would you like?" Kenneth asked.

Pondering, Monica finally said, "I'll have a Crown and cranberry."

"Crown and cranberry, coming right up!" Kenneth did his best bartender act, tossing the glass into the air and catching it.

Mark walked to the bar where Monica sat, sipping her drink. "I hope that you brought enough of those chitlins for a Mississippi boy."

Monica smiled at Mark. "Of course I did. But you have to check with Mr. Mann about that."

Mark looked at Kenneth, who was standing across the bar. "Shit. I ain't worried about K Mann. I'm getting me some of those chitlins."

Kenneth laughed at his friend. "Boy, you know damn well you can have some chitlins. Don't even trip."

After Monica finished her drink, she said goodbye to Kenneth's friends. Kenneth walked her to her car, and they shared an intimate kiss.

"I wish you could stay the night with me," Kenneth wanted to convince Monica to stay. But he understood that Monica had plans with her daughter, niece, and sister.

Monica's body screamed for Kenneth's touch, but it would have to wait for another time.

When Kenneth walked back into the house, Bryan followed him to the kitchen. "That's a beauty you got there, Ken. Seems like a really nice girl," he complimented his friend as Kenneth tossed him a beer.

Kenneth gave Bryan a look of appreciation. "Thanks, Bryan. She is something special. Beautiful inside and out."

When Kenneth and Bryan walked back to the living room, Mark and Fred were still focused on the football game. Mark and Fred had made a bet on the game, and Kenneth knew that the shit-talking would be very intense between the two. Kenneth looked at Fred and knew that his team was winning. Mark's face spelled anger and disappointment. And Kenneth knew that Mark hated losing against Fred. Each time Fred won, Mark would have to hear major bragging for days on end.

Fred Harris played college football with Kenneth. He was from Flint, Michigan, and had made it out of the projects on a football scholarship. Kenneth and Fred hit it off right away, developing a life-long friendship. Fred graduated and was now working on his master's degree in psychology. He coached and taught at a high school in Atlanta and loved inspiring young kids. Fred had decided to devote his life to young black children, helping them to avoid the pitfalls of the hood life.

After Bryan and Fred left, Kenneth and Mark sat at the bar, drinking, and talking. Kenneth hadn't told Mark that Monica was married. He avoided sharing that detail with his friend because he knew that Mark would sound his warnings about being involved with a married woman. Mark had been in relationships with several married women and had even fallen in love with one that had a terrible ending. But Kenneth had to tell Mark so that there would be no surprises.

Kenneth looked at his friend and said, "Mark, I have to tell you something."

"What's up, K. Mann? Everything okay?" Mark asked.

Attempting to downplay his feelings, Kenneth responded, "Oh, yeah. Everything is good." Kenneth took a sip from his drink. "You know you my boy, and we tell it like it is, no matter what."

Mark stared at Kenneth, a puzzled look on his face. "Yeah… yeah we always keep it on a hunnid. What's up?"

Kenneth came right out with it. "Monica is married. But she's separated."

Mark stood up and turned his back. Rubbing the back of his head, he said, "Oh no, K. Mann! Why? There are so many beautiful single women here in the ATL."

"Well, it just sort of happened. You know? The station answered a fire alarm, and she was home alone, and things just happened. I really can't explain it. It just happened."

Mark turned around and asked, "So is she talking about a divorce?"

Kenneth leaned back in his chair, realizing that the conversation about divorce had never come up between him and Monica. "No, we haven't talked about that yet."

Mark sat back in his seat. "Well, let me ask you this. Did she leave him, or did he leave her?"

Kenneth looked away and then back at his friend. "He left her for another woman. One time she went to his office, and the woman was there."

A pensive look on his face, Mark warned, "Oh, I see. But I just ask you to be careful with this. Don't let your heart get involved with this shit. I'm telling you, my brother. Just hit it and keep it moving. If he left for another woman, he still has the power. He can drop that other woman and return home. I'm just telling you that. Don't let your heart get involved."

Hoping to convince his friend, Kenneth said, "I believe it's over between them." Reflecting on the times he and Monica went out on dates, enjoying each other's company, the hot passionate lovemaking, and intense fucking, Kenneth felt that he had made his mark. He believed that he and Monica vibed well together and shared similar interests and sense of humor.

Mark looked Kenneth straight in the eyes. "Listen to me and listen to me good. I felt the same way. I rocked this married woman's world. You remember Yolanda? Her husband just up and got ghost on her ass. Left her ass lost and devastated. Found himself a new toy and threw the old one away." Mark started to laugh through the pain his memory brought, "Well, I started to ride that old toy real good and hard. Having the time of my life! Her old man found out and wanted that old toy back."

Kenneth nodded his head. "Yeah, I remember that. He wanted to kick your ass."

Mark laughed and said, "Yeah, he wanted to, but he knew he couldn't handle me." Mark shook his head and continued. "My point is. . .now listen to me, K. Mann. Remember when you were a kid? Say, around four or five? You had a friend or cousin over at your house. Mamma bought you a new toy. You were playing with that new toy like a mothafucka!" Mark took a sip of his drink, shaking his head. "Then all of a sudden, you look over at your friend or cousin, and they are enjoying your old toy, laughing and riding it like it's the best damn thing in the world. Suddenly, you get off the new toy, and now you want that old one back. You be screaming, 'Mine! Mine! Mine!' Why? Because he is riding that motherfucka and enjoying it!"

Kenneth's mind went into deep thought, knowing what Mark was saying made sense. He was in love with Monica, and there was no denying it. He had been there for her through her difficult times, and she had become the focal point of his life. What if her husband found out and wanted her back?

Chapter Thirty-Three

That Friday afternoon, Kenneth and Bryan were getting the house ready for their gathering for that night. Bryan was excited about the post-New Year's party, telling Kenneth that he had met a fine and beautiful nurse while taking a prisoner to the hospital. Kenneth knew that Bryan was always meeting some fine honey, enjoying his freedom as a single man. And Bryan had no problem catching himself a fine black Sistah in the ATL. Being white wasn't the reason. Bryan had a certain charisma and disposition that all women loved.

Kenneth and Bryan took a break from setting up the house and decided to sit outside at one of the patio garden umbrella tables. It was a bright sunny day, and the temperature had risen to 70 degrees. Kenneth enjoyed Bryan's company, but their schedules hardly allowed them to hang out. Kenneth could talk to Bryan about anything, and so could Bryan to Kenneth. Both had become extremely close over the years, something that Captain Franklin welcomed.

Kenneth started to think about the first time he and Bryan met. Bryan had come by the fire station to get some barbeque. Captain Franklin was on the barbeque pit that day and had told Bryan to stop by while he was patrolling. Kenneth knew that there was something different about Bryan. He had a certain kind of swag about himself and was very approachable and easy to talk to. The two hit it off right away and started to hang out.

Kenneth said, "Man, it's been some years since we first met and started hanging out. I remember saying, 'This is a cool white dude.'"

Bryan laughed and countered, "And when I got to know you, I said, 'This is a cool black dude.'" His laughter came to a halt as he stopped and said, "Kenneth, you know that I don't see color, man. For some reason, I just didn't see things the way my father and his friends did regarding race. They were taught that shit, and unfortunately, they couldn't accept other races as being equal."

"Yeah, but Captain made some positive strides. His heart has changed, and I definitely can tell," Kenneth said.

Bryan held his beer up, looking at it but not taking a drink. "Yeah, I know. But as we talked about before, he thought that I was being rebellious when I got to high school." Bryan took a sip of his beer and continued. "I wasn't being rebellious. I just got to know people. Sure there are evil people of all races. But I just refused to believe that white people were the least evil of them all."

Kenneth always appreciated Bryan's openness regarding race. He knew his feelings were genuine, and Bryan was very compassionate. "Well, my brotha, you turned out to be an alright dude."

"You're not a bad fella yourself, my brother. And Pops loves you like you were his own son. Now, how that came to be, I don't know." Bryan started to laugh at loud.

Kenneth started to laugh as well. "Shit, you know how. His prejudice had to go away once he met Da Mann! If the head of the KKK got to me, his ass would change too."

Bryan started to laugh uncontrollably. When he gathered himself, he warned, "You better not try. Keep that shit on the safe side." Bryan looked away, and his mind began to reflect on when he played Little League baseball. "Ken, I remember when I played Little League baseball. The team was diverse. But mostly white kids. I became friends with a black teammate named Lewis McCutchin, who now plays for the Oakland A's. He was the best player on the team, and some of the white parents couldn't stand it. But getting to know Lewis and his parents, I liked him and vowed to stand by him. That was the first time I stood up to my father and didn't back down." Bryan looked at Kenneth and took a deep breath. "Not too long after getting cool with him, Lewis began coming to the house and sometimes spending the night on weekends. That was when I started to see a change in my father, especially when he got to know Lewis and his parents. Lewis and I still talk on occasion."

After Bryan and Kenneth finished their trip down memory lane, they headed inside to complete some finishing touches to perfect the setup. Bryan hooked up the karaoke system. Kenneth was sure to tell their friends to be ready for the karaoke fun¬¬—there would be a prize for the winner. Karaoke was Mark's idea. He was a great singer and wanted to show off for the guests. The theme for karaoke would be all old-school songs.

Bryan left just before 4 O'clock that afternoon to prepare for the night. Kenneth went back outside and sat at the patio table. He texted Monica just to compliment her.

Hey, Beautiful!

Kenneth looked up to the sky and admired the beautiful sunny day. Prince's, Insatiable played in the background as he thought about Monica. He envisioned her gorgeous smile, closing his eyes and keeping it inside his head. He smiled, thinking of the day that he first met her. So damn sexy!

Deep in thought, his cell phone rang. He looked down, and it was Monica. "Hey, you!"

"What are you doing, Mr. Mann?" she asked, her voice full of energy.

"Sitting out back thinking of you."

"Oh, really! And what are you thinking about?"

Kenneth stood up and started to walk around the backyard. "Just your beauty. Inside and out."

"Oh yeah? And what else besides my booty. . .I mean, my beauty?" Monica laughed as she teased Kenneth.

Kenneth joined her in laughter. "You know you crazy, don't you?"

"And you love it, too. Don't you?"

Kenneth giggled a little more and said, "You better know it. Can't wait to see you later on."

"Well, I'm getting dressed. So, you better let me finish so I can be on my way."

Kenneth walked toward the house. "Okay, I'll do just that. See you around six. Have your singing voice ready."

"I'll do my best for you, Daddy."

"Girl, get off this phone and get dressed." Kenneth loved the way she called him Daddy. She stirred that fire inside of him again. A fire that she would have to put out after the party.

Chapter Thirty-Four

Kenneth and Monica sat at the bar, passing the time, laughing, and joking as they waited for the guests to arrive. Monica wore a short, tight red dress that stopped at her sexy thighs. Kenneth lusted for her the moment she walked into the house. But he knew that his dessert would have to wait until after midnight. Kenneth sat with his elbow on the bar, resting his head in the palm of his hand. He was in awe of her beauty, admiring her gorgeous smile. Monica was the type of woman a man could easily fall in love with. And Kenneth was just that. In love.

Mark and his date arrived a little after 7 O'clock. He introduced his date to Monica. "Monica, meet Tina. Tina, this is Monica."

Monica stood up and gave Tina a friendly hug. "Nice to meet you, Tina."

After their brief hug, Tina stepped back with a smile and said,

"Nice to meet you too, Monica." Tina looked Monica over with admiration. "Girl, that is a gorgeous dress, and you are wearing that thing!"

"Thank you," Monica responded. "Girl, that outfit you have on is something too. I love that Columbia blue dress!"

Monica and Tina hit it off immediately, leaving the guys at the bar to get better acquainted. Mark looked at his date walk off with Monica, shaking his head. The girls settled on the couch, talking about where they both loved to shop. They had the same taste in clothes and places they liked to shop. Monica learned that Tina was from New York City and had lived in Atlanta for five years.

Bryan and his date arrived at 7:30 p.m. He walked into the house, giving his friends high fives, and talking loudly. "What's up, fellas! Let's get this shit going!" He looked back at his date and said, "Hey, y'all! This is Whitney! Come on over here, girl, and meet my boys!" Bryan introduced Whitney to Kenneth and Mark and then poured himself a drink.

Monica and Tina came over to introduce themselves to Bryan and Whitney. They all gathered around the bar, drinking, laughing, and joking. Monica and Tina asked Whitney to join them in the living room to get better acquainted with her. Whitney seemed a little shy but very approachable. Monica and the girls laughed as they listened to Mark and Bryan sing along to Case and Joe's, Faded Pictures. For a white guy, the girls thought that Bryan held his own against Mark.

Mark asked Kenneth, "Where the hell is Fred? That dude is always running late."

Kenneth shook his head and said, "Yeah, you know Fred. Always love to make his grand entrance."

Fred and his date eventually arrived a little before 9 O'clock. Fred walked into the house with a bottle of Remy Martin VSOP. "Fellas, fellas, fellas! What the fuck is up?!" His date stood behind him, her arms folded as she laughed at Fred. Fred turned around to his date. "Oh, shit! Who is this fine-ass woman who followed me in here? I didn't see you come in behind me! Damn, you fine!"

Feeling put on the spot but joyously embarrassed, she told Fred, "Boy, you crazy! Just introduce me," she said, shaking her head.

Fred hugged her and planted a kiss on her lips. "Come on in here. You know Ken, Mark, and Bryan. My boys." He looked over at Monica and the girls. "Hey, y'all! Come on over here! I want you to meet Michelle. She's from right here in Da ATL!"

Monica and the girls walked over and introduced themselves to Michelle. They all joined the men at the bar for a drink. Everyone seemed relaxed and at ease while getting better acquainted. Monica was enjoying Kenneth's friends, noticing their strong bond. She couldn't take her eyes off Kenneth. He looked sexy in his tailor-made pinstripe grey suit and red tie with a grey design. She noticed that he would often take a flirty glance at her too.

After everyone ate and had a few more drinks, they all settled in the front room. Each man sat next to his date while Mark Morrison's Return of the Mack played at a subdued level in the background. There were discussions and debates about relationships, sports, religion, and politics. The ladies were hyped when the discussion was on relationships. Kenneth and Monica sat back and observed the talk show scene.

Mark's enthusiasm for the discussion grew when Tina started to talk about marriage and religion. Mark was not interested in marriage but didn't knock those who believed in it.

"Marriage is nothing but an image in most cases. Very seldom does love have anything to do with marriage. It's all about security and convenience," he argued.

Tina stood up and started waving her hand back and forth. "No, it isn't! Mark, people do marry for love."

Mark looked up at her and refuted, "Oh, yeah? Then why do women put stipulations on what a man has to have before they even think about dating the man? What do these women say nowadays? 'A man must have a degree. A man must have his own house. A man must make one-hundred thousand dollars or more, a year!" Mark stood up and faced Tina. "Now, all I'm saying is. .

.she's not marrying the man. She's marrying his credentials. His possessions. His title. Marrying his money." Mark walked around the room and then turned back to Tina. "The man could be a good man. But she ain't trying to hear that if he doesn't meet those criteria."

Tina argued her case, "Yeah, he does have to bring something to the table. I can love him. But if we are not financially compatible, why should I settle? I don't want a bum for a man!"

Mark started to laugh. "A bum. So, what you are saying, if a man doesn't possess money at the time you meet him, he's a bum?"

She squinted at Mark. "No, that's not what I'm saying. I'm saying that if he doesn't have any ambition, he's a bum."

Monica and the rest of the guests were enjoying the heated battle between Mark and Tina. The discussion made Monica think. It was a good debate with interest and intrigue. She looked over at the other two ladies, who were also mentally engaged. Both Whitney and Michelle had a look of curiosity and surprise on their faces.

Mark admitted, "Well, I don't believe in marriage anyway. Marriage doesn't work. Over 50% of couples end up getting a divorce. And those who do remain in the marriage, 99% of them are unhappy. Just going through the motions for the kids and convenience."

Whitney jumped in the conversation. "No, that's not true! Many people are happily married. I happen to know some happily married couples."

Mark turned to Whitney and thought for a few seconds. He rubbed his chin and then said, "Most of it is out of image. Yeah, around others they seem like they are the happiest couple in the world. But behind the scenes there's a lot of fighting and fussing. And they are not fucking anymore."

A curious look on her face, Whitney asked, "Mark, how do you know that? You seem so pessimistic about marriage."

"No, I'm not pessimistic. I'm realistic. What does marriage give that one can't have by themselves? I have everything that married people have. I can cook and clean for myself." Mark was on a roll and there would be no stopping him.

Whitney became more aggressive in her debate. "So you don't believe in God, I guess."

With a dubious look on his face, Mark asked, "What does believing in God have to do with this conversation?"

"You don't think having sex without being married is a sin?" Whitney asked.

Excited about that question, Mark yelled, "Oh, hell no! That shit was put in the Bible by man! How could it be a sin to use something that God gave you for that purpose? It doesn't make any sense! Adam and Eve wasn't married."

Bryan started to laugh as he stood up. "Mark, I need another drink on that one, man. You killin' it, my brother."

Whitney looked at Bryan and exclaimed, "Shut up, Bryan! This is your friend, so you are going to agree with him regardless."

Bryan stopped and looked back at Whitney. "Well, it does make sense. People do act like having sex is more egregious than murder, robbery, abuse of children and the elderly. We wasn't put here on earth to commit those type acts against one another. But we were put here to be fruitful and multiply."

Mark walked over to Bryan with his hand in the air. He gave Bryan a loud high five and yelled, "Play that funky music white boy! Tell the damn truth!"

Whitney started laughing as she shook her head. "Men! You are all the same. Thinking with the other head."

Kenneth stood up and demanded that the subject be changed. "Hey, I think we should get off of this and enjoy the rest of the night." He looked at Monica, who was laughing at Whitney. Kenneth didn't want the rest of the night to be about discussing sex before marriage, especially considering his plans with Monica once everyone finally left. Kenneth told them that it was time to have some fun, singing and dancing.

Chapter Thirty-Five

It was two thirty in the morning when Mark and Tina finally left. Kenneth and Monica walked them out to Mark's car and said their goodbyes. They then decided to sit out back and talk more. Monica had enjoyed herself that night and thanked Kenneth for inviting her. She found out that Kenneth could really sing, giving a good rendition of Barry White's *Can't Get Enough of Your Love*. Kenneth's singing surprised her as she sat listening while being turned on by his baritone voice.

Rose Royce's *I Wanna Get Next to You* played as Monica and Kenneth sat talking. Monica was very relaxed but not sleepy or tired from all the laughter and fun that the night had brought. Monica loved the song, remembering when her mother played it when she was a little girl. She noticed that Kenneth was silent as she looked at him. His mind seemed to be someplace else, his gaze looking off and far away.

Monica interrupted his thoughts. "Kenneth? You look like there's something heavy on your mind."

Kenneth had to refocus his attention on Monica. "Oh, I'm sorry. Did you say something that I missed?"

"No, I was actually listening to that song. Reminds me of when I was a young girl. My mother would play it all the time."

Kenneth nodded his head. "Yeah. . .yeah. Rose Royce was one of my mother's favorite groups growing up. I remember listening to that song as a young kid, too."

Monica held a seductive gaze on Kenneth, beginning to lust for his touch and his amazing sex. She wanted him and she wanted Kenneth to know it. When his eyes met hers, she said without hesitation, "Kenneth Mann, I want you to take me to your bedroom and have your way with me."

A fire ignited inside of Kenneth as he stood and walked over to her. Her voice and her unexpected demand turned him on. He reached out his hand to her as she sat looking up at him with a striking gleam in her eyes. Tonight, he would go above and beyond to pleasure her. Tonight, would not be about him, only Monica's satisfaction and desires mattered. Whatever she wanted, she would get it that night.

In the darkness of his bedroom, Kenneth kissed Monica's neck as he slid the zipper of her dress down her back. She held the back of his head as she moaned seductively in his ear. He started his tongue downward from her neck to her breasts and then down to her stomach as he began to kneel. When he was on his knees, he slid her panties off, still kissing and licking her stomach. She held his head, looking down at him, she stepped out of her panties as soon as they hit the floor.

Kenneth rose to his feet and without hesitation, Monica began unbuttoning his shirt. Kissing him with fervor, she peeled off his shirt and began kissing and sucking his chest. Fire burning inside of her, she quickly unbuckled his pants and ripped his zipper down. Kneeling, she pulled his pants to the floor and grabbed what was rock hard. He stepped out of his pants as she held on to his dick, looking at it with great admiration.

Wanting badly to taste him, she placed her mouth around it and began giving it her all. She wanted to show him that she had skills in the head department, wanting to be the best that he ever had. As her head went back and forth, she knew Kenneth was enjoying it. His legs began to shake as he grabbed her head, letting out strong, loud moans. She knew he wanted more when he turned around and lay at the foot of the bed. She held on tight as she looked at his body lay on the bed with his legs hanging over the edge, and his feet on the floor.

Monica continued her mission of pleasing him. Circling her mouth vigorously around the tip of his manhood, listening to him weakening and shouting, she was turned on.

"Ohhhhhh, shit! Ohhhhhh, shit!" Kenneth shouted.

Monica paused and leaned back, keeping her grip on his long solid dick, she stared at it with lust in her eyes. She raised up and stood at the edge of the bed and without saying a word, Kenneth rose and started to kiss her. He lay her on the bed and went straight down on her.

He started to taste her, licking and sucking her hot, wet, luscious juices. Her screams made him dig in more, causing her body jerk.

"Kenneth! Kenneth! Ohhhhh, Baby! Shit!"

He vowed not to stop until she came. The more he tasted her, the more her juices flowed. He began to work his tongue on her clitoris. She held on to his head as she screamed with desire.

"Ohhhhhh! Oh, Baby! I'm cummin'! I'm cummin'! Ohhhhhhhh, shit!" He knew that he had accomplished his mission when she threw his head back and jerked away, as she screamed, "Stop Baby! Stop!"

Kenneth stood over her, looking at her rub her breasts. Her eyes closed tightly as she moaned. When she came off her orgasmic high, she looked up at him and said, "Come here." He lay in the bed and rolled gently on top of her. She opened her legs and held them in the air. "Fuck me tonight, Baby", she whispered in his ear.

He rose on his knees, grabbed both of her ankles, and lifted her legs back. Her knees line up with her head. Monica held her gaze on Kenneth as he positioned himself to enter her with his big and long mule.

"That's it, Baby! Fuck me hard! Give me that big dick, Daddy!"

Kenneth pushed inside of her and began to move up and down, hitting her with powerful thrusts.

Monica screamed, "Yeah! Yeah! Ohhhhh, shit! Fuck me! Harder, Baby! Yeah!"

He looked down at her as she held her ankles and said, "Is this what you want! You want this dick?!"

Monica looked down and watched his stroke. The vision of his dick going in and out of her wet pussy mesmerized her. She was fully opened now, taking all he gave to her body . She loved it. Looking up at him, Monica had an epiphany; Kenneth was the best lover she ever had.

Kenneth and Monica woke up the next day at noon. They lay in bed talking for a while. Kenneth told her that he wanted another gathering at his house before returning to work. He had taken a week off and wanted Mark to help him smoke some meat on the barbeque pit. He looked at Monica and asked, "Do you think you can make it on Monday?"

Flattered that Kenneth wanted to have her over with his friends again, Monica responded, "Sure. I would love that." She looked down, her back up against the headboard, and asked, "Would it be okay if my sister came by with a date?"

Kenneth smiled and answered, "You don't have to ask. Of course, it's okay."

Monica had talked about Tasha to Kenneth. And now it was finally the time for him to meet her funny-but-take-no-jive sister.

Monica pulled her knees up close to her breasts, resting in the fetal position . She looked at Kenneth and said, "I'll tell her about it when I get home. She's at my house with girls."

Kenneth leaned over and kissed Monica. She looked into his eyes and reciprocated his kiss. He began sucking her breasts, then moving his head down and kissing her belly. Monica's excitement welled, and her juices began to flow. Kenneth lay on his back and pulled her on top of him. She leaned forward, slid her hand down, and grabbed his hard, waiting manhood. Monica guided him inside of her and began to rise up and down on him. She wanted all of him and wanted to give him all of her.

Chapter Thirty-Six

Kenneth and Mark sat in Kenneth's backyard on a bright Monday morning. Kenneth wanted everything to be perfect for the gathering. He was excited that the University of Georgia had made it to the National Championship game. Guests were to arrive at 3 o'clock that afternoon. He and Mark vowed to live life to the fullest while on vacation, and what better way to enjoy it than by his alma mater representing in the College National Football game? And they had a blast on Friday night. Kenneth also anticipated that Mark couldn't wait to spark engaging discussions about dubious topics with the guests. Mark loved to prove himself right all the time, and their friends found his point-of-view entertaining.

Turning the chickens over, Mark looked at Kenneth and exclaimed, "Man, this is a lot of meat. Do you think we will be done by at least two? Shit, I have to shower and get cleaned up."

Sid eyeing Mark as he mopped his secret liquid base on the ribs, he said, "Man, don't worry. We started way ahead of time. You should be able to head home in a couple of hours, get ready and still have time to relax."

Monica and Tasha were at Monica's house getting dressed for the gathering at Kenneth's. They were both in Monica's bathroom, putting on lipstick and makeup. Brianna's father agreed to keep her after Tasha had made her demands for him to spend more time with his daughter. Tasha was thrilled to finally meet Kenneth, and she couldn't contain her excitement. She hounded Monica to meet her prince charming, and now the time had finally arrived.

Looking in the mirror, Tasha said, "Anthony is supposed to be here to pick me up around three o'clock, and we should get there around three thirty or so."

"Okay, that's fine," Monica answered. "I'll leave here around two; Kenneth wants me to help finish setting up. He's so excited that Georgia is in the National Championship game."

Tasha looked at Monica and said, "Girl, this whole city is going crazy!"

Monica walked out of the bathroom and called Kenneth. "Hey, Babe! How is everything going?" She talked to Kenneth until it was time for her to go to his place.

Monica arrived at Kenneth's at 2 o'clock as planned, and she could smell the aroma of the smoked meat. "Kenneth, that sure does smell good! I guess you know what you're doing when it comes to good barbeque," she teased.

Kenneth rubbed his palms together and smiled. "I guess I know a lil' something, something." He watched as Monica walked to the kitchen, her tight jeans gripping her round ass. Damn!

To Kenneth's surprise, Fred and Michelle arrived promptly at three on the dot. "Man, I'm shocked! I just knew that you would get here later, just before kickoff."

Fred walked past Kenneth and went straight to the beer cooler. He retrieved a beer and looked back at Kenneth. "K Mann, don't start that shit." He looked over at Monica, who was making potato salad. "Hey, Monica. How are you?" He looked back at Kenneth and yelled, "Let's rep, baby!" Both men had on their University of Georgia jerseys.

"I'm doing great, Fred. And yourself?" Monica answered.

Fred walked over to Michelle who was standing in the middle of the living room. "I can't do any better than this gorgeous, fine-ass Sistah!" He reached around Michelle and slapped her on her ass.

Michelle laughed and walked to the kitchen where Monica was. "Hey, girl! How are you?"

Monica put down the potato, went over to Michelle, and gave

her a friendly hug. "Girl, I'm doing just fine." She looked Michelle up and down and said, "Girl, you know you are wearing those jeans!"

Michelle looked at Monica with a wide smile. "Girl, I can say the same about you! You have the nicest shape!"

Fred shook his head, listening to the women compliment each other. He looked at Kenneth and said, "Ain't it funny how women can get away with that shit?"

Tasha and Anthony finally arrived at 4 O'clock. They walked through the door with Kenneth trailing after welcoming them. Tasha turned quickly around to face Kenneth. "So you're Kenneth! Nice to finally meet you!" She extended her hand.

Kenneth took her hand and held it. "Naw, naw. Meeting Monica's sister requires a greeting hug." He pulled Tasha closer and gave her a big hug. "Now, we have officially met."

Tasha smiled up at Kenneth and said, "I guess we have." She turned to Anthony and introduced him to Kenneth. As Kenneth and Anthony got acquainted, Tasha introduced herself to Fred and Michelle.

As Monica stood over the stove, checking the potatoes, she looked back and saw her sister walking towards her. "Hey, girl. I see you finally made it."

"Yeah, we were running a little late." Tasha looked at the potatoes boiling in the pot and asked, "Do you need me to do any-thing?"

Monica answered, "No, I got this. I've already chopped up the onions." She looked at Kenneth and Anthony, who were laughing.

Tasha's eyes followed Monica's to Kenneth and Anthony. She looked back at Monica and said, "Kenneth is really a handsome man. And he seems very nice."

Feeling proud, Monica replied, "Yes, he is a very nice and caring person."

Mark and Tina arrived around 4:30 p.m. and introduced themselves to Tasha and Anthony before saying hello to the rest of the party. Michelle and Tina sat on the couch and talked. Mark joined in conversation with Kenneth and Anthony; they were having a gentlemen's chat about the football game. Tasha hung out in the kitchen while Monica finished preparing the potato salad.

At five thirty that evening, Bryan and Whitney walked into the house adorned with their University of Georgia jerseys. Bryan held up an open palm and gave Kenneth a high five. "Let's get that ass, Georgia!"

Whitney headed over and found a spot on the couch with Monica and the other ladies. Monica and Tasha joined the group, talking about the usual girl things: shopping, movies, and men. Monica looked over at Kenneth and the crew, the men oblivious to what the women were talking about. She smiled as she watched Kenneth flaunt his college jersey. She was so happy for him that his alma mater had made it to the championship game. But more than that, she was so happy that he asked her to share in his day. with him. No matter the outcome of the game, Monica would be there to cheer Kenneth and his college team on .

It was an hour before kickoff, and everyone was sitting in the living room discussing the Bible and marriage. Kenneth knew that Mark would be fired up about the two subjects. Mark had a mind of his own and was always thinking outside of the box. But Kenneth always thought that Mark was a deep thinker and had legitimate points regarding the Bible and marriage. And Mark didn't believe in holding any punches back to get his point across.

Whitney went in right away on Mark. "So, do you believe in God and the Bible?"

Mark was sitting next to Tina. He looked at Tina and then at Whitney. "I do believe in God. But I don't believe in man." He went on to explain. "You see, the Bible was written by man. And the King James Version has contradictions in it."

Whitney's face grew with curiosity. "What contradictions?"

Mark looked at Whitney and paused before he answered. Knowing that the debate could easily become hostile, he said, "Before I answer that question, I'm not trying to get you to change your beliefs or anything like that." Mark stood up and walked to get Kenneth's Bible from the bookshelf. He found the scriptures he was looking for and read them to Whitney and the group. He looked around the room, and then his eyes locked onto Whitney. "Here in first Timothy verse six, it reads, 'Slaves, obey your earthly masters with respect and fear, and with sincerity of heart, just as you would obey Christ'."

A surprised look came over Whitney's face as Mark read the scriptures. She had never been taught what Mark was reading. It was all new to her. The entire room focused on Mark, anxious to hear where he was going with the subject. Kenneth already knew how Mark felt about the English version of the Bible, and he and Mark had had this discussion many times before.

Mark began to flip the pages until he stopped where he found the next scripture he was looking for. "Now, here it says in Matthew 6:24, 'No man can serve two masters, for either he will hate the one, and love the other, or else, he will hold to the one, and despise the other, Ye cannot serve God and man.'" Mark looked around the room at the other guests before he continued. "You see, the scriptures on slavery in the New Testament are very different from those about slavery in the Old Testament. The New Testament condones slavery, telling the slaves to obey their earthly masters with respect and fear. Those scriptures were not supposed to be in there. They were put in there so the slaves would learn them and not revolt against their owners. And again, Matthew says one cannot serve two masters. So, how could slaves have an earthly master and God as their other master? Think about that."

Whitney had looked forward to the battle with Mark from the last debate. But to her surprise, Mark had a point that she did not want to believe. She had grown up in the church and had never learned those particular scriptures. She looked up at Mark and said, "I'll have to ask someone who studies the Bible what those scriptures mean."

Mark frowned at Whitney and asked, "Did you go to school?"

"Yes, I did," she snapped. "What does that have anything to do with it?"

"Well, they taught you to read and comprehend English, didn't they?" Mark placed the Bible back on the bookshelf and sat back down. "I don't need anyone to explain to me what I just read. I can comprehend that myself, and it's quite self-explanatory."

The discussions continued about the Bible and marriage until the game came on. Ten minutes before kickoff, Kenneth insisted that it was game time, and the conversations would have to continue another day. Monica could see Kenneth's excitement and hoped his team would come out victorious. She didn't want him to be disappointed and hurt. She knew how fans could react to their favorite teams winning or losing. Monica thought whatever the outcome, she would make sure that Kenneth was satisfied before he went to sleep that night.

Chapter Thirty-Seven

Marcus and Taylor sat on the couch watching TV. He let her pick out her favorite movies, and tonight would be The Lion King and Pocahontas. He had agreed to keep her for the night while Monica and Tasha spent time together. Marcus was in no mood to watch the football game and had told Ed that he would spend time with his daughter. Ed had insisted that Marcus join him and the boys to watch the game, but this time, Marcus had a perfect excuse not to join them.

Marcus had tried to call Kyra several times since New Year's Eve, but she never answered. He felt like a fool, leaving his family thinking that she was the one for him. He had never in his life felt so low and despondent. Not only did he feel like she made a fool of him, but he also knew that he made a complete fool of himself that dreadful night. Now his world was turned upside down and inside out. How am I going to recuperate from this disaster of a situation?

His thoughts were interrupted by Taylor.

She looked up at her father and asked, "Daddy, when are you coming back home?"

Marcus rubbed her head and hugged her, bringing her closer to him. He looked out toward the balcony. "Daddy don't know that right now, Baby girl." Marcus didn't want to discuss any of this with his daughter, so he attempted to change the subject. "I see you still love watching The Lion King. It's a good movie."

Not letting her father off the hook, Taylor said in a sad voice, "Daddy, I miss you and Mommy being together. I'm scared when you are not home. Please, Daddy. Come back home with me and Mommy."

Marcus took his arm from around Taylor and stood up. He looked down at his daughter, who had the saddest look on her face. He reached his hand to her and said, "Come here, Baby girl." When Taylor stood up, he picked her up and hugged her tightly. "How about we talk about this some other time, huh? Daddy will always be here for his little princess. Don't you worry."

Midnight fell as Marcus sat on his balcony puffing a cigar. Taylor had gone to bed at eleven o'clock, which gave Marcus time to himself. His daughter's plea for him to return home stuck in his mind. Can I return home? Or better yet, would Monica accept me back in her life? Is it really over between Kyra and me? Has Kyra been sleeping with that basketball player the whole time? Was she sneaking behind my back and giving up the goods? Questions with no answers ran through his head like a raging tornado.

Something inside of Marcus forced him to call Kyra. She mostly answered him when he called her after midnight. He listened as the phone rang. Eventually, it went to voicemail, leaving him with a feeling of misery and despair. Damn! How could she do this shit?! He had left her messages every time he called, but he decided not to this time. Anger began to resurface as he stood up and reached out to the balcony rail, gripping it with his head down. "Shit!"

Marcus sat back down and rubbed his head, looking down. Monica's face entered his thoughts. And then her smile and laughter. Marcus started to reflect on when they first met and how they enjoyed each other from the moment they began dating. She was a devoted woman. She was always committed to her man and her career. And when Taylor was born, she was just as committed as a mother. Marcus started to think of his unfortunate consequences. What made him stray from the woman who truly loved and admired him?

He lay in a dark room, looking up at the ceiling. In complete silence, his dilemma wouldn't allow him to fall asleep. Kyra's mystique and freaky sex caused him to wander away from home. Then it hit him like a ton of bricks. Kyra was not a better lover than

Monica. It had to be the mystery about Kyra that intrigued his curiosity. Kyra exuded a fantasy that spread across a room when she walked in. And Marcus had gotten caught in her web like a fly landing in a spider's web, ready to be eaten inside out. Leaving him to ignore what he had dedicated his life to.

The following day, Marcus and Taylor sat at The Beautiful Restaurant, waiting to order breakfast. He had a few more hours to spend with her before taking her home and heading to his office. It was a sleepless night for Marcus, trying to figure out where his life was heading. His mind was going in every direction, back and forth, from Monica to Kyra. While Taylor ate her breakfast, he sat at the table going through his cell phone. He looked up and watched his lovely daughter, who was a striking resemblance to him, and a joy inside of his soul awoke. A smile began to form as he admired his beautiful daughter.

Marcus took Taylor home at 1 O'clock that afternoon. He sat in the kitchen with Monica, admiring her beauty. The subject of that New Year's Eve never came up, and it started to bother Marcus. Why hasn't she brought it up? Why is she walking around glowing like that? he thought to himself. Monica talked about how good the football was and how she was so happy for the city of Atlanta that Georgia had won the game. Marcus could not comprehend why Monica seemed so happy.

Marcus couldn't fight the urge to ask Monica if she was seeing another man. "Monica, can I ask you a question?" He leaned back and raised both of his hands. "Now, you don't have to answer if you don't want to."

Monica sat across the bar from Marcus, placed an elbow on the table, and rested her chin in her palm. Looking him straight in the eyes, smiling, she asked, "What is it, Marcus?"

Marcus kept his lean back on the bar stool. He ran a finger up and down the coffee cup and looked down. "Are you seeing someone?"

Monica kept her position and laughed. "Marcus, that's none of your business. And I don't have to give you answers to anything that's going on in my private life."

Throwing up his arms, Marcus replied, "Okay, okay. I was just curious, is all." A feeling of envy and jealousy began to boil inside of him. Marcus decided to finish his coffee and head to his office. Had she already moved on? Is that why she is smiling and glowing? Marcus left what was once his home feeling even more sad and confused than the night before. Where was his life taking him?

Chapter Thirty-Eight

Marcus and Ed sat on the balcony, puffing on their cigars and sipping scotch. All was forgiven between the two friends, and both vowed to forget the night Marcus kicked Ed out of his condo. Ed was there to comfort his friend, not to pile on Marcus' guilt. And Marcus appreciated his friend for his support. Marcus wanted things to return to normal if that was at all possible.

Marcus looked at Ed with sincerity in his eyes. "Ed, I really appreciate you being here for me. It really means a lot, my brother."

Ed smiled at his friend and nodded his head. "You got it, my brother. And I really do mean my brother."

Marcus turned and took in the view of Atlanta. It was seven thirty in the evening, the sky clear but a slight chill on the late January night. It had been two weeks since Marcus had asked Monica if she was seeing anyone. He looked back at Ed and said, "I asked Monica if she was seeing someone when I took Taylor home a couple of weeks ago. Man, she brushed me off like it wasn't shit."

A serious expression came over Ed's face. "Marcus, does it matter if she started seeing someone? You've been gone for a while now." Ed paused before he continued. "You are the one she married and had a daughter by. Shit happens in this life." He looked away from his friend and said, "You just have to accept what happened in the past, acknowledge it and move on. Go get your family back."

Marcus stood up and walked to the edge of the balcony. Without looking back at Ed, he said, "Shit! I still don't understand how Kyra could handle me like that!"

Ed sat in his chair, shaking his head. "Marcus, that's who she is. Accept that, man! And move the fuck on! She's going to be who she is and can't nobody change that. She'll be out there wandering around, not caring who comes in and out of her life. But you have a chance to get back what you've lost, and you still love Monica."

Marcus turned around to face Ed. "If I wanted to go back to Monica, it wouldn't be that easy."

"Well, go through the struggle of getting her back. Remember, it was you who left. But if it's one thing I know, Monica still loves you. No doubt about it." Ed took a sip from his drink and raised his glass. "It could be M&M back together again."

Marcus started to laugh. "Yeah, I remember you always called us the M&Ms. Just like that damn candy."

"You know, my brother. That's my sister! And I miss her ass." Ed stood up and walked over to his friend. "Whatever I can do to help, you know your boy is there. I know that I can get her to talk to me. I just want y'all back together."

Marcus sat on his couch, flipping through channels. Ed had left at 11 O'clock, leaving a sense of confidence and comfort behind. Marcus really appreciated having a friend like Ed. Ed was always real and honest when it came to life situations and issues, and he always told people what they needed to hear and not what they wanted to hear. Something Marcus had to get used to and accept from his best friend.

Marcus began to think about how Monica walked around with a radiant smile and a glow about herself. He thought about what he had learned about women whose hearts had been broken. Most women would often take on the spiritual role; going to church and praying all the time, telling themselves that God would get them through their hurt and pain. Maybe it was some spiritual being and belief that Monica had experienced to get her through her pain. Besides, Taylor hadn't mentioned another man coming around. Marcus knew that his daughter would have told him of another man coming around.

His mind went back and forth between Monica and Kyra. If Monica was involved with another man, that meant that he had two women who were getting on with other men. The thought sickened him as he stood up and walked to the kitchen to fix a stiff drink. He found out about Kyra and the basketball player. But the mystery about Monica made his head spin out of control.

It was a late Friday night, and Marcus decided to call Monica. Something burned inside him to try and open the line of communication with her that night. Nervous and ashamed, Marcus spoke into the phone when she answered. "Hey, Monica. I hope I didn't wake you."

"What is it, Marcus?" she asked, sounding like she didn't want to be bothered.

"Nothing," he said, lying. "I was up late and just wanted to call and see how you were doing."

"Oh, now you want to call me and see how I'm doing. Why is that, Marcus?"

Marcus heard a tone in her voice that he had never heard before, and he knew he may have to accept his loss limitations. "Hey, I hear in your voice that you don't want to be bothered. So hopefully, we can talk soon."

"Marcus, if it's not about Taylor, we have nothing to talk about. You made that clear when you left me for that other woman." Monica hung up before Marcus could respond.

His heart dropped when he realized that she had hung up. Feeling defeated, he went and lay on the couch. She was obviously very angry with him, and Marcus knew that if he tried to get back with his wife, it would take some time for her to accept him. . . if she accepted him back. As he lay looking up at the ceiling, decisions and questions crowded his mind. Monica's rejection encouraged him to fight for what he felt was his. And that night, he decided he'd do just that.

The next day around 3 p.m., Marcus sat alone inside Donetto's Restaurant. He was seated next to the window, looking at the people walking up and down the street. The weather had been very unpredictable; the temperature was now in the low 70s. West Midtown was always busy, especially on Saturdays. But Marcus wanted to get out of his condo to free his mind of his dilemma.

He couldn't get Monica and Taylor off his mind. Guilt filled up inside of his soul, painfully aware of his actions. Concluding that he had let the smaller head take over the bigger one, shame and embarrassment were deeply embedded in his consciousness. He took a bite of pasta, then a sip of beer. His eyes followed people going in and out of restaurants and retail stores.

To Marcus' miserable surprise, the answer about Monica seeing another man was answered. Marcus stood up when he spotted Monica and a tall, dark-skinned man walking inside the seafood restaurant across the street. The sight of Monica with another man delivered a crushing blow to Marcus' macho ego. It felt like a hard punch to his gut.

Chapter Thirty-Nine

Monica and Kenneth sat at a table in the back of the restaurant, Monica hoping to avoid seeing any of her friends or people that she knew. Kenneth was always understanding and considerate when it came to Monica wanting to be inconspicuous. He knew it was best not to be noticed when they were out. Although he loved her, he would give her that respect. Kenneth believed that his time would come when their relationship wouldn't be a secret anymore. Something that he looked forward to.

As usual, Monica wore her radiant smile, staring at Kenneth while he feasted on his salmon. "Mr. Mann. You really can eat."

Kenneth looked up at her and laughed. "Ms. Sexy. You better eat and stop worrying about my appetite."

Monica leaned back, rolling her neck, she said, "Well, if you don't know, a woman loves a man with a hefty appetite. A real woman, that is."

Kenneth straightened up in his chair and stared at Monica. "Oh, you don't have to tell me that you are a real woman. I knew that the moment I saw you."

"Oh yeah? And tell me, how did you come to that conclusion so fast?" she said as she folded her arms.

"Something inside of me just knew. It's hard to explain. Hell, I can't even figure that out myself. I just knew that there was something special about you."

Monica looked around the restaurant and then back at Kenneth. She leaned forward, placing her elbows on the table. She looked into his eyes and said, "You want to know something? I honestly felt the same about you. That's why I stopped to talk to you at the fire station." She leaned back. Her gaze still fixated on him. "It didn't have anything to do with my situation. I really wanted to get to know you. And I'm so glad I did."

Feeling flattered, Kenneth admitted, "You have no idea how glad I am. My life has been wonderful since you came into it."

After their late lunch and a few drinks, Monica and Kenneth decided to go to his place. They had wanted to go to the movies but decided against it. Monica wanted Kenneth, and he wanted her. They could feel the electricity in the air as they flirted with each other. Monica telling Kenneth to take whatever he wanted gave him a rise. Her professionalism, her sexiness, and beauty complimented her freaky side.

Kenneth walked Monica to her car, walking behind her and looking at her perfect ass. They had to park a block away from the restaurant because so many people flooded West Midtown. Monica suddenly stopped when she noticed Marcus standing by her car. She quickly turned around to Kenneth and told him to stay where he was. She stood there with Kenneth; her arms folded. Surprise and anger boiled up inside of her.

Monica turned to Kenneth and spoke with displeasure. "That's Marcus! Why is he standing by my car?!" She looked Kenneth in his eyes, furious, and said, "Kenneth, go on home. I'll be over there as soon as I can."

Feeling protective and thinking that something bad may happen, Kenneth said, "No, I'm not going until I know that you are okay."

Monica pleaded with Kenneth. "Please, Kenneth, just go. I'll be fine. Trust me."

Not wanting to leave Monica to a potentially angry husband, Kenneth told Monica, "I'll be sitting in my truck just to make sure nothing goes wrong." He looked Monica in her eyes and continued, "I don't know what state of mind he's in. And I don't want anything to happen to you."

Monica threw up her hands and looked down. "Okay, okay!" She caught herself before she spoke any further. "I'm sorry. It's just that I wasn't expecting this. Damn!"

"I know. But I'll be sitting in my truck. I can't just leave you here like this." Kenneth walked to his truck and stared at Marcus, standing across the street at Monica's car.

Monica walked across the street to her car. Marcus was leaning back on the car with his arms folded. When she got closer, she yelled, "Marcus! What are you doing standing by my car?!"

Marcus stood straight up and unfolded his arms. "So that's who keeping you all smiling and shit." Marcus shook his head and watched Kenneth get into his truck. "So, how long have you been seeing this dude?"

Angry to the highest level, Monica yelled, "None of your damn business, Marcus! And I'm not going to discuss this out here! So move out of my way so I can leave!"

Marcus grabbed Monica's arm and spun her around to face him. "Monica, we need to talk!"

Monica pulled away from his grip and took two steps back. "Don't you touch me again, you bastard! Now get out of my way!"

Marcus noticed that passerby's stopped and looked at the commotion. Not wanting to draw any more attention, he looked at Monica and said, "We really need to talk. I'll meet you at the house."

Monica didn't say a word as she got into her car and drove away. Tears of anger streamed down her face as she drove. She pulled over in a grocery store parking lot to gather and compose herself. She knew she had to call Kenneth and postpone visiting his house. She knew that he would be upset but understanding. But Monica knew she had to go home and deal with Marcus. And she was ready to set him straight.

Marcus was standing by his car when Monica pulled up in her driveway. She pulled beside his car and jumped out. "What the hell was that all about, Marcus?"

Marcus looked up and down the street and then looked back to Monica. "I don't want to discuss this in the yard. I really don't want our neighbors to hear us. So can we please go inside our house?"

Trying to keep her voice at a minimum, Monica responded, "Hell fucking no! You left this house for another woman. Remember?"

Marcus rubbed his face and started to walk toward the front door. "Monica, let's go inside and talk."

"I'm not going in there with you, Marcus!" her voice rising without care. "Now, why don't you just leave?!"

A vision came over Marcus as he turned and looked at the sky. "Answer me this. You haven't brought another man into our house, have you?"

Monica stretched out an open palm, her head down, and said, "Marcus, I don't have time for this shit! And no, I haven't had any other man in this damn house." She paused and said, "As a matter of fact, you can have this goddamn house! Fuck you and this house! When I move out, you can go and beg that slut you were with to move in here with your ass! How 'bout that!"

Marcus' voice became low as he pleaded for Monica to come inside and talk to him. "Monica, please, let's just go inside and talk. That's all I want to do. Please hear me out."

Monica put both hands on her hips, rocking her body in anger. She said, "You can go in. I'm leaving." Monica began walking towards her car when Marcus ran up to her. She looked at him as he stood between her and her car. "Marcus, please get out of my way."

Realizing that he had lost the battle, Marcus stepped aside and let Monica get in her car. As she drove away, Marcus stared until it disappeared. He stood in front of the house, looking at it. He was free to go inside if he wanted to. Should I go inside and wait for Monica and Taylor to come home? Or should I just go to my condo and try to talk to her another time? Believing that he had made the best decision, Marcus got into his car and drove away.

Chapter Forty

Monica made it to Kenneth's just before 7:00 p.m. Feeling embarrassed, she sat in her car, reluctant to face Kenneth. Gripping the steering wheel, she leaned forward; questions raced through her mind. *Why now, Marcus? Why did you have to see Kenneth and me? Why do you want to talk now?* She took a deep breath and laid her head back. She knew she had to face Kenneth, knowing he was shaken and caught off guard by her husband standing by her car.

She finally gathered enough strength to get out of the car. The walk to Kenneth's front door was a series of hesitant steps. *Should I just turn around and go back home? Should we just talk about it on the phone?* She stood at the front door looking up, trying to force her mind to push her to ring the doorbell. *Shit!* She finally reached for the doorbell and then took a step back.

Kenneth opened the door, and Monica walked inside with her head down. She walked to the bar and sat down on a stool. Kenneth could tell she was mixed with emotions and didn't want to make her uncomfortable. Her coming over gave him a sense of security. He had hoped she would still come over after the scene in West Midtown. Kenneth vowed to put her worries at ease.

Kenneth walked over and sat across from her at the bar. He took in a long, deep breath and looked at Monica. "Hey, Beautiful. Would you like something to drink?"

Monica's head slowly rose, looking Kenneth in his eyes. "Sure. I could use something strong."

"How about Crown?" he asked.

Monica looked down and answered, "Yes, that will do."

Kenneth poured her a glass of Crown on ice and sat it in front of her. Wanting to be considerate, he said, "Monica, if you need time to be alone and think about things, I'll understand."

"Kenneth, I don't know what to do," Monica replied. "I don't know what to think." She paused before continuing. "After you left, Marcus insisted I meet him at the house. I knew he would probably follow me if I came straight to your house, and I didn't want him to know where you lived. So I met him at the house and talked to him in the driveway. He finally left, and I drove around for a while, trying to see if he was following me. But he wasn't."

Not knowing what to say, Kenneth sat in silence. He wanted her to get her head together and think things through. He didn't want any added pressure to her already vulnerable state of mind, so he suggested that she go home and clear her mind.

"Monica, it's okay if you want to go home and clear your head. Relaxation and meditation could be a big help."

Monica looked up at Kenneth, appreciating his understanding. "Yeah, I may just do that. Taylor is at my sister's for the night, so maybe the privacy will help."

Kenneth walked Monica to her car after she finished her drink. They stood by the car, staring into each other's eyes. Kenneth finally managed to pull Monica close to him, hugging her and trying to assure her comfort. He stepped back, his hands on her shoulders, and leaned down to kiss her lips. He then pulled her close again and held her. She squeezed him tight, not wanting to let go of the man that had brought her out of misery.

Monica made it home just before 9 O'clock that night. She had driven around Interstate 285 after leaving Kenneth's house, listening to music, hoping it would clear her head. But her mind was still cloudy and unsure of what lay ahead for her future. Her husband had left her for another woman, and she found the perfect man in Kenneth. But she was still married with a young daughter who cried and often worried, wishing for her father to return home.

Monica sat on the edge of her bed, looking down at the floor. What have I done to deserve being put in this whirlwind of a life? Why am I feeling like my world is falling apart? The questions kept coming, with no answers to follow. She took off all her clothes and lay under the covers. Knowing how Taylor felt, wanting her father to come home, Monica knew that she was in for a perplexing battle. A battle between a young daughter who wanted her father, a husband who had abandoned them for another woman, and now not wanting to return home.

Unsure of when she had dozed off, Monica opened her eyes, sat up in the bed, and pulled her knees up to her breasts. She looked over at the clock, which read, 11:55. She reached for her cell phone to check for any messages. She touched the text messaging icon, and Marcus' name popped up. She opened the message and began reading it.

Monica, I just want to talk. Please just hear me out. I don't want to communicate through phone calls and text messages. What I want and have to say, I would prefer it be face to face. Please, Baby. Consider.

Monica slammed the phone down on the bed. "Shit!" She looked up at the ceiling, patting her foot on the bed. What the fuck do you have to talk to me about, Marcus? Why should I listen to any damn thing you have to say! Anger in her body and soul, Monica got out of bed and put her robe on. She went to the kitchen and slammed her cell phone on the counter. She made a cup of coffee and sat on a bar stool. She was supposed to stay the night with Kenneth and spend the day with him.

After drinking her coffee and thinking about Marcus' text message, Monica decided to call Kenneth. "Hey," she said softly.

His voice deep and sounding like he had just woken up, Kenneth replied, "Hey, Beautiful. How are you feeling?"

"I could be better." She paused for a few seconds. "Kenneth, I would like to go to Canoe for lunch if you don't mind. I really could use getting away from this house."

"No problem, I would love that. What time do you want to go?"

Monica stood up and went to the kitchen window. Looking out of the window into the backyard, she asked, "How about three? Would that work for you?"

"Sure," Kenneth answered. "I'll meet you there at three."

Feeling a sense of not giving a damn, Monica responded, "Kenneth, if you don't mind, can I come to your place, and we go together?"

"That'll work for me, sure."

Monica hung up the phone and sat at the bar. She was determined to spend the day with Kenneth and enjoy her time with him. Nothing was going to ruin her desire to be with the man who saved her from a misery. that had started to eat her inside and out. Kenneth didn't deserve to be put on hold, and Monica was going to uplift her spirits and do whatever she pleased with him. She rose from the stool and walked to her bedroom. Fuck you, Marcus!

Chapter Forty-One

Marcus sat on his couch, flipping through the channels on the TV. The vision of Kenneth stayed in his mind. I have seen that dude somewhere before. Marcus tried to figure out where he had seen Kenneth. He knew that he recognized his face, and trying to recall from where drove him crazy . And the thought of Monica being sexed crazy by another man intensified his anger.

Trying to extricate the thought of Monica being with another man from his mind, Marcus got up and started to pace around his condo. His cell phone rang, interrupting his thoughts. Rubbing the back of his head, he walked to the table and saw Ed's name. "Hey, Ed. What's up?"

"Just checking on you. How are you, my brother?"

Marcus gave a laugh of disgust and answered, "Man, I wish I

could tell you that I'm doing good." He paused, took a deep breath in, and then exhaled loudly. "I saw Monica with another man."

"What?!" Ed yelled into the phone.

Marcus sat on the couch and leaned his head back. "Yeah. I saw it with my own eyes."

"Well, it was probably nothing. She does have all kinds of clients. Remember, she does have her own real estate franchise. Maybe she was with one of her high-dollar clients."

Wanting to agree with his friend, Marcus' intuition told him that Monica had gotten involved with another man. "I kind of doubt that. She did come to my office and encountered Kyra there with me. And she knows about the New Year's Eve incident." Marcus leaned forward and looked down at the floor. "I tried to talk to her earlier, but apparently, she's still upset about all of this."

Offering his advice, Ed told his friend, "Marcus, just give it some time. I'm sure she knows that you and Kyra's relationship is over. And I know that she loves you still. So just continue to text her, letting her know that you want to open communication. Don't try and rush anything."

Standing up, Marcus walked to his balcony and slid the door open. "Damn! I can't believe how stupid I was."

Marcus and Ed talked for 30 minutes about Monica. After talking to Ed, Marcus texted Monica, hoping she would respond with an answer that he would be pleased with.

Monica, whenever you are available, please let me know. If we sit down and talk, I'm sure that you would understand. Please consider.

He closed the balcony door and went back to the couch. Looking at his phone, he was hoping to get an immediate response to his text. He looked for a response that never came.

Trying to occupy his mind with other thoughts, his cell phone rang. To his surprise, it was Kyra. Reluctant to answer, Marcus picked up the phone. "What's up, Kyra?"

Sounding remorseful, Kyra answered, "Marcus, I'm sorry for what happened. I got your messages, but I couldn't bring myself to answer."

A boiling anger began to stir inside of him. "What the fuck do you mean you couldn't answer?! Ain't that some bullshit!"

"Marcus, I just called to say that I'm sorry, that's all. I feel like I at least owe you that much."

Standing up with rage, Marcus yelled into the phone, "You owe me that fucking much?! I went to fucking jail! And you left with that motherfucker?! Oh, yeah! I know all about that shit!"

Her voice low and apologetic, Kyra said, "Okay, Marcus. I understand your being upset. I just wanted to call and apologize and say goodbye." And then the phone went silent.

Marcus tossed the cell phone on the couch and stood still with his head down. The vision of Kenneth's face resurfaced in his mind. Trying to forget that he had just talked to Kyra, Marcus switched his focus back to Monica and Kenneth. Was he really a client? Was that a business meeting? Marcus tried his best to convince himself that perhaps the man with his wife was a business proposition. But Marcus knew that he had seen the man before. Where have I seen him before?

The Atlanta Hawks were getting ready for an early-day game. Because of the New Year's Eve assault on the basketball player, Marcus couldn't bring himself to watch the game. He checked his cell phone for any text messages from Monica. But there was still no response. Disappointed and angry, he felt compelled to call her. Her phone rang until the voicemail came on. Listening to her voice, Marcus breathed heavily in and out. In a low, desperate tone, Marcus said, "Monica. I texted you, and you didn't respond. So I'm leaving you this message, hoping you read the text and will consider seeing and talking to me. Please get back with me."

Laying on the couch, a brilliant thought entered Marcus's mind. Why haven't I thought about this before? Taylor! Marcus leaped to his feet and began to put his plan together. He and Monica did have a young daughter who missed her father. Taylor would be his leverage to get Monica to open up to him. A sad, crying daughter, longing for her father, would surely help get Monica to talk to him.

Chapter Forty-Two

Monica sat across from Kenneth, trying to concentrate only on him. But her phone kept ringing with Marcus' name popping up on it¬¬—text message after text message. She apologized to Kenneth about the disturbance and said, "Let me put this damn thing on silent. Once again, I'm sorry."

Understanding, Kenneth replied, "No, no. You are a businesswoman. That phone will never stop ringing. It doesn't bother me at all."

Monica put the cell phone on silent and put it inside of her purse. She looked at Kenneth and said, "I wish it were business. That's Marcus, who keeps calling and texting me. That's why I had to apologize." She looked Kenneth in his eyes and told him, "Kenneth, I am not going to lie to you. I'm going to be straight up with you. My husband got into trouble with the woman he left me for."

She paused and continued. "New Year's Eve, he found out that the woman he was with was involved with an Atlanta Hawks basketball player. So, his dumbass assaulted the dude, and they took his ass to jail."

Shaking his head, Kenneth said, "Wow! That's heavy."

After taking a sip from her wine, Monica said, "Yes, it is. And now I have the feeling that he wants to come crawling back to me because he lost his girlfriend on top of facing assault charges." Monica started to feel a sense of guilt, knowing that she had entertained the thought of the possibility of reuniting with her husband. She was hoping that Kenneth wouldn't ask about it and that they would just enjoy the day.

Kenneth looked away and stared out at the view of the lake. The restaurant was crowded with people inside and out. The temperature was in the 50s—too cool for Monica's blood to sit outside. The thought of Monica getting back with her husband began to cross Kenneth's mind. Thinking of what Mark had told him about the old toy and new toy analogy stuck in his head. Her husband lost his new toy, and now he wants his old toy. Is this a possibility now?

Monica stared out at the lake in deep thought about her and Kenneth. Lately, she had begun to think of Kenneth as an auspicious soulmate. His timing couldn't have been any better, coming to her rescue in her time of need. When she was with him, it was as if their hearts were one. She looked at Kenneth, who was staring out at the lake himself. "Kenneth?" She watched him as he turned his head slowly toward her. "Do you believe in soulmates?"

Kenneth looked into her eyes with a serious look on his face. Thinking about her question, he looked down at the table and twirled his finger around his drink. Gathering his thoughts, he answered her. "Soulmates have to have the same hearts, whether good or bad. Both hearts have to be the same for that to work." He rubbed his chin and leaned forward. "If a person has a caring heart, that person cannot become a soulmate to someone who is malicious and evil. It just wouldn't work as soulmates. Even the devil must have someone with the same evil heart as he does to be a soulmate. So do I believe in soulmates? Yes, I do." Kenneth leaned back. "Soulmates love unconditionally no matter what happens."

Monica listened to Kenneth, processing his analysis of soulmates. Kenneth was like no other man that she had ever known. He was so intriguing to her. His life was a mysterious success, given his background. He had told Monica of the violence that he had witnessed in Arkansas. Friends being shot and killed. Drugs and crime destroyed his community. But somehow, he managed to escape the vicious streets of a small city in Arkansas, made it to college, and became a fireman. And after losing a mother and sister to cancer, he had shown an undeniable strength.

Feeling horny and ready to give her body and soul to Kenneth, Monica smiled at Kenneth. "I want you so bad right now."

A serious look on his face, Kenneth looked Monica in her eyes. "God knows that I really want you too."

Monica took a sip from her drink and crossed her legs. Holding the glass near her lips, she said, "Well, let's go back to your place." A seductive look came over her face. "I want you to take all of me. I am feeling so damn freaky, and I want to try something that we haven't tried before."

Kenneth and Monica pulled into his driveway just before the sun had set. Monica placed her hand on Kenneth's. She looked him in his eyes as they sat staring at each other with desire. Kenneth leaned over and started to kiss her. She pulled up her skirt and placed his hand between her legs. She was hot and wet, and she wanted him to know it. She wanted to show him the effect that he had on her. She wanted him to have all of her, leaving nothing to be desired.

Monica and Kenneth stood by his bed, undressing each other while kissing passionately. She was turned on by his hard dick pressing up against her body. She wanted him to enter her without foreplay. She was soaking wet and ready. She pulled Kenneth on top of her as she lay on the bed. She opened her legs, grabbed his dick, and let it inside her. Screaming with passion, her legs flew wide open, taking every inch of him.

Monica began to lick his ear, her tongue going in and out. She then whispered, "I am so wet. My juices got my ass so wet." She held his face and looked into his eyes. "I want you to fuck my ass."

Kenneth rose and stood on the side of the bed. He watched as Monica turned over while looking back at him. She got on her knees, lifted her round ass, and arched her back down, laying her head on the bed. Kenneth went inside her wet pussy, stroking her as he fingered her ass. Her moans and screams excited him more and more as he stroked her from behind. He was ready to give her what she had asked for.

Kenneth slowly slid himself out of her hot, wet pussy. He stepped back, admiring her beautiful, sexy body. Her ass was so perfect, her legs so long and sexy. Kenneth eased closer to her and placed his dick on her ass. He began to ease the head of his dick inside her ass. He felt her tighten, and then he held his position. When she relaxed, he eased more inside of her ass.

Monica kept her back arched and her head on the bed. "Ohhh-hh, shit! Fuck my ass! Deeper!"

Kenneth had eased half of himself inside her ass, loving how Monica wanted him to please her in every way. Surprised and willing, Kenneth eased more of his dick inside of her ass. "Oh, yeah, Baby. You want me to fuck that ass!"

Her eyes closed and mouth wide open, she yelled, "Yes, Daddy!

Yes! Fuck my ass!"

Monica loved the feeling of being freaked by Kenneth. She hadn't been fucked in her ass in a long time and wanted to feel it again. She and Marcus had tried it on occasion, her loving the adventure of stepping out of the regular sexual box. Now, Kenneth was rocking her erotic world that had lay dormant for quite some time. And she wanted Kenneth to have all of her that night, enjoying all of him. Monica would let tomorrow take care of itself.

Chapter Forty-Three

onica and Taylor sat at the food court in Lenox Mall. Taylor was telling her mother about the fun she had with her father. Marcus had picked Taylor up from school that past Friday and took her out for dinner. She smiled as she told Monica how much fun she had at the Hippo Hopp, meeting friends and playing all the games. Monica listened as Taylor's excitement about spending the weekend with her dad poured out.

It was a beautiful Sunday afternoon, and Monica wanted to take Taylor shopping after Marcus had brought her home. Monica had no choice about talking to Marcus regarding their daughter. But she continued to brush him off each time he tried to talk to her about meeting him to talk about giving him a chance to make up for his mistakes. She could hear the frustration and desperation in his voice as he tried to convince her to hear him out.

After eating and shopping, Monica and Taylor made it home just before 8:00 p.m. Monica put a pizza in the oven for Taylor before getting her clothes ready for school. Taylor sat on her bed and watched as her mother picked over outfits in her closet. After deciding what Taylor would wear to school, Monica walked out of the closet and placed the clothes at the foot of Taylor's bed. She noticed that her daughter had a sad look on her face, and she knew right away why.

Not wanting to talk about Marcus, Monica rubbed Taylor on the top of her head. "Okay, let's go take this pizza out of the oven. You have to eat and get ready for bed in a few minutes."

Without saying a word, Taylor got up and walked downstairs. Monica stood with her arms folded, knowing that she would have to have a continuous conversation with her daughter about her father. Why me, Lord? Monica finally walked downstairs to her daughter, sitting at the table with her head down. The sad look hadn't left her face, and Monica wanted to do anything to change her daughter's mood. But it was not going to happen that night, and she knew it.

Avoiding the topic of Marcus, Monica gently rubbed her daughter's face as Taylor took small bites from her pizza. "I really like the clothes that you picked out today," she told Taylor, trying her best to bring some kind of joy to her daughter. Taylor didn't say a word as she put the slice of pizza on the plate. Monica pulled Taylor close to her and hugged her. "Mommy loves you so much." Loving the hug that Taylor returned made Monica feel good inside.

After putting Taylor to bed, Monica sat in her office looking over papers for potential deals. She wasn't focused on her, although she tried her best to shake the thoughts of Marcus and Kenneth. She needed to clear her head in the worst way. She leaned back in her chair and folded her arms, looking up at the ceiling. A million thoughts clouded her mind. She was interrupted by her cell phone. She looked down, and it was Marcus. Shit!

"Hello, Monica," he said in a low voice.

Monica took a deep breath and gave a long sigh. "What is it, Marcus?"

"I guess the little princess is sleeping now. She had a great time this weekend."

"Yeah, she told me how much fun she had." Not wanting to talk to Marcus, Monica asked, "Is that why you are calling me? To talk about Taylor?"

Marcus' voice rose slightly. "Of course. And to ask if you have at least thought about meeting with me so we can talk."

Monica rubbed her head and closed her eyes. "Talk about what, Marcus?"

"Monica, I don't want to talk about it over the phone. I really think that it would be better if we sat down to a meal and discussed things."

Sadness began to run through her soul, making her feel weak and sickened. Her world was in a tumultuous whirlwind again, knowing that her husband wanted to return home and her daughter longed for her father. "Marcus...I..." She leaned forward with her head down. "I just don't know," her voice weak. "It's not that easy for me to talk to you. I did nothing wrong, and you left me for another woman."

"Look, Monica. Please just meet with me. A nice private dinner of your choice," he pleaded.

Reluctant to agree, Monica said, "Marcus, I will think about it. Just give me some time. That's the least you can do."

"Okay. I don't want to rush you, but I really hope that you don't take too long. There's nothing that can't be made right again by two people who love each other."

Not wanting the conversation to go any further, Monica said, "Goodbye, Marcus. I'm working."

The following day, Monica drove Taylor to school, looking at her daughter, who hadn't said much that morning. Monica didn't know how to get her daughter to open up to her. She knew that Taylor had only one thing on her mind. She wanted her father to return home. But there were things that Monica could not explain to her daughter. She knew that a young girl should not know certain details about grown people's actions and decisions.

After dropping Taylor off at school, Monica went to her office. She stood looking out the window at the cars and people passing by and wished she could just go someplace far away. She began wishing she could leave Atlanta for a while and leave her life behind. She was trying her best to maintain her sanity. But Marcus' and Kenneth's voices stayed in her head. She was caught between her separated marriage and a man that had come into her life and rocked her world.

Sitting at her desk, fighting to eradicate the thought of Marcus from her mind, her cell phone rang. She picked up the phone and saw Ed's name. "Fuck!" She knew why Ed was calling. Feeling angry, she answered the phone. "Hello, Ed."

In a happy and loud voice, Ed said, "What's up, Sis! I'm just calling to check on you!"

"How are you doing, Ed?" Monica asked, her voice low.

"Can't be better. How's my little niece?"

"She's doing good. Missing her father being at home, of course."

"Yeah, I figured that. Marcus told me."

Not wanting to drag on the conversation, Monica got straight to the point with Ed. "Ed, I know why you are calling. You and Marcus discussed it and he had you call me, knowing that you and I are like brother and sister."

"You are right. Marcus wants to make things right with you. Sis, he is really sorry."

Monica yelled into the phone. "His ass ain't sorry about leaving me! His ass is sorry that he went to jail behind that damn slut who left his ass! So don't give me that bullshit! Please!"

"Okay, okay. All of that shit did happen. Can't deny that, and he fucked up big time. And I mean big time. But you can't tell me that you can't at least meet with him and listen to him."

"Ed, I don't want to meet him and talk about shit!" She stood up and walked to the window. "I don't owe Marcus a damn thing!"

"Wait...wait! Please, Sis! Just hear me out! Please!" Ed paused for a few seconds. "Now you know I love you. And I love my little niece. I know you and Marcus once had a beautiful thing. I was there, and I know what I saw. If a man is willing to beg for forgiveness, that should mean something."

Frustrated and confused, Monica finally agreed with Ed. "Okay, Ed. I'll meet with his ass. But he shouldn't expect nothing else."

Monica sat at her desk and began to cry. She started to think of Kenneth and his kindness. She knew that Kenneth loved and cherished her. She could feel his love by the way he looked at her. The way he held and caressed her. The way that he made her feel with his unselfish lovemaking. And now she had agreed to meet with her estranged husband. Guilt ran through her as she thought about her meeting with her husband. What has my life turned into?

Chapter Forty-Four

Monica had decided to meet Marcus the following Friday at Cooks & Soldiers for dinner. Marcus waited at a table near the front entrance. Monica spotted him when she walked in. Her emotions were running high, and she wanted to get the meeting over with as soon as possible. She knew Marcus would not give up his pursuit to meet with her. So she figured the sooner she met with him and told him what was on her mind, the better.

Her face exhibited agitation as she sat at the table across from Marcus. She folded her arms and looked around the restaurant. She could feel Marcus' eyes on her, making her uncomfortable. She managed to turn her head and look him directly in his eyes. She noticed that he had a pitiful look on his face, and for a second, she wanted to laugh out loud. But instead, she kept her gaze and shook her head. She was definitely not going to start the conversation.

Marcus lowered his head and stared at the table. He had practiced what he wanted to say, but the words would not come out. He managed to look up at Monica and then said, "You look beautiful."

Monica turned her head without saying a word. The thought of going to his office and seeing Kyra there made her furious. She had been faithful to him, dedicated to her marriage, and wanted to be the best wife she could be, and he betrayed her with his careless temptations. She turned her head and began to stare at him again. She wanted him to feel uncomfortable. She wanted all the guilt that he felt to pour out. She wanted him to hurt the same way she was hurting.

Trying to break the ice, Marcus asked, "How is work going?"

Monica looked at him and rolled her eyes before she looked away. Without looking at Marcus, she replied, "Work is going well."

Keeping his eyes on her, Marcus said, "That's good. I know you are a dedicated businesswoman, and I always loved that about you."

Monica opened her mouth and squinted her eyes at him. "Marcus. What is it that you want to talk about?"

Marcus leaned back and took a sip from his beer. He looked up at the ceiling and took a deep breath. "Monica. . .I. . .I. . ." He stuttered his words.

Monica leaned forward and placed her elbows on the table, lacing her hands together. "I what?"

Marcus looked at her and said, "I want to make things right. I want you to just think about what we had before and get back to what we had."

Monica laughed sarcastically and asked, "Marcus, what did we have before?"

"We had something special, and you know that." Marcus looked away, trying to keep his composure. "I believe you know that."

Monica leaned back and responded, "If what we had was so special, why did you start seeing that slut?"

Marcus said, ashamed but determined, "Monica, I know that I fucked up. But now I'm going to give it my all to convince you that I can make things right, and I'm willing to do whatever it takes."

Leaning back and folding her arms, Monica said, "If you had not found out that slut had been with that basketball player and your ass had not gone to jail, you wouldn't be here tonight. So you can spare me with that make things right bullshit."

Marcus placed both hands on his face and slid them down slowly. He looked at Monica, feeling captured with no way out. But he had to keep trying; no matter what blows she landed, he was determined to keep fighting. "Monica, you can say whatever you want to, but all I know is that I'm not going to give up on my family."

Monica stood up and put her jacket on. "Marcus, you gave up on your family when you started sleeping with that slut." She looked around the restaurant again, her face full of anger. "I'm going home now. You have a great rest of the night." She walked away and looked back at him before walking out of the door.

Monica made it home shortly before 11:00 p.m. She had cried all the way home, feeling confused and lost. Why did I have to meet Marcus? Why couldn't I just say no and let him suffer? Mixed emotions and sadness came over her. She started to think about Taylor and how she missed her father being at home. What was she to do? She knew her daughter would blame her if she didn't allow her father to return home. And she didn't want to cause her daughter any more confusion and sadness. Shit!

Monica lay across the bed, staring at the ceiling, and began crying again. Her cell phone rang as she was sorting through her thoughts. She raised up and picked up her the phone from the nightstand. It was Kenneth. Her heart dropped and felt heavy with guilt. She composed herself before she answered. "Hello, Kenneth. How are you?"

"Hey, Beautiful. You sound a little tired. Hope I didn't wake you," he said.

Monica stood up and walked around the room. "No, no, you

didn't. I was just relaxing on the bed."

"The reason that I was calling was to see if you wanted to take a trip to the Virgin Islands next month. I would love for you to find time to get away with me for four days." Kenneth blurted out.

A feeling of excitement came over Monica. "Do you mean for Spring Break?"

"Yes. I figured if you didn't have plans with Taylor, maybe her dad or your sister could keep her, and we have a getaway."

"That sounds great, Kenneth! Let me check, and I'll let you know in a few days."

"Okay, I really hope that it can work out. A romantic getaway would be nice."

Smiling at the thought of going to the Virgin Islands with Kenneth, Monica said, "I would love that! I could really use that right now! Thanks for the invite!"

Chapter Forty-Five

Marcus was on his way to get Taylor for the day. It was a beautiful Saturday afternoon, and she had begged her dad to take her to her favorite place to play games. Marcus drove slowly through the neighborhood, reflecting on when he and Monica had purchased their home. When he stopped at the stop sign near the fire station, he noticed Kenneth standing outside talking to another fireman. Marcus looked away and then quickly turned his head and stared at Kenneth. *I knew I had seen that mothafucker before!*

Knowing that he wanted to desperately reconcile with his wife and not want any competition, he made a turn and parked his car across the street from the fire station. He watched Kenneth as he laughed and talked with the other fireman. Marcus' ego was roaring in full motion, and he wanted to let Kenneth know he needed to stay away from his wife. Marcus got out of his car and stood next to it. He hoped Kenneth would notice him before he called him. And Marcus got what he wanted when Kenneth stopped laughing and stared at Marcus.

Kenneth remembered Marcus from the incident the other night, and now he wondered why Marcus stopped by the fire station. Kenneth watched as Marcus leaned against his car with his hands in his pockets. Not wanting any drama at his job, Kenneth excused himself from talking with the other fireman. "Excuse me for a few minutes. There is someone who wants to talk to me."

Marcus watched as Kenneth crossed the street. He could tell that Kenneth worked out and must have been an athlete at some point and time. Marcus stood up straight as Kenneth came closer. He stared at Kenneth, who was now standing a couple of feet away from him. Looking Kenneth straight in the eyes, Marcus said, "I was passing by and noticed you. So you are a fireman?"

Feeling uncomfortable because he was at his job, Kenneth said, "Yeah, I am." Kenneth squinted his eyes and continued. "Why would you stop by my job? This is not the time nor the place for any discussion."

Marcus rubbed his nose with his thumb and smiled. "My wife hasn't told me anything so I was hoping that maybe you could tell me something." Marcus waited for Kenneth to respond, but he just stood there staring at Marcus. Wanting information about Kenneth and Monica, Marcus asked, "Is there anything going on between you and my wife?"

Not taking his angry stare off Marcus, Kenneth said, "I think you should leave."

Frustration started to build up inside Marcus. Jealousy and envy filled his soul. He knew that there was a probability that Monica was sleeping with the man standing in front of him. Marcus pointed his finger at Kenneth and paused before saying, "Look, I'm getting back with my wife. So I want you to stay away from her."

"You need to get in your car and leave," Kenneth gritted his teeth.

Marcus' voice began to rise. "Look, mothafucker! You heard what the fuck I said! Don't make no mistake about it. I'll kill your ass if you don't stay away from my wife!"

Still looking Marcus straight in the eyes, Kenneth said, "I run into burning buildings for a living. Do you really think that I'm afraid of death?"

Feeling intimidated by Kenneth's disposition and stern look, Marcus got into his car without saying another word. He watched as Kenneth turned his back and walked across the street to the fire station. Marcus was both disappointed and relieved that he did not get the information he had stopped for. But if Kenneth and Monica weren't involved, any man would have come right out and denied the relationship. There was something definitely going on between his wife and the fireman.

Marcus sat in the driveway staring at the house he and Monica had purchased. That son of a bitch works right in this neighborhood. Shit! He could have been inside my house! Boiling mad, Marcus got out of the car and walked to the door at a fast pace. He rang the doorbell, angry that Monica had changed the locks when he got his own place. This is still my goddamn house! When Monica opened the door, without saying a word, Marcus pushed past her and went and sat at the bar.

Monica closed the door and stood still as she watched Marcus disappear into the kitchen. She knew that he was upset about something by the look on his face and his body language. She wasn't in the mood for any drama, and she was going to let him know that from the start. But she was going to let him talk about whatever was on his mind. She walked to the kitchen and sat at the bar across from Marcus. She noticed his lips were tight, and his fists were balled up.

Marcus sat at the bar, unable to speak. He shook his head as he stared at Monica. His meeting with the fireman ate at him, and he wanted to let out all his frustration. He wanted Monica to know that he had talked with Kenneth and didn't give a damn how she felt about it. But Taylor was in the house, and he didn't want to start an argument, as he remembered how his daughter had cried when he blew off the handle and left the house before.

Monica let the silence continue, not knowing why Marcus was acting the way he was. She picked up her phone and noticed a text message from Kenneth.

Hey. I'm just letting you know that your husband stopped by the fire station. I guess he recognized me when I was standing outside talking to a co-worker. If something goes wrong with you two, I'm sorry.

Now understanding what was bothering Marcus, Monica got up and fixed herself a cup of coffee. She was in no mood to entertain the conversation about Marcus stopping by the fire station. She looked over at him and asked, "Do you want some coffee while Taylor finishes getting dressed?"

Marcus looked up at Monica and said, "No, I do not."

She took a sip from her cup and said, "Okay. Let me go and see if Taylor is ready."

Marcus watched as Monica started for the stairs. "Wait a minute."

Monica turned around and asked, "What is it, Marcus?"

Shaking his head and laughing sarcastically, Marcus said, "I recognized ol' boy that you were out with when I seen you two. He's a fireman in this neighborhood."

Monica put one hand on her hip and said, "Let me go and get Taylor."

Marcus stared into Monica's eyes, trying to hold in his anger. "I told him to stay away from you. And I mean that. I just wanted you to know that."

Monica shook her head and walked up the stairs. You bastard!

Monica walked Taylor out with her dad. She waved goodbye to Taylor as Marcus got into the car and started it. She noticed that Marcus hadn't closed his door as he stared at her. Would you just leave?! I don't have time for this shit!

Marcus got out of the car and closed the door. He started to walk towards Monica, looking at the frustration on her face. "Monica, we need to talk. I'm not giving up on getting my family back."

Monica rolled her eyes and looked up. Without looking at Marcus and shaking her head, she said, "Marcus, just leave. Have fun with your daughter. She's really looking forward to spending time with her father."

Determined to get his wife to give him another chance, Marcus demanded that she talk to him about it. "Monica. I'm not giving up. So you are going to have to talk to me. I'm not taking no for an answer." He lowered his head and said in a convincing voice as he tried to convince her, "I love you so much. You have to realize that."

Not wanting her daughter to witness any drama, she turned around and walked into the house. She stood inside with her back against the front door and arms folded. Monica looked up and shook her head, shoulders heaving as she began to cry. She couldn't stop the emotions from flowing. I love you so much. You have to realize that.

Chapter Forty-Six

Marcus and Taylor sat outside on his balcony. It was the first of March, and the evening weather was perfect. Marcus enjoyed watching his daughter having a great time at her favorite place. He knew that Monica would bring her there whenever Taylor asked. He began to reminisce about when he and Monica would sit back and watch her play with other kids, running around for hours. Memories of him and Monica invaded his thoughts once again. How could I be so damn stupid?!

Marcus' curiosity began to get the best of him. Was there a chance that Taylor had seen Kenneth? Had he been over to the house? He looked at Taylor, who was enjoying her ice cream. He wanted to be very careful not to make his daughter uncomfortable about him asking about the fireman. "Hey, Sweetheart. Daddy has to ask you a question."

Taylor looked up at her father with a curious look on her face. "What is it, Daddy?"

Marcus took a deep breath and asked, "Has any other man that has come to the house since Daddy's been gone?"

Taylor shook her head and said, "No, Daddy. You are the only man that comes to the house." With a puzzled look, she asked, "Why do you ask that, Daddy?"

It was now time for Marcus to put his plan together. His daughter was going to be his ally, and he was determined to get back with his wife by any means necessary. "Well, Sweetheart. Mommy has a new friend that is a man. That's why I haven't been back home yet."

Taylor shook her head vigorously. "No, Daddy! Mommy doesn't have a new friend that's a man!"

Marcus rubbed his daughter's head and looked at her. "Yes, Sweetheart. Daddy saw them out one day."

Taylor started to cry as she went to her father and hugged him. "Daddy, please come back home."

Feeling his daughter's pain, Marcus held her tight in his arms. "Shhhhh. Hush now. Daddy will be home soon."

Taylor looked up at her father with tears flowing down her cheeks. "You are? When Daddy? When?"

"Soon, Sweetheart. Soon."

That Sunday afternoon, Marcus and Taylor sat in the driveway when they arrived at the house. Marcus tried his best to convince Taylor that he would come home soon. His heart sank as he watched his daughter cry. Guilt overcame him as he began to think about why he had left home. He had abandoned his family for Kyra. And now he was the fool that had lost the people who meant the most to him. Marcus was determined to get all that he had lost.

Marcus rang the doorbell as Taylor clung to him. She was still crying. "Taylor, you need to stop crying now, baby girl. I don't want your mother to see you cry."

Taylor looked up at her father and said, "But Daddy. I can't help it. I want you and Mommy to live in the same house with me."

Monica opened the door to discover her daughter crying. Taylor ran into the house and went upstairs to her room. Monica knew that her daughter was hurting, wanting her father home. She couldn't help but feel a sense of guilt and confusion. She looked at Marcus standing on the porch outside the front door. "I guess she talked to you about coming back home. I can see that she is crying and upset."

Marcus looked down, knowing that he had planted the seed of his daughter confronting Monica about seeing another man. "Look, I'll talk to you later. I have to run. I have some business to take care of."

Monica looked at Marcus as she closed the door. Hesitant to go up to her daughter's room, she took a deep breath and leaned her back against the front door. She had to figure out what she was going to say to Taylor. How could she convince her daughter that her mother was not to blame for what had happened? She didn't want her daughter to know that the reason her father left was behind another woman. She felt that young children should be left out of what happens between adults.

Monica went to their daughter's room and found her crying on the bed. She walked over to her daughter and said, "Come here, Baby."

Taylor jumped up and screamed, "No! Daddy told me that you have a new friend! And he's a man! I want my Daddy!"

Taylor's words pierced, almost as if someone had punched Monica in the head. She looked at Taylor, trying to process what she had just heard. "What did you say?"

Looking at her mother with an angry look on her face, Taylor yelled, "Daddy said that you have a boyfriend!"

Trying her best to calm her daughter, Monica asked, "Baby, can Mommy talk to you?" She reached for her daughter and pulled her close to her. "Honey, there are things that you should understand. Mommy loves you very much."

Taylor laid her head on her mother's chest while still crying. "Mommy, you have to let Daddy come back home."

Monica was furious that Marcus would stoop so low as to tell their daughter about Kenneth. *How could he?! That bastard!* Feeling that there was no other choice but to confront Marcus face to face, Monica told Taylor that she had to go and talk to her father. "Baby, I have to talk to your father. I'm going to take you over to Auntie Tasha's while me and your father talk. Okay?"

Monica and Taylor arrived at Tasha's house and sat in the driveway. Monica looked at her daughter and said, "Baby, I'll be back soon. Me and your daddy have to figure some things out." Monica's blood was boiling, and she wanted to get to Marcus as soon as possible. She walked Taylor to the front door and rang the bell. Tasha opened the door and Monica told her sister she would return in a few hours.

Monica drove as fast as she could. She didn't give Marcus any warning that she was coming over. It was going to be an unwelcome surprise—a rude awakening. She was going to be sure to put him in his place. Son of a bitch! Monica was still in disbelief that Marcus would tell their daughter about her personal life. She would never think of telling her about Kyra.

Monica rode the elevator, the fury rising as it ascended. She got out of the elevator and walked to his door. She took a deep breath before ringing the doorbell. Monica folded her arms and tapped her foot, ready for battle as soon as Marcus opened the door. She rang the doorbell again and then knocked hard on the door. Open this damn door, you son of a bitch!

Marcus opened the door after looking through the peephole. He was surprised but knew why she had come. He stood there looking at an angry woman who stared him in the eyes. "Come in, Monica."

Monica walked inside and turned to face Marcus. "You bastard! Why would you tell Taylor that shit! You stooped too damn low!"

Marcus walked to Monica and stood face to face. "I told her because I wanted to."

Without thinking, Monica slapped him across the face. "Fuck you! I would never have told her about you and that filthy slut that you were fucking! That bitch who had your sorry ass leave your damn family!"

Marcus rubbed his face, wanting to strike back at his wife, but held his composure. He looked Monica in her eyes and said, "I'm going to get my family back by any means necessary." He lowered his hand from his face and grabbed Monica by her arms. He held her tight and said, "I love your ass! And ain't nothing going to change that!"

Monica looked at his hands on her arms and yelled, "Get your goddamn hands off me!"

Marcus pulled her close to him and held her tight. Feeling her trying to pull away, he said in her ear, "I love you, Baby. And I'm not letting you go."

Monica yelled, unable to release herself from his grip, "Marcus, let me go! Let me the fuck go!"

Marcus held on to her tightly as she tried to fight herself free. He waited until her body weakened and eased his grip but still held her close. She started to cry, her head lying against his chest. Marcus rubbed her back as he hugged her. Suddenly, he felt her pain, and he wanted to comfort her. Without knowing it, tears began to stream down his face. Marcus held her tight, crying with his wife again, hoping that she could understand that his guilt was killing him inside.

Marcus released his hug and stood back, looking at his crying wife. "Monica, please try and understand and forgive me."

Monica looked at her teary-eyed husband. She had discovered a look on his face that she had never seen before. A look of sadness. Is he really sorry for what he has done? Should I give him a chance to make things right? She looked into his eyes and said weakly, "I have to go and get Taylor. I have to get her ready for school tomorrow."

Wiping the tears from his eyes, Marcus asked, "So can we try?

Please?"

Monica looked down at the floor and then back up at her husband. "We'll talk about it later. Okay? I just have too much on my mind."

Understanding his wife's feelings, Marcus said, "Okay. I'll be here whenever you are ready." Marcus watched as Monica walked to the door. Before she opened the door, he asked, "Baby, can I have a hug before you leave?"

Monica turned around and looked at her husband. Without saying a word, feeling compelled to honor his desire, she walked to him and put her arms around him. She held on to him, his arms holding her tight. She couldn't stop the tears from flowing as her body jerked. With all that happened and all he had put her through, she realized she truly loved the man who caused her so much pain.

Chapter Forty-Seven

The crew at the fire station decided to throw some steaks on the grill that afternoon. Kenneth volunteered to go to the neighborhood grocery store and pick up the steak. He hadn't heard from Monica in two days and was worried about her. She hadn't even returned his text messages. He knew he could not just show up at her house and wondered if he should go by her office to check on her. The one thing he did know was that her husband wanted back in her life.

While walking out of the grocery store, Kenneth spotted Marcus walking toward the store's entrance. Shit! What fucking odds! Kenneth's truck was parked near where Marcus was walking. Bags in his hands, he started to walk to his truck. Marcus noticed him and stood still. Kenneth looked at him as he walked toward Marcus, seeing an agitated look on his face. Marcus rubbed his face as Kenneth approached him. Jealousy aroused the male machoism inside of Marcus. He had to say something to Kenneth. It was something deep down inside of him that wanted to know what Monica felt for the fireman and if he was the reason for the glow and vibrant smile she exuberated. The more he thought about Monica being sexed by the man near him, the angrier he became. Marcus stared at Kenneth, and Kenneth kept his eyes on Marcus.

His eyes still glued to Marcus, Kenneth asked, "Looks like you have something you want to say."

"Maybe I do have something to say," Marcus responded.

Kenneth nodded his head slowly. "Well, by all means. Say what's on your mind."

Marcus laughed and said, "I don't know why Monica would want a damn fireman."

Intensifying his gaze at Marcus, Kenneth responded, "You see a fireman. Monica sees a real man."

"A real man?" Marcus asked. "Who pulls down what? $60,000 a year?"

Kenneth chuckled, still with a serious look on his face, and said, "Money doesn't make a real man. If I made six dollars a year, I would still be more of a man than you could ever dream of being." He paused and then continued, "And besides, firemen's salaries are public record. I advise that you go and do your homework. You may be surprised."

Marcus was speechless. He wanted to punch Kenneth in the face but knew that it wouldn't be in his best interest. There was something about Kenneth that intimidated Marcus. But his male ego would not let him reveal the respect that he had for the man who was sleeping with his wife. Marcus also knew there was a great chance that Kenneth would win the physical fight. Kenneth had been with his wife, and there was no chance that Marcus wanted to risk getting his ass kicked by the man that made his wife smile and glow.

Kenneth made it back to the fire station, feeling sad and defeated. He loved Monica and had put his hopes on her not giving her husband a chance to return. He felt that he had made an impression on her and knew she loved him too. He could feel it in his soul when she smiled at him and how she held him. She had given him all she had when having hot, passionate sex with her. And now he hadn't heard from her in two days. Hurt and pain ran through his mind, body, and soul.

Kenneth made it home after 11:00 p.m. Monica had been on his mind the whole time he was at the station. Each time he tried to think of something else, her smile would invade, locking the image of her beautiful face into his awakened dream. It had been the longest two days he could remember. The unknown bothered him. Was she working things out with her husband, not wanting to tell him? Or was she trying to figure out how to get her husband to leave her alone?

Something told him to call her. Kenneth wanted to know if she was doing okay, wondering if her estranged husband threatened her. Kenneth let the phone ring until her voicemail came on. Choked up on his words, he finally said, "Hey, Monica. I'm just worried about you. I'm hoping all is well with you. No matter what is going on in your life, I would just like to know that you are doing okay. Please let me know."

Kenneth lay across his bed, thinking about the times he and Monica spent together. His mind would not release her face. His desire for her burned inside of lustful emotions. He couldn't shake the thought of her soft, sweet body. Monica had come into his life and rocked his world. Becoming the only woman that he desired to be with. It was only two days that he hadn't heard from her, but the loneliness consumed him. They had talked every day since the first time they had rocked each other's world. Now Kenneth felt that he was left out in the cold.

Since being with Monica, Kenneth had it all. With Monica, Kenneth had experienced nothing as he had with any other woman. For the first time in his life, he had the perfect woman—a woman with the best personality and natural beauty. She was the most unselfish woman he had ever been with. Monica was the woman who had the hottest pussy that a man could experience. She set a fire inside of him, unlike any other woman.

She had the silliest laugh that, in its own way, was the sweetest laugh he had ever heard. Her smile always turned him on. Everything about her, he loved. Her talk, her walk, stayed in his mind. Monica was a man's dream. Kenneth could not understand why any man would deliberately neglect the best woman in the world.

Chapter Forty-Eight

Monica had decided to go to her office that evening. She wanted to get away from the house. She allowed Marcus to come over; he was playing video games with Taylor. She had listened to Kenneth's messages from her voicemail and had read his text messages. It saddened her that she did not respond. Listening to Kenneth's sad voice made her tear up. Kenneth told her he loved her in his voicemails and text messages. Monica's life was a big ball of confusion, wishing that something would come and pop it and free her mind.

Driving in her car, she became agitated, thinking about Marcus asking her where she was going. He had a suspicious look on his face. His ass should be grateful and appreciative that I let his ass come over. But she had to talk to Kenneth. She owed him an explanation, even though she knew it would break his heart. Kenneth had to know that her decision to let Marcus reenter her life wasn't an easy one. Taylor needed her father, and Monica didn't want her daughter to have any psychological damage because of her mother and father not being together.

When Monica got to her office, she sat at her desk and poured herself a glass of Crown. She sat back and tried to clear her mind. Her cell phone rang, interrupting her thoughts. It was her sister. "Hey, girl. What's up?"

Tasha's voice was loud and angry. "Monica! We didn't complete our talk! Yo' ass hung up on me!"

"Tasha. I did not want to discuss my marriage with you. I told you that."

Lowering her voice, trying not to get her sister upset, Tasha said, "Monica, listen to me. Taylor will be just fine. Shit. Look at Brianna. She's doing just fine."

Monica stood up and began to pace around her office. "Tasha, I didn't want to take that chance. Taylor is having a difficult time with this separation. She's really taking it hard. And I just don't want to chance it."

Tasha's voice rose again. "Monica! His sorry ass only came back because he found out that skank was fucking someone else, and he went to jail!"

Monica wanted her sister to understand and not be so critical, "Tasha, please try and look at it from my point of view. Believe me.

It is the right decision for Taylor. I don't think I could live with myself if she grew up and had issues because I didn't allow her father to come back home. That is the last thing I want to happen."

"Monica! Marcus has put you through a lot of heartache and pain! How do you know that he won't do it again?"

Interrupting her sister, Monica calmly said, "Tasha, I know that you want what's best for me. But I have to take that chance of getting my family back together. I have to give my husband the benefit of the doubt."

Not wanting to hear what she believed were her sister's excuses, Tasha said, "I'm not trying to hear that shit. Bye, Monica." And she hung up the phone.

Monica sat at her desk, trying to gather herself before she called Kenneth. She had practiced the words over and over again, but for some reason, she couldn't put them together in her head. She knew it would be one of the most difficult conversations she's ever had. She knew Kenneth didn't deserve the heartache she was about to cause him. She loved Kenneth, and the last thing that she wanted was to hurt him. But it was a phone call that she had to make.

Monica took another sip of Crown for courage. She dialed Kenneth's phone and leaned forward, resting her head in the palm of her hand. "Hello, Kenneth. How are you?"

Worried about Monica and her well-being, Kenneth replied, "Monica! Are you okay? I have been worried about you!"

Hearing the care and concern in Kenneth's voice, Monica started to cry. "Yes," she said in a weak voice. "Yes, Kenneth. I'm okay."

Hearing Monica crying, Kenneth didn't believe her. "What's wrong? Please tell me!" He was worried, hoping she and her husband hadn't gotten into a physical altercation. Or that he hadn't threatened her. Kenneth had his run-ins with Marcus and was worried about what he was capable of doing to Monica. Anger came over him as thoughts of Marcus hurting Monica ran through his head. Kenneth swore he would kick Marcus' ass if he laid one hand on her. "He didn't hurt you, did he?"

Monica shook her head without saying a word. She couldn't stop the tears from flowing, and she couldn't make her words come out. How could she tell Kenneth that she was allowing her husband back into her life? How could she expect him to understand? She began to cry louder, her eyes closed and still shaking her head. She finally managed to let out, "Kenneth! I'm sorry!"

When Kenneth heard her, his body went numb. Her words stung him deeply as he listened to her cry uncontrollably. It was a reality that he wasn't ready for. In his heart of hearts, Kenneth knew that her husband had returned, and Monica was going to allow him back into her life. Shit!

Chapter Forty-Nine

Kenneth sat out back on his patio. He sipped on his Crown on the rocks as he thought about Monica. The Kings of Leon's Sex on Fire resonated profoundly in the background of his memories. He remembered Bryan introducing him to the rock group several years earlier. And the song reminded him of Monica. He listened to the lyrics, not wanting to let go of what he and Monica had experienced.

"Hot as a fever. Rattle of bones. I could just taste it...taste it. If it's not forever. But there's just tonight. Oh, we're still the greatest... the greatest. Yoooooouu! Your sex is on fire! "

Monica's decision to let Marcus back into her life had Kenneth's head spinning out of control. Kenneth felt Monica was his true destiny when he held and felt her love. She had become the reason for his existence. And now he was like a lost child wandering around in a freezing blizzard and walking through the wilderness. Kenneth was now climbing the slippery slope of love, trying to maintain his balance, only to slip constantly when Monica entered his thoughts.

He could not get her off his mind. He craved her touch. He craved the taste of her sweet, hot juices, desiring to make her scream his name when she came. He grew aroused at the thought of her cumming from below, rising to the surface and pleasing her more by giving her a long, hard throbbing dick. He loved pleasing her. Now his love was stuck in neutral with no indication of ever being moved.

It was the week he and Monica were set to be in the Virgin Islands that Monica broke off all communication. She refused to answer his phone calls and texts. Kenneth knew deep down in his heart that Monica loved him. He refused to believe the contrary and hoped that she would recognize his love for her and realize that going back to her husband was a mistake. But how could he convince her? He had sent a CD with songs to her office, hoping that she would listen to them and that they would make a difference. But there was no response.

Monica had become the soulmate that he couldn't have. As fate would have it, she entered his life, gathered all his soul, and unlocked and released all he held inside, only to walk away and return to the life that awaited her return. Her marriage. Her daughter. Her commitment, which she had once stood before an audience, made a promise, "Til death do us part."

If she was in front of him, looking him in his eyes, she could not truly deny her love for him. But the vow to fulfill the family life extracted her from the man who loved her more than anything. He reflected on the ride of his life. The precious memories that Monica had provided. Her adorable sense of humor. The romantic dinners and the walk in the park stuck in his mind. Her dark, soft, sweet skin always mesmerized him. And most of all, the fiery sex that he had never experienced before. Monica was his fire.

The thought of Monica returning to her husband made Kenneth feel angry and sad at the same time. He had vowed to stand by a wounded and confused woman who needed the strength of a caring man. Kenneth knew that Monica's pain was not warranted. He would stand by a woman he had let into his guarded world. She tore down the walls of his reluctant will to let a woman inside. But she tore down those walls and had gotten to know the man that he had hidden from so many women.

His love for Monica had weakened him. So much so that he had forgotten how to stand strong in a time of loss. For some reason, he couldn't remember what had given him the strength to keep going after the loss of the two women that he had cherished the most. And now he needed that strength once again; the strength to pick himself up and face the reality that people you love come and go in this life.

Needing something to take his mind off the woman he loved, Kenneth decided to call Captain Franklin and ask to work the rest of the week. He refused to just sit around the house, filled with memories of the woman that had entered his world, only to leave him devastated. Being at the fire station and fighting fires is where he needed to be. Being there wouldn't totally remove Monica from his heart, but it would be a start. And oftentimes, the fire station was his sanctuary.

Chapter Fifty

It was after seven that evening, and Monica was still at her office. She wanted so much to answer Kenneth's phone calls and text messages. But giving her husband a second chance to return home held her back. She felt Kenneth's relentless pursuit, knowing that he truly loved her and that she truly loved him. His voice on her voicemail penetrated her weakened emotions. She wanted to pick up her cell phone and call him back so badly. But she didn't want the phone call to lead to Kenneth holding and caressing her and leading her to his bedroom for the thrill of her life.

Marcus tried his best not to bring up Kenneth, but his ego wouldn't allow him to just not go there. Every time Marcus would sneak Kenneth's name into their conversation, Monica would change the subject to his affair with Kyra, shutting down his intentions. She would not be outdone in the battle of the guilt game. But she knew that Marcus' mind was always on Kenneth, wondering if she was still secretly seeing him when she left the house.

Staring at her cell phone, Monica knew that she owed Kenneth an explanation. She had been unfair to the man that had saved her from a deep, miserable depression. Kenneth had entered her life at a time when she needed someone to lean on. If her situation had been different, she could have started a life with Kenneth. But the reality was what it was. And that reality began to make tears form and roll down her cheeks. Her crying uncontrollably resurfaced with no way of stopping the flow of tears.

Monica looked at the clock on her office wall. She had been at her office for two hours now, still fighting the tears and the urge to call Kenneth. She finally managed to stop crying and took a deep breath before picking up her cell phone. As the phone rang, she hoped Kenneth was busy and couldn't answer. But he answered, his deep voice low and saddened. What would she say to him? Would he believe her if she told him that she truly loved him? Would he understand her decision to give her marriage another chance because of her daughter?

"Hello, Kenneth." Monica's voice was low and weak. "I guess I shouldn't ask you how you are doing." A long pause and silence were all Monica heard.

Kenneth took a deep breath before he spoke. "Monica, I really don't know what to say."

"I know, Kenneth. I called without knowing what to say myself. But I just had to call you." Tears started to roll down her cheeks again.

Kenneth knew she was crying, making it that much more difficult to understand why she took her love away from him. "Monica, I'm really trying to put things in perspective. I have been trying to put myself in your shoes, but my love for you overshadows my ability to do that."

Hearing the sadness in Kenneth's voice pierced through her regrettable soul. She knew that there was no way to make him feel better, as much as she wanted to. "Kenneth. Just know that I do love you very much. But my daughter was having a difficult time with the separation, and I didn't want it to affect her mentally. Please understand that's the reason."

"Are you sure that's the only reason?" Kenneth asked.

Monica's voice rose as she tried to convince Kenneth. "Yes! Believe me! Please!"

"Well, it doesn't make me feel any better. I love you, so that means that I have to accept your decision. And because I love you so much, I really wish nothing but the best for you. I enjoyed every second that we spent together. It's funny, you know? I have never loved a woman as much as I love you."

Kenneth's words made Monica feel ecstatic and sad at the same time. "Thank you, Kenneth. Your words mean so much to me right now. I want you to know that I enjoyed every second with you."

After hanging up the phone, Monica sat at her desk, looking out her office window. Memories of Kenneth stuck in her mind. She loved his laugh, his smile, his kisses, how he smelled, and most of all, how he treated her. Kenneth was the ultimate gentleman. He was classy and very intelligent. She loved his caring heart. She had never been taken so high sexually, an erotic experience that she would never forget. Now Monica had to readjust her mind to accept her husband's touch, his kisses, and his desire to please her sexually.

Monica made it home just after eleven that night. Marcus sat in the formal room drinking Crown on the rocks. Monica walked past the room, looking at him as he stared at her with a suspicious look on his face. She knew that his mind was on Kenneth and didn't want to get into a conversation about it. She went up to the bedroom and began to undress. She turned around to a husband with that same suspicious look, leaning against the bedroom door entrance.

"So, how was work at the office?" Marcus finally asked.

"I got some work done," she answered, her nude body standing before her husband as he looked her up and down.

"So, are you about to shower?"

Staring Marcus right in his eyes, her eyes squinted and serious, Monica answered, "Yes, I am about to take a shower."

An insidious smile on his face, Marcus stepped out of the doorway and walked toward Monica. "Can I join you?"

Monica shook her head and started to walk to the bathroom. Without looking back, she replied, "No. I prefer to shower alone, thank you."

Watching Monica's round ass and getting aroused, Marcus asked, "Are you sure you are not trying to wash off that fireman's scent?"

Irritated and disgusted, Monica turned around and faced her husband. "Don't ask me no shit like that! Remember, I wouldn't have been in that situation if you hadn't moved out of the house to be with that tramp! Now, I'm about to shower." She walked into the bathroom and slammed the door behind her.

When Monica was done showering, she walked into the bedroom to a naked husband lying on the bed. She looked down at his aroused dick. He was holding it and stroking it up and down. She was in no mood for his advancements, nor was she in the mood to have sex with him.

"You can stroke it until you cum. Because I am not in the mood." She looked him in his eyes, a look that said, And I'm not in the mood for your bullshit!

Marcus jumped up and yelled, "What the fuck is wrong with you?"

Monica put on her nightgown and turned around to face an angry husband. "Stop yelling! You'll wake up, Taylor!"

Marcus rubbed his head, standing there with an erection. "I can't believe this shit."

"Well, believe it. I'm tired, and I am going to bed." Monica got underneath the covers and turned off the table lamp. Without looking at Marcus, she said, "Call that tramp and have phone sex."

Marcus put on his pajamas and went downstairs. The thought of Kenneth was embedded in his thoughts. Was she out with that fireman? Did they fuck? The thoughts were driving him crazy. The thought of Monica being pleased by Kenneth before she came home infuriated him. And there was nothing he could do to get the thought out of his head. This was another insufferable blow to his male ego. And now he was back in his house with a wife who seemed not to give a damn about his feelings.

Chapter Fifty-One

Kenneth volunteered to work the week he and Monica were supposed to be on their romantic getaway. He was trying to start getting over the woman he had come to love more than any other woman. And being at work would help him begin to heal. Mark would be a great help, making Kenneth laugh, giving him advice, and keeping it real. Now more than ever, Kenneth needed his friend and the fire station.

It was a warm March night, and Kenneth and Mark sat at the back of the fire station. Marvin Gaye's Get to This played in the background. Kenneth remembered his mother playing the song when he was a young kid. And it always reminded him of his mother, cooking and cleaning to her favorite music. Kenneth and Mark puffed on their cigars, thankful for a slow and quiet evening.

But the quiet evening came to a sudden halt when the alarm

blared. It was time to go and put out another fire. Captain Franklin yelled out to Kenneth and Mark as both rose to their feet. "Okay, men! Let's mount up!" Captain Franklin yelled. "It looks like we got a big'un!"

Mark had driving duty that week, and Kenneth was on the firefighting team. The men quickly put on their gear and jumped into the fire engine. Kenneth's adrenaline kicked in when Captain Franklin told the crew that the AT&T Midtown Center Building downtown had caught fire, and the fire registered a five-alarm, which meant that multiple fire stations had to respond. Kenneth hoped that everyone had gotten out of the building. He had seen the horrific after-effects of those left behind in a large fire.

The fire engine arrived to meet three fire engines from other stations, their ladders high with men hosing the fire. Captain Franklin gave his commands as the men leaped from the truck. He turned around to a yelling captain from another station. "Franklin! The fire started on the 15th floor! My men have cleared people from the 15th floor and are searching the building for others!"

Captain Franklin yelled back, "Has the fire spread to any other floors?"

The short, round, black captain shook his head. "We are not sure! My crew is on the floor beneath the fire! Looks like it's going to spread!"

Captain Franklin looked at his crew and then back at the burning building. "Okay, men! Let's get to work! Let's get ready to go in!" The ladder from Captain Franklin's fire engine had already begun to ascend upward. He kept his eyes on the rising ladder and yelled, "Grab those axes and head on up to meet the hoses!"

There were six firefighters in Kenneth's crew, and he knew that all six would be needed. He had battled enough fires to know that the fire could get out of control very quickly. But he was ready for battle. The six firemen ran up the stairs as fast as they could. The men were in excellent physical condition, displaying their strength as they climbed the stairs with Scott air packs on their backs.

Kenneth and his crew arrived on the 14th floor and met eight firefighters from other stations. Kenneth yelled at a fireman battling the flames with a water hose coming from outside the window. "Is there anyone inside?!"

The fireman turned around and yelled back, "I sure hope not! We've been fighting this damn blaze, trying to get it under control!"

The other fire station's lieutenant was leading the charge. He was tall and dark with a huge frame. "Okay, boys! 69! Tell your men to hurry up with those hoses! We have to push through this damn beast! Hurry!"

The hoses from Kenneth's fire engine arrived as the lieutenant was yelling. Kenneth looked at his friend Mark who was pulling a hose, eager to get to the fight with the fire. Feeling proud to be side by side with his friend, Kenneth's strength and motivation rose to an all-time high. He grabbed a hose and caught up to his friend. Each looked at the other, reading the other's mind. Let's kick ass!

The men from the other fire station finally cleared a way for Kenneth's crew to go inside an office. The lieutenant yelled his command to the firemen. "Go! Go! Two men now! Go!"

Kenneth and Mark ran into the office without hesitation. They began to search for anyone left behind. Kenneth yelled to the lieutenant, "All clear!" He looked at his friend, who had just looked underneath a desk near the door to the office. "Okay, Mr. B! Let's get out of here!" Just as Kenneth took his first step, a large steel pole came crashing through the ceiling and knocked him to the wall, pinning him against the wall.

Mark turned around when he heard the loud noise. He looked up to a large blaze that was coming through the ceiling. He tried to reach his friend, but the blaze was too intense. "Help! Man down! Get those hoses in here! Now!" Mark didn't hear any response from the firemen outside of the door. "Get me a damn hose!" Before Mark could get another word out, three men grabbed him and pulled him out of the office.

Knowing that his friend was trapped between a large steel pipe and the wall, Mark fought vigorously to free himself from the three men. "No! Let me go!" But the three men pulled Mark with all the strength they had.

One of the men yelled at Mark, "The fire is coming down from above! We have to retreat!"

Something inside of Mark wouldn't allow him to go that easy. He fell to the floor and turned on his back. Two men grabbed his legs and began to pull Mark towards the stairwell. Mark kicked and yelled, but the firemen held on until they got him to the stairwell. The other firemen were there waiting and assisted by grabbing Mark and dragging him down the stairs. The firefighters had barely pulled Mark from the inferno, but Kenneth was trapped inside the office.

Kenneth lay trapped beneath the heavy steel pipe, his back against the wall. The blow had rendered him weak and helpless. The flickering flames looked like they were teasing him. The fire would come closer and then back away. He kept his eyes on the fire, wanting to let the fire know that he wasn't afraid. "Come and get me, you son of a bitch," he said in a weak whisper. His body was aching from broken ribs, battered arms, and shoulders.

He began to envision his mother and sister as he watched the flames inch closer to him. He closed his eyes as he saw his mother's smile. His body weakened as his sister's voice talked to him. "Kenneth, I love you so much. You are going to be somebody." Flashes of his mother and sister cascaded inside his head. He managed to open his eyes, looking at a hungry fire with an evil grin. He wanted to lift the heavy steel pipe from his weak body, but he didn't have the strength.

Monica's face appeared while his eyes opened and closed. He could see her lovely smile. He could hear her silly laugh and see her sexy walk. If only she had gone to Jamaica with him, he wouldn't be lying helpless, facing an evil fire slowly coming to devour him. If only he could have tried harder to convince her that he was the man that truly loved her.

Kenneth looked up for the last time as the fire inched closer and closer. He swore that he could hear the fire laughing and talking to him. I'm going to eat you alive. Kenneth managed to gather enough strength to yell, "Is this what you want?! You motherfucker!" Before he could get another word out, the fire blazed all over his body. Kenneth let out a loud roar as the flames consumed his body.

Captain Franklin quickly turned around and saw the other firefighters holding and dragging Mark from the burning building. Mark yelled and fought, trying to go back into the burning building. Captain Franklin came running up to Mark, who was crying uncontrollably. Captain Franklin didn't want to believe the undeniable truth of why Mark was fighting to run back into the burning building. He fell to his knees, his head bowed, and started to cry as his entire body shook.

The crew from Station 69 came running to Captain Franklin and Mark. Mark had kneeled with his arms around his captain. The men lifted Captain Franklin up to his feet and pulled the two men to their fire engine. All the men were crying, trying to console each other. They knew that they had lost their favorite man of Station 69. And the gut-wrenching feeling would live with them forever.

Chapter Fifty-Two

The morning after Monica and Marcus' disagreement, she sat on her bed with her back against the headboard. Marcus was sitting next to her as they watched TV. She hadn't been in the mood for his sexual advances, denying him every time he tried. There was something inside of her that wouldn't allow her to give herself to him. The hurt and anger ruled over her decision to try and start the process. She needed more time to figure herself out and get her mind back into her marriage. Most of all, she missed Kenneth.

While sitting in total silence, her show was interrupted by breaking news. Thinking it was another Atlanta shooting, she waited until the news broadcaster came on. "We have breaking news from a fire at the AT&T Midtown Center. Firefighters battled a five-alarm fire which took a turn for the worst. They managed to get all the workers out of the building, but Fire Station 69 lost one of their most beloved firemen." Monica's heart began to pound when Kenneth's picture appeared on the TV screen. "Kenneth Mann was trapped inside of an office on the 14th floor and could not be rescued."

Monica lowered her head and began to cry. She could feel Marcus looking at her. She stood to her feet, her body weak and shaking. She walked downstairs to her office and sat at her desk. She started to cry uncontrollably as her body began to shake. She couldn't think straight and didn't know what to do next. She felt trapped inside a claustrophobic haze, trying to escape her mind. She wanted to be free from the thoughts of her husband and the man that had rescued her from her deep depression. And now he had died in a fire, leaving her more confused and saddened.

Monica looked up to an angry husband standing in the doorway. Tears rolling down her face, and she stared straight up at him. She wanted to curse at him but held it in. She knew he was angry because she was crying over the man she had been with while he was gone. And she didn't give a damn how her husband felt. She was hurting, and there was no way of hiding it.

Marcus put his hands in his pockets while leaning against the door rail. "So you are crying because he died? What the fuck?!"

Monica slowly rose to her feet. She gathered herself before she walked toward the door. She stood in front of her husband, not knowing what to say. She tried walking out of her office only to be grabbed by her arm and spun around to face her angry husband. She looked down at his hand on her arm and then back up at him. "Marcus, please let me go," she said in a low voice.

Marcus pulled her close to him and looked down at her. "So that's why you won't let me touch you!" he yelled. "Because of that mothafucka!"

Monica looked at him, her face showing extreme anger and frustration. "If you don't get your fucking hands off of me. . .Let me go!"

Unwilling to let go of his grip, Marcus responded, "Hell no! What the fuck is wrong with you!"

Monica heard Taylor crying upstairs and knew she was listening to her parents argue. "My child can hear us. And you are not going to put her through any more pain," she said in a low voice. "Now get your goddamn hands off of me."

Realizing that he could cause more harm to his daughter's psyche, Marcus eased his grip from her arms. "Monica, we have to talk about this," he said in a low voice.

Without saying a word, Monica walked upstairs to her bedroom. She needed to get out of the house to clear her mind. There was no way that she could stay in the house with her mind spinning out of control. Marcus would stay with Taylor until she returned. And she wasn't going to be denied. There was nothing

Marcus could say or do to make her stay. He had to respect her feelings and her decision to go somewhere and clear her mind.

Monica drove to the fire station, hoping to see Mark. She sat inside her car crying, trying to compose herself before getting out of the car. She got out and stood by her car. She saw a skinny white fireman standing at the fire station entrance. She recognized him from New Year's Eve when she brought Kenneth something to eat. She waved and yelled for the fireman to turn around. "Hello!"

The fireman turned around and stood still, trying to figure out who Monica was. He walked to the edge of the open entrance and asked, "Yes, ma'am. How can I help you?"

Monica started to walk towards the fireman with her arms folded. "Is Mark here?" she asked.

"No, I'm sorry. We had a loss, and he is taking it hard." The fireman finally realized who Monica was, and a sad look came over his face. "I suppose you know?"

Monica started to cry. She nodded her head, unable to speak. The fireman walked to Monica and put his arms around her. Monica held onto him tight, unable to stop the tears from falling. She didn't know the fireman, only meeting him the night she had brought Kenneth food. But she didn't mind him hugging and consoling her because she knew he also needed comfort.

Monica asked the fireman for Mark's phone number. She just

had to call him because she wanted Mark to know she would be there for him. She didn't know what she would say to Mark, but she knew she had to talk to him and hoped that he wouldn't mind her calling him at a time when he had just lost his best friend.

Monica made it to her office that afternoon. She called Mark, hoping that he would answer his phone. Monica heard a somber tone in Mark's voice when he answered the phone. "Hello, Mark?"

"Yeah," he answered.

Monica started to cry, trying to get herself together. "Mark, this is Monica. I went by the station to see if you were there. I got your number from one of the firemen."

Mark's voice rose as he started to cry on the phone. "It's hard! It's hard! My boy is gone! And I couldn't save him! Dammit!"

"Mark, I just had to call you. I don't know what to do." Monica's body started to shake as she cried. "I just had to call you. I know that you are hurting, and I understand. I'm at a loss for words. I loved Kenneth so much."

Mark cried as his voice got lower and lower. "I couldn't save my friend. My brother. How could I just leave him like that?"

Monica did her best to console Mark while looking for consolation herself. But both were weakened to the core by the loss of Kenneth. And Monica knew by talking to Mark that he blamed himself for Kenneth's death. She knew that he was second-guessing himself about what actions he should have taken during the fire. She felt sorry for Mark, not knowing if he would be able to rebound from losing his best friend and not being able to help Kenneth. And then she started to wonder if she could recover from losing Kenneth.

Monica sat at her desk, thinking about the times she and Kenneth had spent together. Her cell phone rang, and she hoped that it wasn't Marcus. She looked at her phone and was glad that it was her sister. She picked up, "Tasha! I'm hurting so bad!"

Tasha's voice was sad but comforting. "I know, Sis. Is there anything that I can do for you?"

Monica's voice started to crack as she begged her sister. "Tasha, please come to my office. I need you. Please."

Without hesitation, Tasha answered, "Girl, I'm on my way."

Tasha finally arrived at Monica's office, rushing through the door to hug her sister, who was crying at her desk. Monica stood up and met her sister, and they embraced. Tasha held her tight in her arms, hoping to comfort her sister. Tasha didn't know what and how to feel, but she knew her sister cared for Kenneth. She was in a complicated situation trying to pick up the pieces to a marriage that had been broken. And no matter what, Tasha was going to be there for her sister 'til the end.

Tasha released Monica and stood back, looking at her sister, who was obviously in great pain. "Monica, you have to be strong," she managed to say. "I know that this is a difficult time."

Monica interrupted her sister and screamed, "Tasha! You don't understand! We were supposed to be in Jamaica ! If I hadn't let Marcus come back, Kenneth would still be alive!" Her legs felt weak and unsteady, and Monica fell to the floor on her knees. Her cry became louder as she held on to her sister's hand. Her grieving of Kenneth was unexpectantly interrupted when she heard her husband's angry voice.

Marcus stood inside the door, furious at what he was seeing. "What the fuck! You are on your damn knees crying for that son of a bitch!" Marcus rushed over to Monica, grabbed her by the shoulders, and lifted her to her feet. "Enough of this shit! Get your ass home now!" Marcus had no sympathy for the man who had been with his wife. "I could give a rat's ass about that mothafucka!"

Monica pushed away from Marcus with all she had, stood back, and glared at him with piercing eyes. "Fuck you, Marcus! Go to hell!"

Marcus was filled with so much rage his mind went blank, not knowing what he was about to do. He rushed to Monica, grabbed her by her neck, and started choking her. All he could see was Kenneth's face, and he wanted revenge that would erase Monica's lover from her memory. Marcus' temper had reached an all-time high, and his wife was going to have to snap out of her sadness for a fly-by-night fireman.

Before Marcus could get another word out, Tasha jumped on his back and put her arm around his neck. "Take your goddamn hands off of my damn sister!"

Barely able to breathe, Marcus released his hand from Monica's neck and tried to pull himself free from Tasha's grip. When Tasha released her grip, Marcus turned around with his fist balled, wanting to punch her. Marcus was furious and wanted to release his anger on something or someone. His male ego had sent his mind spiraling out of control, and he had no way of containing it.

Tasha stepped back and put up both fists. She looked Marcus straight in the eyes and challenged him. "Come on, you sorry mothafucka! I ain't never turned down a fight!"

Monica rushed to her sister's side, ready for battle. "Marcus, if you don't leave now, we are going to fuck yo' ass up! Now get out of here with your bullshit!"

Marcus stood in front of the two sisters, contemplating his actions. A calmer head prevailed, and he opened his hand. He looked down at his fist and then back up at Monica. His voice low and glum, he said, "Monica, I'm trying. Believe me, I'm trying." He looked at the wall and said, "I guess I deserve all I am getting right now. But still, a man has his pride." Marcus walked out of Monica's office, his injured pride not wanting to accept that Monica was distraught over another man.

Chapter Fifty-Three

Monica sat on her sister's bed, trying to gather the strength to go to Kenneth's funeral. Something inside her told her that she needed to be there, and she didn't want to be at her house with Marcus fussing and being inconsiderate about her attending the funeral. So, she told Tasha that she would bring her clothes to her house and get dressed there. Tasha was more than happy to have her sister come by before the funeral. Tasha insisted that she attend the funeral with her sister and Monica was glad to have her sister with her.

Monica and Tasha settled at a spot and stood watching as the firefighters' funeral procession started down Peachtree Street. Monica watched as hundreds of firefighters stood still, lined Peachtree, facing the street as three Atlanta Police Department cars appeared first with their flashing lights. Monica listened as the bell rang three times, and then she watched as the Honor

Guard passed, holding the American flag and the Atlanta flag. She was impressed with how well all the firemen were dressed, their long dark coats, blue ties, and white hats. She envisioned Kenneth in his formal uniform, knowing he would have been handsome.

The firemen playing the Bagpipes came marching down the street with two fire engines creeping slowly behind them. Monica saw Mark and Captain Franklin holding on to the second fire engine as they marched in rhythm with the other firefighters holding on to the fire truck. Monica looked up on the top of Fire Engine 69, saw the casket with Kenneth inside it, and clutched her sister's arm. In her mind, it seemed like a nightmare that would never end. A feeling of guilt overcame her as the tears began to flow again. Watching the hundreds of firefighters walk behind the fire engine carrying Kenneth's body sent Monica to her knees. Tasha kneeled beside her, comforting her sister as best she could.

After the church service, Monica and Tasha went to the cemetery for the conclusion of the service. It was a comfortable sunny, 75-degree day, and Monica started to think about her and Kenneth on their romantic getaway. She knew that they would have had the time of their life. An opportunity that she would never get to experience with the man that had brought her so much joy. The thought saddened her as she watched the firefighters standing at attention as six firemen carried Kenneth's casket to his burial place.

Captain Franklin stood at a podium, preparing to give Kenneth the final call. Monica could see the pain and hurt on his face. She knew by looking at him, he would have to gather all the strength possible to give his speech. She watched as Captain Franklin's head dropped down, him holding on to the podium as tight as he could. Mark and the rest of Station 69 stood around their captain, trying to stand strong while grieving for their fallen comrade.

Captain Franklin lifted his head and looked around at all the firemen. He cleared his throat and gave a long pause. When he finally spoke, he said, "Fellow firemen. We have lost one of our brothers who was as brave as they come." Tears started to roll down his face. He looked around at his crew standing close to him. "Fire Station 69 has been a learning experience for me. And my men know that. But Fireman Mann was a difference-maker for me. I learned so much from him. To be honest, he opened my eyes and heart to become a better man." He began to choke up, stalling and trying to catch his breath. He was determined to make it through his speech for Kenneth. "My fellow firemen. This is the final call. My son. Our son and brother has gone home." He gave a salute, and the rest of the firefighters followed.

Monica watched as two firemen folded the flag in honor of Kenneth. She wished she could have the flag, giving her the last memory of his life. She wished it was all a bad dream and that she would wake up to Kenneth's kisses and radiant smile. But the reality began to set in as she continued watching as the flag was folded and then the 21gun salute, the shots making her cringe at each firing. She felt her sister grab her arm as she lowered her head and began to shake, tears falling down her cheeks.

Monica went to Tasha's house after the funeral, not wanting to face the life that awaited her. Marcus was so angry that she attended the funeral and stormed out of the house. Tasha asked a friend to keep Taylor and Brianna while she and Monica attended the funeral. Monica knew that when she and Taylor went back home, Marcus would be there waiting with rage and unwillingness to understand. But Monica didn't care. She felt she had done the right thing by attending Kenneth's funeral.

Monica and Taylor arrived at the house, but Marcus wasn't home. Monica knew that he was somewhere drowning his sorrows at a bar. She went to her room and sat on the bed. She looked around the room and began to think of how she had arrived at a place in her life. She was filled with so much confusion and pain. The room started to close in on her, thinking about her marriage, her daughter, and Kenneth. Where was she to go from here? How could she begin to fix a marriage that her daughter depended on? Could she and Marcus start all over and get back to the way things used to be?

So much confusion clouded her mind. And at that moment, Monica decided to get away from it all. She was going on a two-week hiatus, and Marcus would have to keep Taylor while she went to Los Angeles and Vegas. Monica was going to clear her head and regain her peace of mind while letting her hair down. She had made up her mind that she was going to party her ass off, gamble, and if she wanted to, get freaky!

The End?

ABOUT THE AUTHOR

Richard L. Willard, was born in Lubbock, TX. Although Richard chose a career in Law Enforcement, he has a passion for writing fiction novels about relationships, marriage, sex and drama. He has written two novels, I Broke my Heart and Reason. In his spare time he enjoys sports and listening to music.